PRAISE FOR RAISING PANIC

"*Raising Panic* presents both a fearless exploration of a rural family riven by alcoholism and a resounding affirmation of hope. Rhonda Zimlich is the rare author who can render the interior lives of children and adolescents with nuance and elucidate the bonds children forge with each other to survive and thrive in a world where adults too often fail them. Zimlich's keen insights into the emotional lives of children, coupled with her gorgeous descriptions of California's desert landscape, testify to the refuge and healing power friendship and natural beauty can provide, even in the direst of circumstances."
-Alice Hatcher, author of *The Wonder That Was Ours*

"Years ago, a writer lamented the wait for the great San Diego novel. I nominate *Raising Panic*, a startlingly affecting story about two young sisters, PJ and Panic, who are in a quest for personal and family identity. Their ache and hope is on every page, daring even to outweigh the historical tragedy of a commercial airliner plunging into a quiet San Diego neighborhood. You won't want to let these girls out of your sight as they come to understand a world far beyond their years."
-Brian Leung, author of *A Terrifying Brush with Optimism*

"*Raising Panic* resonates with the evolving emotional coming-of-age of the resourceful PJ, desperate to protect her vulnerable younger sister from natural dangers as well as the emotional storm that is life with their mercurial mother, Betsy. Rich with sensory details, from the opening paragraph, Zimlich presents Nature as a beautifully wrought character. This poignant story of family loyalty, misguided intentions, and two devoted sisters' bond keeps the reader cheering for PJ and Panic as they hone their survival skills in both the physical and emotional realms."
-Liza Nash Taylor, author of *Etiquette for Runaways* and *In All Good Faith*

" *Raising Panic* by Rhonda Zimlich is that rare wonder, a book that knows its human and non-human landscapes inside and out, and renders them with tender care. I fell hard for Panic and PJ, and for the chaparral broom and brush sage and sycamores and arroyo willows who sheltered these children, offering them protection and solace from a damaged world—when the adult world could not. This story of resiliency, spirit, and sibling love touched me to the core."
-Robin MacArthur, author of *Half Wild* and *Heart Spring Mountain*

"A deeply felt coming of age story, a meditation on grief and shared trauma, and an endlessly rich and detailed evocation of the landscapes of childhood, all in one."
-Tom Howard, author of *Fierce Pretty Things*

"A tender, lyrical portrait of two young sisters forced to reckon with loss and longing; set in the unrelenting California desert, Rhonda Zimlich evokes a time and place marked by tragedy and questions what it means to sacrifice for the ones we love most."
-Patricia Park, author of *What's Eating Jackie Oh?*

"Rhonda Zimlich is a rare talent who compassionately and critically examines rural American communities for their hope and humanity. Through tragedy, sister bonds, and family secrets, Raising Panic reveals the tension between our origin stories and the rocky path of leaving home to save ourselves. This book is astonishing!"
-Melissa Scholes Young, author *Flood and The Hive*

RAISING PANIC

RHONDA ZIMLICH

STEEL TOE BOOKS
est. 2003

RAISING PANIC

for

PSA Flight 182

September 25, 1978

For small creatures such as we the vastness is
bearable only through love.

- Carl Sagan

CHAPTER ONE

September 24, 1978

El Cajon was named for dead horses; her dad had told her. Translated from Spanish, El Cajon meant 'the box' because the valley was box-shaped, but PJ liked the reference to dead horses. The historic marker along the old coach route, Los Coches Road, described large boxes found there—boxes big enough to bury horses—with thick, plaster walls to keep scavengers out. The marker remained, though the boxes were gone.

PJ's dad was also gone.

When she thought of those boxes, she imagined a wagon train atop La Cresta, their view west all the way to San Diego Harbor. But they never got there. Instead, El Cajon became the valley that beat that band of westbound settlers—deprived them of their destination. They were so close to the paradise of the coast, with its jeweled, flowering plants and semi-tropical riches; they were almost there! Then the sepia horses failed the steep descent down those deteriorating marine terraces. After a time, the walls hemmed them in, and they forgot they could climb free. A township grew from the dust of their devastation. Then the rough escarpment stood as a barrier to their freedom and a monument to their loss—to the loss of everyone for generations that followed, eking out a life in the wastelands of arid chaparral and crumbling granite. El Cajon Valley became a coffin to them all. They were trapped in that barren inland, surrounded by the walls that kept them, that defined them, that restricted their destinies. PJ feared that valley could trap her, too, maybe bury her by some landmark along Los Coches Road, unless she could find a way to claw and scrape out of El Cajon, past the outlines of dead horses and lost dreams.

Though she wanted to escape that valley more than anything, it wasn't the land PJ wanted to leave. No. She always felt a kinship with the wild that surrounded her rural home. She liked the smell of sagebrush and the hum of fat bumblebees lulling on the breeze, the crunch of the granite grit beneath her feet, the tall live oaks that flanked the front of her house offering cool shade and privacy in the heat of summer. PJ even liked the snakes and tarantulas. She often hiked the hills, along fire roads and washes. She'd walked deep into the chaparral rehearsing her retreat, sometimes stashing needed things like water and food. She wanted to know if the wild could offer her a sanctuary. But PJ walked distances she knew her little sister couldn't make. When Panic tagged along with her, PJ always knew when the younger girl was tired, when she'd had enough, long before PJ would give up.

"I'm hot," Panic would say before collapsing in the shade of a sycamore or folding near towering stacks of granite boulders.

If the wild offered PJ respite and reasons to stay in El Cajon, Panic solidified those reasons. If not for Panic, PJ would have left when their dad left. Sure, Panic was stronger than most kids her age, but she was only nine then. PJ couldn't expect Panic to walk south into the desert, or east up into the hills, with no plan. Instead, PJ waited. She knew one day Panic would be old enough to go. Until then, she would practice her outdoor skills, measure how far she could hike in half a day, and try to formulate a plan.

But PJ didn't spend all her time on long walks and survival skills. She also cooked and cleaned, took care of their mother, Betsy, and went to school. She and Panic also built forts in the hills and spent extra hours adding to those odd structures with corrugated steel and particle boards. They collected interesting rocks and caught lizards. They even caught a scorpion once—brought it home in a Mason jar—but Betsy was fuming mad about it. She said it could have killed them both with one sting, which made Panic laugh, probably because Betsy hardly gave notice to the girls outside of housekeeping. They ran wild much of the time, spent more time away from home than there, and enjoyed freedoms that young girls should not have—or so their neighbor, Mrs. Stanislaw, often remarked. And they found themselves in trouble many times. But they were also resourceful, fed themselves, and worked hard for the things they needed. They collected bottles for dimes, raked yards, and helped with the harvest in Mr. Minkus' avocado groves. They had learned to be practical. By their mother's neglect, the sisters became independent, and, too, by Betsy's wrath, the sisters became resilient. If their mother was the reason PJ wanted to escape that dry valley, she was also the reason PJ needed to stay. If she left on her own, PJ knew Panic would become Betsy's new target. As often as PJ could, she took the brunt of Betsy's anger, always mindful to keep Panic safe.

By the time PJ was fourteen most of what she did either prepared the girls to run away or else kept Panic from harm. Even PJ's made-up games took on these goals. A favorite game, a version of hide-and-seek, focused on how long Panic could remain hidden. Calm and quiet were not her default.

"Try to stay absolutely still," PJ said. Her sister's eyes were wide and attentive. "Even if you think I might never find you, it's important that you stay quiet. Stay hidden."

Panic nodded and said, "but you will find me."

"Yes, I will always find you even if you become the best hider, better than me. Here, let me show you," PJ said, switching it up because she didn't think Panic understood. "Close your eyes and count to twenty. I'll hide."

As soon as Panic started counting, PJ scouted the chaparral for a hiding spot. She could scoot beneath the toyon berry or duck behind the sage, though her head would remain conspicuous.

She was taller than Panic by nearly a foot, and five years her elder, but other than that, PJ was a teenage version of her younger sister. They had the same brown hair, wild and unruly, same dots of freckles along the rise of their cheeks and nose, big feet, long fingers, and dark eyelashes. And, until recently, they looked like twins with a five-year age difference. But the changes in PJ's body, in both size and curve, had become harder to hide. To her chagrin, the resemblance PJ shared with her sister transformed away from the younger girl that was Panic and more toward the woman that was Betsy. PJ hated this change. To hide her rounding breasts, PJ wore the same baggy sweatshirt, one that had belonged to her dad. She kept her shoulders slumped forward and her chin tucked, especially at school or in town, a different form of hiding. But outdoors, away from all of that, she could still be more like Panic.

Their game took place in a wash, a dry riverbed that had long since guided water, surrounded by arroyo willows, tall and spindly, with light green leaves. A few high sycamores towered over the willows, fanning out their flat leaves. The shade felt cool in the wash, but the deep sand also lent itself to tracks. So, PJ made a full circle tiptoeing around Panic, around a rock then between a cactus and a yucca, before slipping into a thick shrub.

As she hid, PJ watched her sister. Panic's hands clasped over her eyes as her wild hair bounced with measured beats. She counted, "One… two…three…" She called out each number for PJ's benefit. When she reached twenty, Panic pulled her face free from her hands. She spun on her heel scanning all around.

PJ stifled a laugh to see the younger girl spin with such earnestness. She clasped her own hands to her mouth to keep from laughing out loud from deep within the shrub. She watched Panic pause between the withered prickly pear and towering yucca, spindly and sharp with its spikes pointing at a rainless sky. From the shade of the bush where PJ hid, the toyon berry's thick waxy leaves of dark green and berry clusters offered her the camouflage she needed. It was important to remain hidden, the lesson she tried to teach her younger sister was imperative. Still, as PJ watched Panic poke around in the underbrush with a long stick, then look inside a tree trunk, she could tell Panic's fortitude waned as the little girl grew tired of their game.

"Olly olly, oxen free!" Panic yelled, the universal cry of surrender, the I-give-up call of hide-and-seek games everywhere. Her eyes swept the canopy of a nearby Sycamore.

PJ heard her own words in her head, "remain hidden no matter what." So, PJ stayed quiet and watched her sister scrunch up her face as her gaze traveled around the tops of the leafy sycamores. Did Panic really think she'd be up a tree, she wondered, appreciating her unconventional thinking. Then the lesson lost its traction. Too tempted by childhood whimsy, Panic's attention homed in on a Western fence lizard on the trunk of a eucalyptus tree. It seemed the game was up. So, PJ decided to give the younger girl a clue. She whistled in the high voice of a black-bird's call, a trilling noise which they often joked sounded like "poke your neighbor!" As luck would have it, or perhaps nature had joined the game, a red-winged blackbird perched on the branch of a sycamore tree. Panic looked from the lizard to where PJ had issued the call. With hands on her hips, she turned in place and PJ caught her scowl as she turned to watch the bird. A breeze lifted the sycamore's branches, and the black-bird sprang to the air. Panic turned to watch it go.

A slash of bright red beneath its wing reminded PJ of the hidden beauty in the world, how a touch of something lovely could bring joy. She reached in her pocket and thumbed the soft rabbit's foot keychain she hid there.

How at peace she felt then, there in her wild backyard. PJ always felt great comfort in the world of her outdoor home. She never felt like she had to be more of anything there, surrounded by the flattop buckwheat and bunch grasses. Where eerie brush and broom jutted up from the tawny earth, she and Panic made play-castles and hideouts into real and protective domains. PJ always felt right-sized there, surrounded by the smell of earth and dirt and sagebrush. At their house, she felt small and helpless, sometimes awkward, but in the chaparral, she felt like a warrior, like Wonder Woman. She fit perfectly there in the wild unlike anywhere else. At home, the crashing noises and rough sensations made her long for the cover of sumac, the shade of lemonade berry, the soothing smell of the soft purple bloom on black sage—salvia mallifera, she'd learned that year in school—salve, like a protective covering for an injury. When necessary, PJ would turn her thoughts to the puffs of dry silt kicking up in clouds beneath Panic's feet as they ran from the house into the open and welcoming landscape, even when such visions could only exist in her imagination. A walk among shoulder-high sagebrush, or artemisia, lent her its perfume. Brushing its fragrant filaments with her fingers, the spicy scent would stay with her long after she had returned home. She could conjure the thought of its touch when she needed it most. She could smell the deep perfume of its hunger, its need to connect by emitting a stout fragrance, calling bees to carry its kisses to petals and leaves out of reach. And she soon learned, in more meditative moments, she could return there always, revisit that memory whenever she chose, close her eyes to return to that place where her fingers grazed the long spires of California sagebrush, or imagine herself tucked into the toyon berry, spying on Panic as she lost interest in their game of hide-and-seek.

"Poke your neighbor," PJ called out this time with words. Panic turned her head right to the toyon bush and saw PJ peering out, a sister's grin telling her no blackbird could speak with such ridicule. Then PJ rushed out from her hiding place and scooped Panic in her arms. They collapsed in the sandy, dry streambed, a fit of giggles overtaking them both. Nearby, a cluster of blackbirds shook free and took the sky in a frenzy. A stand of gold straw—avena or some other invasive grass—waved its long arms in the warm Santa Ana breeze. It seemed to welcome the girls for the afternoon, lapping lazily at the wafting air. And there they stayed and rested, talking and laughing until their sides ached and they ran out of absurdity, at last lying motionless, staring at the cloudless sky.

Tree limbs framed their view of the firmament, which always seemed big when PJ looked at it from her back. She recognized something of its vastness because she had flown up there once, like a bird only without the promise to fly again. Their dad, Chet, had always wanted to fly, to pilot airplanes. He took PJ flying once during a lesson. He said that flying gave him a feeling like heaven was a real place. PJ was six years old then, but she remembered when he said it, how the words had lifted his eyes to the sky. "Heaven's real up there, PJ. And you're gonna see it all today." Her eyes had followed his to that blue sky, the same blue she saw then from her back lying next to her sister in the grass. His words, especially the word "heaven," rang like a bell in her thoughts. She told herself then she needed to memorize his words and his actions, the details of that day, somehow carve the colors into her mind in deep grooves that could not be worn down by time. But some details were already forgotten. Or was it later that she told herself to remember that day and its details? Did PJ search for the memory after Chet had gone so that she could recreate it in her thoughts, only then cementing the colors and sensations in her mind? Each time she replayed the memory, she redoubled that commitment, recounted the buttons on his shirt, traced the lines along his knuckles where his hands were jammed into pockets of blue jeans. Or was it the corduroy he wore that day? She settled on jeans and clearly pictured them. She even saw, in her mind's eye, the turkey vultures circling above him, teetering in flight, their slight wobble in the slow spiral upward against the sky, the unyielding blue there, an invariable blue—the same blue that did not relent even when PJ felt sad or ashamed and wanted the sky to match the grey of her melancholy.

She pulled her thoughts away from their dad, away from the memory, and back to the sandy wash where she lay next to Panic. That afternoon—all of it, from the smell of the sage in the air to their laughter in harmony with the dancing leaves—became another moment for her to memorize, perfect and wonderful. She told herself to hold it silently like a photograph in her mind. Then she had to spoil the memory with her words.

"Our hill looks a lot different from up there, from an airplane," PJ said as she nodded at a small airplane crossing the sky.

"Not this again." Panic said. The small girl rolled away from her sister.

PJ ignored her. Panic usually complained or sulked when PJ brought up their dad. But on this particular day she couldn't help herself, and so she went on. "And it isn't just that everything's tiny, either."

"PJ. . ." Panic twisted so that PJ could see her profile.

"Can I tell it, please?" PJ asked, examining the bridge of Panic's nose.

Panic rolled back to her. PJ caught the kaleidoscope of warmth in her sister's eyes. The sun highlighted each dapple of freckles upon her nose. Her thick, brown eyelashes curled away from her brown eyes. A ruddy scar marked her cheek, about the same size as the rim of her pinky nail and the same shape, too—a tiny crescent. PJ stared at the scar often but couldn't remember where it had come from. The shape of it bothered PJ, like something familiar, but the moon never triggered the right memory. Chickenpox had come and gone, but this injury left a much larger souvenir than those from chickenpox. As she examined the scar, PJ wondered how long it had even been there. She almost asked but instead repeated her question, "Can I tell it?"

Panic relented. "Sure."

"You don't even know what I'm going to say," PJ said.

"You're gonna tell the story about flying with Dad. You don't need my permission. You're gonna tell it anyway."

"I wasn't even," PJ lied. "I was going to tell you about this dry creek." She gestured at the wash without sitting up or looking at it.

"Go on then. Tell it."

"Well," PJ gathered her thoughts. "Well, from up there, the washes that we see down here look like the lines of water that run down the bathtub wall when you set the wet washcloth on the edge of the tub. Do you know what I mean?"

"No."

"Or like the way the water runs off in branches when we play in the sprinkler."

"Is that why they call it 'a wash?'" Panic asked.

"I don't know about that, but it's like miles of tiny rivers rolling across the gravel, all joined together."

Panic plucked a tall grass blade and rolled it between her forefinger and thumb. The grass twirled. "Tiny rivers, like the ones you can stop with your foot?" Panic asked.

"Sure, only, imagine if our gravel driveway didn't run along that gully."

"Like when the water has nowhere to go so it branches out spreading everywhere," Panic said. A clever look formed on her face.

"Let me tell it." PJ shook her head. "Because the driveway has that rut, the water runs down in one long stream, right? But if it didn't, it might spill out and spread everywhere, like . . . the branches of a tree."

"An upside-down tree," Panic said.

"Right. Now imagine that the tree runs along a bigger part of the earth, down the slopes of hills and valleys." PJ held her hand up and raked her fingers through the air mimicking water flowing over an invisible plane above their heads. "Imagine we are tiny specks on one of those enormous branches. And I mean tiny, smaller than ants. And the tree is enormous. I'm talking huge branches, Panic." She turned all the way to look at her sister. "Like, miles long for just one branch, only each wash has thousands of branches."

"They don't have thousands of branches," Panic argued.

"They do."

"No," she said. "There are cities that would get in the way."

PJ could see she had thought about this.

"No, Panic." She propped herself up on her elbow to make her point clear. "There's so much wild that these great, big washes go for miles and miles and even more miles; like when we take the bus to the mountains. And there are no cities that get in the way. They just keep going."

From PJ's upright vantage, she looked around at where they had been resting. The grasses continued to wave, and the leaves of the sycamore and eucalyptus fluttered as the afternoon winds increased. She saw a blue-bellied lizard sunning on a large rock nearby. The lizard saw PJ, too, and it pressed a few pushups, a warning to her.

"There's so much wild that you could get lost forever, even walking out there for a day—a half a day, even. Maybe less—you could get lost without a trace."

"No kidding?" Panic asked, now with her eyes on PJ.

"No kidding," PJ answered.

She shrugged. "I wish I could see it all."

"You will someday," PJ said harkening back to the words of their dad. She stood shifting clumsily in the sand. "Come on. I want to show you something."

Panic sat up. She brushed the gravel from her arm and felt the texture of her skin from the indentations. How strange, it seemed the world wanted to pull her into itself and keep her close while PJ wanted to pull her out of it, away from this beautiful land. A nap right there in the grass would have been divine. Still, she stood and followed PJ up the game trail hoping she could keep up and thinking of ways she could impress her big sister.

Panic reached forward to brush stickers and seeds off PJ's back. The hill was not steep, and they'd climbed most of it before, but Panic had never really seen the top. Sure, she'd asked, but there were so many wonderful things to see along the way. Panic especially loved seeing the desert cottontails that hopped around this part of their neighborhood, rare sighting for sure, but thrilling when one happened along. The snakes were fine but also scary, after one of her friends got bit last year and had to go to the hospital. Since then, Panic tossed rocks at snakes to clear them from the path, but she also loved looking at their scale patterns, their stacks of rattles, the deep slits of their eyes. She knew a coiled snake should be regarded with great caution and she gave them plenty of room. The flowers, too, were amazing along this slope, more so after a rain, another rarity. Even the wild oats captured her attention. PJ called the wild oats "avena," but Panic liked the "wild" part of their regular name. As they climbed the hill, Panic noticed the wild oat stalks as they waved in the breeze, begging to be plucked.

Panic noticed PJ glance over her shoulder, knew that look of impatience urging her along, so she kept moving. Everywhere, wild oats bobbed in the breeze. She reached out as they walked and ran her hands over the tall, blond oatgrasses and stems. Before long, she pinched a stem and ran her fingers up a single stalk, sliding her pinched thumb and index finger along the slender stem. Seeds popped off in her pinched grip, gathering into a cluster of pointed oats. She removed and held these bunched oat seeds in her fingertips. With her other hand, she found another stalk of avena. She grasped these too, mid-stem, then closed fingers gliding upward along the length of blond straw, popping the seeds off while gathering them in her pressed fingertips as she pulled. Each seed lined up with the others forming a spikey ball in her pointed grasp, a starburst of oats.

By then, PJ stopped walking and turned around. Panic had not noticed her own stalled motion until PJ had turned. She held both hands out toward PJ showing off the miniature pompoms of dried seed clusters fanned out from the tips of her pursed fingers.

"What are you going to do with them?" PJ asked.

"I don't know. Maybe tie them with grass. Make them into decorations to hang in the fort window, or from a tree, or something like that." She felt pleased with her quick thinking. "They look like sea urchins when they're gathered like this; don't you think?" She held the pinched cluster closer toward her sister. Panic remembered a school field trip to the tide pools at False Point. Groups of spikey purple sea creatures piled in the deepest recesses of the pool appeared more like bull thorns or spearhead thistles than sea animals.

"Yep." PJ nodded. "But how will you tie them? You have your hands full now, and if you set one down . . ." She wiggled her fingers in the air then made a sweeping gesture to indicate the oats would blow away.

"Well, maybe I'll scatter them for the birds. I haven't decided." She cocked her head at PJ. "Are we still walking or is this the place you wanted to show me?"

"We're still walking," PJ said then turned to continue up the hill.

After what seemed like a long while, Panic dared to ask, "Are we there?" Her legs burned and she needed a rest. Already, they were higher than they normally went. Panic caught her breath. She took in a protruding granite boulder ahead, wondered if she had noticed it before. They were much farther beyond their fort and in a place Panic where had never been. Even if she had, she'd never been there under Santa Ana conditions.

The dry winds of a Santa Ana could blow up to forty miles per hour; every kid knew that. The winds kicked up in the fall, often in September, and in some years blew on through the new year. The Santa Anas had been strong that year. They brought thirsty air as the wind ripped over the mountains and pushed toward the ocean, bringing higher temperatures from the eastern desert. They learned about Santa Anas in school. Panic loved their magic and their threat. Santa Ana conditions were so dry that if a fire started it could burn all the way from Mt. Laguna to the coast. Places like the El Cajon Valley were tinder in the path of a wildfire, gone in an instant of smoke and flame. But the upside of a Santa Ana meant that strong winds would clear the air, blow all the smog and smoke out to the Pacific Ocean. Then from the right vantage, you might see as far as the Los Coronados Islands across the blue Pacific, southwest of San Diego. Maybe that was what PJ hoped to show Panic when they reached the top of Le Cresta that day. They tried to hike up to the top of the hill the year before, but Panic had been too young. The escarpment was too steep. The day, too hot. Since then, with the experience she'd gained hiking over that last year, she could go to new places—with PJ there to guide her, of course.

They reached the granite boulders; Panic noticed they were a lot bigger than she thought when she spotted them from below.

"This last bit is tricky," PJ cautioned. "I'll give you a boost."

"Betcha I don't need you to," Panic said, dropping the wild oat seeds as she reached for the tall boulder's edge. The seeds dispersed around her. She hoped there were birds nearby. Maybe she'd intended to scatter them all along.

She pushed past PJ scrambling up the large granite boulder. It stood six feet tall, towering over them, skirted on both sides by thick manzanita with red, spindly wood. The rock was misshapen at its base which afforded a step leading up to a crack in the side. Panic placed her foot on the step, wedged her hand into the crack, and pulled herself up the face of the boulder. She jammed her other hand farther up in the fissure and pulled herself up higher. Before PJ could comment on Panic's technique, she was up and over the edge of the boulder calling back, "What are you waiting for?"

Her sister tried to match Panic's technique but could not quite fit her larger hands into the rock's opening. Instead, she stuck her shoe's tip into the crack and pulled herself up with her fingertips. Panic was impressed with PJ's ability to adjust, a slower method for sure, but safe for her form and weight. When PJ hoisted herself over the edge where

Panic waited for her, the two sisters laughed. Then, they sat cross-legged together and faced west, a clear view from La Cresta.

The El Cajon Valley was filled with farms and clusters of neighborhoods connected by arteries of avenues lined with young trees. A patchwork of groves, mostly citrus and avocado, flanked the rambling neighborhoods. In the center of the valley stood the tallest building at five stories.

PJ pointed toward the building. "That's the new civic center and there's the new jail."

These looked like the same building to Panic.

Up the opposite side of the valley, the oldest part of El Cajon's residential sections was conspicuous, the trees there darker and taller obscuring the streets that crisscrossed the hillside.

"That's La Mesa, a name that means 'the table,'" PJ said.

"It looks like a bluff."

"It's just another marine terrace between our valley and Mission Valley. Beyond is the college area, with El Cajon Boulevard to the south." PJ pointed as she talked.

"Wait, El Cajon Boulevard is way over there?" Panic asked.

"Yeah, weird, huh?" PJ shrugged. She pointed out "Uptown" with its brighter, bustling boulevards and neon-lined streets of commerce already lit even in the daylight. Parts of San Diego—Kensington, North Park, and Hillcrest—were not quite visible, obscured by Mt. Helix which rose along the south end of the El Cajon Valley and blocked part of the view. But Mt. Helix wasn't tall enough to blot out the entire cityscape of downtown San Diego or the ocean beyond. San Diego proper, with its grid of roads that stretched the land between the other side of their valley to the coast, was revealed by the clearing, dry wind.

Where the downtown skyline jutted out from the edge of the expanse, a jet approached the airport there. Panic could just make out the blinking lights of the runway and tower at Lindberg Field. She imagined the people in the plane happy to soon see those who waited for them at the airport below. This thought made Panic a little sad. What must it be like to have relatives come visit? Her friends all had large families with people coming and going all the time, but not Panic and PJ. The only had Betsy, their mom.

The harbor was also visible in the distance, and National City extended southward with its boatyards. Above the glinting harbor, the arch of the Coronado Bridge curved up and over the water offering a road in the sky that connected San Diego's downtown with Coronado.

"See there?" PJ pointed to the bridge. "That's Coronado Bridge. You have to pay to drive over it." She described the island of Coronado where the bridge ended. This was not part of the Coronado Islands—protruding along the horizon—in fact, it wasn't an island at all, PJ explained. Coronado was a peninsula made years earlier from dredging the harbor to make way for the naval base. The other prominent peninsula, Point Loma—its striking rise of Ballast Point jutted beyond Coronado—shined pleasantly in the late afternoon light. Panic thought it glowed in an otherworldly way. She wanted to comment that PJ sure knew a lot, but she didn't. The vast denim blue of the Pacific rolled out behind Point Loma and seemed to pulse as the sun reflected on the water. The harbor skirting the point shone with brilliance, more hot-white than deep blue. Beyond San Diego, farther still and out to sea, lay the actual Coronado Islands, easily conspicuous on this clear day, but Panic had already spotted the islands. The vast expanse that stretched out before them became the boon of their great effort to ascend the hill and scale the towering boulder. Sure, she was tired, but it had been worth the effort.

"Wow," Panic said at last. Then, catching on something distinct she asked, "What's that?" She pointed across the valley to the cross that stood atop Mt. Helix.

"It's a cross, like for god."

"For god?" Panic asked.

"You know, a monument."

From where they sat, the monument looked small, but PJ explained that it was big. They'd visited the cross when Panic was little, before their dad left. PJ talked about going there, how Betsy smiled, her long skirt swished in the breeze. She held baby Panic atop her hip, and she laughed at things Chet said. "He joked about the cross and said he was going to climb it. I thought it was too big for anyone to climb," PJ added.

"I remember it," Panic said.

"No. You don't remember because you were too little."

"Maybe I remember," Panic said as she squinted into the distance. "Why's it there? I mean, why a cross?"

"I don't know."

"You think it's heaven?" Panic asked.

"I don't know." PJ laughed then shook her head. "I guess heaven's real up here," PJ said.

"I'm gonna see it someday, PJ." Panic nodded. "I'm gonna see all of the world and heaven, too." She scanned the horizon wondering how far her eyes could see into the distance over the subtle curve of the Pacific, wondering if there were no limits, could she see forever.

"I know you will," her sister replied. "I know you will, Panic."

They sat in silence for a long while, watching the sun move lower in the sky. PJ broke the silence with a sigh then said, "You are braver than most nine-year-olds, totally fearless."

Panic warmed with pride. Even her nickname, Panic, was a designation of bravery, one their dad had come up with, used for so long that everybody forgot the reason for it. Her mom said that when she was little, she used to flinch at sounds, no matter the volume, whether whisper-sweet or blaring. Since then, the nickname became more of a 'Little John' designation.

"You're about the boldest kid I know." PJ said, maybe to her, but maybe to nobody.

Really Panic's name was Josephine, or JoJo, as only their mom could call her in that Marlboro-gravelly voice. But PJ thought the nickname, Panic, fit her sister better than JoJo, and she said she envied her bravado, as well as her ability to blend and adapt. In a moment, Panic could slip unnoticed into the chaparral as well as any horny toad, as well as a skink could disappear against the dry gravel of a streambed. She always knew when danger would come—even before the rattlesnake knew—and she would turn tail and vanish or else stand and yell with a voice like a banshee. Sometimes Panic gave a high screech like the caw of a crow. Sometimes she would tick as quickly as the twitch of a jackrabbit's ear turning toward the approach of a bull snake, keen to the sound of it sliding against granite, or she'd look up toward the hovering flap of a kestrel. The slightest of slight among the chaparral was Panic, slipping unseen past bristles of cacti and bush, moving with grace and ease as if she'd been born among the cholla, evolved along with the wren amidst this severe acreage. With a blink, she glided into the least possible of places—that is, until big danger came. When danger came, she grew herself to match any fierceness of an attack with her own possibility and daring, like an alligator lizard doing pushups on the rocks, like the thump of a jackrabbit, the spray of a skunk, the flash of white canines on the coyote. But one thing still made Panic shrink with such terror, frozen with fear, she'd recede into herself with the same nervous retreat of the kangaroo rat darting into its burrow not daring to move or act or breathe. When their mom, Betsy, raised her voice or hand, Panic would flitter away to invisibility. PJ always seemed to afford Panic the seconds she needed to flee. Always, PJ would stay and face Betsy so Panic could escape; she knew her sister did this for her.

The sisters loved Betsy, sure. But it was PJ who felt an obligation toward her, like she needed to make sure their mom was okay, or at the very least, that Panic was not causing Betsy more grief.

Betsy was thirty-six and tired. She worked at the Best Spot Café on Main Street as a waitress on the dinner shift, then moonlighted as a cocktail waitress after hours at Doc's. Her earnings provided their modest household utilities, groceries, and basic needs—most of the time. The second job, the cocktail job, helped Betsy "stay in her cups," as she liked to say. In recent years, it had become necessary that she have a few drinks to "take the edge off" of seemingly everything. The sisters agreed with this because when Betsy was sober she became the devil. When she ran out of booze or tried to maintain abstinence after a bad spree, Betsy became impossible. Panic and PJ both preferred Betsy drunk, pacified by the booze and beer in a way that nothing else could soothe her.

But she hadn't always been that way.

Before their dad left, Betsy was a calliope of fun and frivolous amusement. Panic remembered times when Betsy would sit close to their dad and whisper his name, "Chet," then she'd giggle like she'd heard the best secret. Even though Panic did not understand the connection of her parents, she felt awkward seeing them blush and touch each other. PJ would leave the room at such times. When their parents were affectionate, with kissing and such, Panic would hide her face in her hands but still peek through her own fingers, conspicuously watching. Their mom would sip wine and sigh, color would rise to her cheeks, and a song would climb into her voice.

She would sing in her best Patsy Cline, "I go out walking after midnight." Betsy had something of a good singing voice, too. Though not perfect, it was enough to make their house light up.

By the time Chet had gone, Betsy's song had also disappeared, and the house dimmed. Panic thought maybe their dad took the light and Betsy's music with him like it was his to take. Along with her singing, the passion disappeared too—also the fighting, and the pushing, and the unease Panic felt around Chet. And though she felt relief with Chet gone, she missed the spark. From then, only PJ brought a spark into their house, always teaching Panic about the animals and plants, about their valley and their home. Not at all the same excitement that came if Betsy ran out of booze or beer. If Betsy didn't have her drink, the house would ignite in a wildfire of rage. If Betsy needed a drink, the craving would ignite an inferno. And what came next shook the walls. But Betsy never once blamed Chet for the change—blamed their dad. She never once let on that Chet had hurt her by leaving. Maybe Betsy thought it best that Chet left. Or there was at least some other resolve, lingering under Betsy's deportment. Nevertheless, Betsy wouldn't say. She would never talk about it. PJ always wanted to talk about it, but she knew better than to bring up her dad's absence to Betsy, and most of the time to Panic.

PJ always thought he would come home someday, but Panic would say. "he'll never be back," like she knew more than PJ. Panic was certain that he wouldn't come back, and that Betsy's song and light and giggle would never come back either. These were lost things, things gone to the ether.

Panic looked at PJ's face then, alight with the warm glow of the setting sun. As they sat atop that boulder looking over the valley, watching the horizon crawl up over the sky, the lights flickered on around San Diego County like secrets revealing themselves. Panic's eyes followed the path of a jet on its approach into Lindbergh Field, and then she looked at PJ again who brought her own hands together with soft applause. Whether she clapped for the show of the setting sun, the lights winking on along with the planets and stars, or to finally break the thick silence that held them, Panic could not know.

Her own eyes scanned the horizon, and she smiled like she knew a secret herself, like a kid without care, like a kid who didn't have to steal avocados sometimes from the neighbor's grove to have a small bite to eat. In her mind, she danced dress-up-style in her mom's high heels and fur-trimmed coat before the full-length mirror, but in her eyes, she watched the world transform to golden beauty.

"I can do better for you, Panic," PJ said.

"I don't need anything."

"Yes, you do. Are you looking forward to school tomorrow?" PJ asked.

"Not really." Panic clasped her hands then and pulled them under her chin. She brought her knees together and curled her body toward her legs. She followed another jet along its path toward Lindberg Field.

"How was it last week?"

"Better, I guess." Her hands came undone, and she traced the rows of worn corduroy along her knees with her dirty fingers.

"How?" PJ asked.

"I told Heidi Hill that I put lizards in her desk," she huffed. "Only I didn't, but she was still afraid to sit there."

"Did you get in trouble?"

"No. Mrs. Brown is on my side. She knows Heidi is mean to me."

"You want me to meet you after school tomorrow?" PJ asked; she'd meet her anyway, regardless of her answer.

"I'm not a baby." Panic reached down and traced a cleave on the edge of the granite with her finger. She thought about the rock's long life, how it might have been scraped by a thousand pounds of pressure a million years ago. "Besides, I think I really will catch some lizards tomorrow and put them in Heidi's desk for real. Then we'll see who's afraid."

"I know you're fooling," PJ chided but laughed anyway. After a pause, she asked, "Panic, did you know today is Dad's birthday?"

Panic felt her heart in her chest. "PJ, don't."

"Don't, what?"

"Don't bring up Dad." She nearly barked. "It's too pretty up here. We're having a nice time. Aren't we? I'll be good at school tomorrow; I promise." Then she pouted a little and PJ wondered if she had somehow lost track of her sister's age. She wondered if Panic might be a manipulative teenager instead of a nine-year-old. Panic didn't like to talk about their dad, PJ knew. This was something she had picked up from Betsy. They never brought up why Dad left or where he might have gone. Any conversation of the sort sent Betsy into a tailspin that included reactions ranging from violent drinking binges to a week without work because her depression was too consuming. Panic had naturally adopted this response, though to a lesser extreme; she simply refused to talk about him at all. Sometimes, after they talked about him, she'd skip school for days.

But PJ persisted when she needed to talk, and this felt like one of those times. After all, it was his actual birthday, and that date was still important to PJ. Maybe she was the one who needed to talk.

"Well, I noticed the date. September 24th," PJ said.

Panic remained silent; her gaze fixed on eternity.

"I always remember his height," PJ said trying to bait Panic into the conversation. "He was really tall."

Panic shushed her.

"He wore a thick mustache that I used to think might open like curtains at a puppet show when he laughed. You know, the way his mouth curved up and away?" PJ bent sideways, to get a better view of Panic's face. She pantomimed a thick mustache with her index finger along her upper lip. Then she said, in a mock puppet voice, "Hello Panic, I'm H.R. Pufnstuf."

"Pufnstuf doesn't have a mustache." Panic scowled and shrugged away from PJ. She folded her arms across her chest and sunk her head and neck down into her shoulders like a turtle into its shell. PJ saw her sister's true age then.

Often, when PJ tried to bring up their dad, Panic would interrupt with something matter of fact to dismiss the topic like, "Mars is our closest neighbor in the solar system" or "male seahorses take care of their babies; not the moms." This time she sat quietly so PJ assumed she could continue.

"He used to say this weird thing about kittens," PJ said, knowing all-things kitten was a welcomed topic. She waited but Panic remained quiet. "Right now, in about a thousand different places around the world, a litter of kittens is being born." PJ looked away from her sister and toward the setting sun. She thought back on Chet's words about kittens. When he brought up kittens, no matter her mood, PJ would shift from fear or sorrow—even terror—to imagine a pile of kittens in a basket or under a porch somewhere warm and safe. And then she would imagine kittens all over the world and she would wonder if a thousand was an accurate number, or how he could have known that number or even estimated it. By then, the idea of kittens everywhere around the world would distract her to the point that she would forget why she was scared or sad.

"I know this already," Panic whispered. "Kittens all over the world."

She'd heard it before.

"Yep." PJ sat upright, encouraged by Panic's engagement.

"How'd he know? I mean, who told him?" Panic sounded defensive. "He couldn't have been an expert on kitten populations. And what about the number? A thousand? Is that even real?"

PJ laughed so loud she heard her voice echo on the house-sized rocks nearby—fat, solid figures looming out of the vegetation. She and Panic had often imagined such rocks were actual giants, with their wraithlike shapes and bent forms, monoliths frozen since mythological times. She could also see their geology, imagine the rocks as liquid masses before they cooled, deep below the Earth's crust, saw in her mind the rocks forming at depth, incubating deep inside the planet, millions of years earlier. Her science teacher, Mr. Manlow, had said these were igneous rocks, solidifying over millennia, a span of time she could not comprehend. These then emerged upward triumphant and regal through the rain and wind of eons, to stand exposed, erect and bold, sending the sound of her voice back to her then. The enormity of it all made her shudder. And yet, what a small joy it was to laugh and to be a witness to the sound of her unbridled amusement rebounding back to her. She loved her sister for gifting her that laughter.

Turning away again to gaze out across the dimming valley, the nine-year-old's face grew staid. "PJ, that's enough," Panic said. And that was how they left it.

They watched in silence as the sun set. Santa Ana sunsets can either be spectacular or simple: spectacular because the smog gets pushed out over the Pacific Ocean causing the sun to take on a deep russet-red hue as it sinks below the vanishing point of endless water, or simple because the smog blows southwestward revealing a pure sun, an artless ball of light. The latter was the case that night. Simple and clear. The sun in its truest form, as Earth's closest star. PJ's eyes burned with the shape of it. And they watched until the last flicker ducked below the horizon.

They made it home before total darkness. Betsy was at work so PJ heated up a can of Campbell's mushroom soup, and they ate dinner by the T.V. They watched "Good Times" and then "The Jeffersons" on the T.V. that once was Chet's prized possession. Afterward, they went to bed.

It might have been another birthday without him, without their dad, but PJ thought it was a good day and she knew not to take good days for granted.

CHAPTER TWO

The creaking of the house spoke its morning whispers, awakening the sisters to the day. They rose and tiptoed around like mice trying not to disturb the sleeping barnyard cat. Betsy's snores hummed from down the short, dark hall.

They got ready for school like any other day. Panic gathered her belongings while PJ packed lunch, cheese sandwiches on dry white bread using the last of the loaf. Panic knew PJ would take the heels for herself. The block of cheese was one Betsy had picked up from the Catholic Church on Garfield. It would last a few more days. PJ gave Panic a dime so that she could buy milk at school, which was less than they could buy it for at Alpha-Beta, the grocery store up the road. Alpha-Beta was also where they cashed in bottles they collected around the neighborhood. The small pile of dimes PJ had stashed came from many months of collecting and recycling those bottles.

As they headed toward the door, Panic hesitated then stopped walking. She held her stomach, wrapping her arms across the center of her blue t-shirt. She doubled over and groaned.

PJ hushed her sister and then asked, after a heavy sigh, "What's wrong?"

"Tummy ache." Panic said, strained. "Tummy ache . . . terrible . . . all of a sudden."

"Does this tummy ache have anything to do with Heidi Hill?"

Panic peered out through her thick hair, which hung down around her face like a curtain. She caught PJ's expression. PJ rolled her eyes and sighed again, this time puffing out her cheeks as she stood upright.

"Well, I'm not waking mom up for this," PJ said.

"She won't care." Panic was right, too; they both knew.

Betsy had left a note saying she had taken the closing cocktail shift at Doc's. She must've not come in until early that morning. This meant it would be PJ's call if Panic stayed home from school.

"Do you want to stay home?" she asked.

Panic felt sorry for PJ, who could never just stay home and lay around all day watching All My Children with Betsy, or else run around outside chasing jackrabbits. Panic would likely end up outside before the day was over. Maybe earlier. But for now, she had to sell it.

"PJ, it really hurts. Don't be mad at me."

"I'm not mad. Put your sandwich in the fridge. Don't wake up Mom." Then PJ gave her a one-armed squeeze and told her to go lay down. Panic nodded and put her sandwich away. As she walked down the hall, she tried to sneak a glimpse of Betsy sleeping through the cracked bedroom door, but the bed was empty.

Her mom's voice called out from the bathroom as the toilet flushed. "Panic staying home?"

Panic ducked into her bedroom and then peeked out as her mom came out of the bathroom, pulling her robe around her. Her greying hair tussled in a fray around her head. Her grey robe was faded and stained.

She heard PJ say, "She's staying home. Says her stomach hurts."

"PJ," Betsy said. "Can you mix her up a little baking soda before you go? I got a batch of Blue-Chip Stamps I want to sort and paste. Lupe gave me a stack last night." Betsy had been saving Blue-Chip Stamps for a new coffee table. The one they had wasn't a coffee table at all but, instead, a few crates covered in an old bed sheet.

"Sure," PJ said.

Panic heard them talk about the drink concoction and she winced—maybe she could get in her bed and pretend to already be asleep before PJ brought in the drink. Still, she appreciated Betsy's concern. Lately, her mom had been working so much that the girls hardly saw her. At home, Betsy drank and often stayed isolated, away from the girls. Sometimes though, if it had been a good night at the restaurant, or if her boss let her bring home leftovers, the three of them would set the kitchen table and have a dinner party. They would make the table look as fancy as they could with what they had: mismatched forks, chipped coffee cups, and paper placemats that Panic made with crayon-drawn flowers. Panic would gather wildflowers and arrange them in a paper cup as a centerpiece. A few times, Panic dressed up in Betsy's sequined shawl, clopping into the room in her mom's espadrille shoes, clunky high heel sandals that Panic thought were the fanciest things in their house. Then they would sit together and talk, eat until their stomachs were full to bursting, and share funny stories.

Usually, the girls told Betsy about their teachers or their adventures in the chaparral, careful not to mention any run-ins with scorpions or snakes. Sometimes Betsy would join in; she was a great storyteller under the right circumstances. She'd share about summers at Aunt Fancy's house in the mountains, or how she and her own mother set out for California, a grandma the sisters never knew, and the idea of Betsy as a child, or even when she was a baby. The sisters thought it hysterical to imagine Besty as a baby. Once, Betsy even described how she met their dad—he delivered groceries to their house when Betsy was a teen before her mother died. Though, such stories only came if Betsy had had enough wine to lubricate her generosity to share.

Nonetheless, the sisters knew a conversation could turn in an instant. Then, the worst came. Once, Betsy flipped the table over without so much as a warning. She paused, mid-sentence. Looked around at the girls, then stood up, placed her hands under the edge of the table, and flipped it over, sending dishes and food sailing. Another time, she looked across the room and plainly said, "I never should have had you kids." This made Panic gasp but then Betsy burst into a fit of laughter and passed out, face down, on her plate. More often, though, things did not go wrong—Panic reminded herself. Usually, these were good times filled with good food, good stories, and good memories. Panic loved these times.

She climbed into bed and pulled the covers over herself as PJ came in the room with the baking soda drink.

"Mom wants you to drink this," PJ said.

"PJ?" she asked her sister's name like a question.

"Yeah?"

"I heard that humans are also animals. Is that true?"

"Where do you come up with this stuff?" PJ laughed.

"We were talking about it at school. We're part of the animal empire."

"Animal kingdom," PJ corrected. "Don't you wish you were going to school today so you could learn more about that?"

"That's not what I was wondering," Panic huffed.

"What, then?"

"Well, are we the only animals that look at stars, do you think?"

"Ha!" PJ said, not at all like a laugh but more a word. "That's a funny thing to think about. Maybe you should ask Mom."

"Oh, I have something for her." Panic sprang from bed and snatched a crayon drawing off the dresser. "I want to show her what I drew." She tried to dash around her sister, but PJ grabbed her shirt.

"Drink this first."

"What is it?" Panic scrunched up her nose at the cup, knowing but pretending she hadn't heard PJ's conversation with their mom.

"Baking soda. It's for your stomachache." PJ said "stomach-ache" with a note of sarcasm.

"Ick."

"If you don't drink it, you might as well put your shoes on for school."

"Fine," Panic said, and she took the cup and swallowed the contents. "Ugh, gross!" She stuck out her tongue. Panic handed the cup back to PJ and then flew out the door to find their mom.

Down the hall and into the kitchen she went. Betsy was at the table with a dampened sponge and her stamps spread out on the table.

"Mom, look!"

"Hello, sickie," Betsy smiled. She reached out and took Panic's drawing in her hand. Panic noticed the slight tremble of the paper but dismissed the tremor for the earnest look in Betsy's eyes.

"Well, would you look at that!" Betsy said. "This is the best dragon I have ever seen."

"It's Pete's Dragon."

"I can see that." Betsy looked directly at Panic then. "But isn't that the problem?"

"What problem?" Panic's heart sank. She heard PJ somewhere by the front door getting her book bag together.

"Well, I mean, Pete's dragon is supposed to be invisible, right? You've drawn him too visible." Betsy winked at Panic and then turned the page over to show the blank side. The paper shook more as Betsy held it up facing Panic. "Ah, there he is," she said, showing Panic the blank side of the paper.

"Oh yeah," Panic said. She took the paper back and hopped into a seat at the table. "Can I help stick your stamps?"

"Sure can," Betsy said sliding a sheet and stamp book over to Panic.

PJ called out from the hall, "Bye."

"See you later alligator," Panic said, and their mom laughed.

"Imagine, alligators here in El Cajon," Betsy said. The sound of the door closing thumped from the hall as PJ left.

"Mom, did you know humans are animals?" Panic asked, setting up the booklet and lining up the stamps.

"Well, we certainly act like animals." Betsy laughed, and Panic joined her, gauging her mood.

Panic pressed, "Do you think other animals look at stars like we do?"

"Oh sure," Betsy said, pressing a section of stamps to the booklet. "I seem to remember something about whales and dolphins navigating the oceans by the stars and currents."

"Hmm," Panic thought about the ocean, big and dark. She remembered the tide pools again, and also how large the horizon had looked last night. She wanted to see it again, that place PJ had taken her. She knew she could get there on her own too; she wasn't so helpless. There was lots she could do on her own.

"That drink helped my tummy a lot." She said, already formulating her plan.

"Good." Her mom thumbed through sheets of stamps, counting under her breath. She'd started over.

"Bet some fresh air would do me some good," Panic tried.

"Uh huh," Betsy said.

"Okay, then." Panic pushed herself away from the table and the chair legs scraped loudly along the floor making her shudder. "I'll just be in the back for a bit."

"Stay close," Betsy said, but Panic was already around the corner and headed toward the back sliding glass door, already tracing the steps along the avena path from the night before. She was certain she knew the way to that outcrop of rocks and the endless horizon.

•

Panic reached the granite monolith on her own, like she knew she would. She shook the avena seeds from her hands and climbed the rock the way she had the night before. Lizards scattered.

As she crested the rock, she took in the full view of the valley that stretched out before her and the mountains to the north and south. She looked behind her and saw the top of Cuyamaca and Mount Laguna looming to the east. Then, back to the west, her eyes settled on the dark blue slice of the Pacific. She imagined whales and dolphins within its vast expanse relying on stars to move up and down the long coast they traveled, how they would teach their babies to travel the same way year after year. PJ had taught her how to find her way among these hills. She knew the landmarks, certain trees and rocks that stood out among the tawny landscape. Their backyard played host to the largest eucalyptus in their parts and was home to a nesting pair of owls. PJ had told her that eucalyptus trees were not supposed to be in California but had been brought here but people hoping to use them for timber. "The weirdest thing about them, though," PJ said, "is that they grew backward here. Twisted."

Was that what she said, Panic wondered as she thought back to PJ's explanation.

"Backwards, like, in Australia, where they belong, they grow straight. And up here, on the other side of the globe"—Panic was sure PJ had used the word "globe"—"they twist against the forces of our side of the planet. Our side is backwards to them." The explanation confused Panic but when PJ pointed out most of the eucalyptus trees in the neighborhood, showing how they grew twisted, climbing in an upward spiral, she plainly saw. Some of the trees were so twisted they looked like cruller donuts, the kind Betsy loved. Even the large eucalyptus in the backyard grew this way. But its unique structure also made it stand out as an excellent landmark.

PJ taught Panic the animal trails throughout the chaparral, too. Plus, Panic felt confident that if she had been somewhere once, she could always find her way back. She prided herself on her navigation skills—no; more like her navigation instincts. After all, she'd made it back to that viewpoint, hadn't she? She felt quite contented with herself. Sure, it had taken over an hour and she had to double back, but she never lost her nerve. Now that she had found the rock and had successfully climbed it, she wondered why PJ had waited so long to take her there in the first place. Wasn't this the best view along the whole canyon?

A jet airplane slowed itself westward toward the San Diego sky-line. Panic could make out the row of small windows along the plane. She imagined the people inside looking out and seeing their hillside and the dry riverbed, the branches of the faded wash, how they spread out as far as PJ had described. She wanted to imagine what it was like in that airplane. Heidi Hill bragged about going on a trip in an airplane. She said they gave her a TV dinner, only better, with Salisbury steak and mashed potatoes, and they brought it right to her in her seat and invited her to pick a beverage—any beverage she wanted. She said she picked cran-berry juice because she liked the color. How stupid, Panic thought. Ev-eryone knew cranberry juice was like medicine. Heidi could have picked ginger ale or Mellow-Yellow, but she chose cranberry juice.

The airplane got smaller as it flew farther west but Panic could still see the dots of windows. "Pick the ginger ale," she yelled and then laughed at herself.

Turkey vultures had found a column of air not far off and they circled upward. Panic watched them for a bit without thinking much at all. She liked the way they glided and climbed, relying on the air to hold them up with hardly any effort of their own.

Another jet plane moved across the sky toward Lindberg Field. This time, Panic imagined the people on board were all on their way to a party, maybe a big festive wedding. They'd dance and have cake and the bride and groom would kiss and drive off in a car with cans tied to the bumper. Panic leaned back deciding she'd stay a while and watch the planes and birds. It felt better than watching game shows or soap operas with Betsy, though Betsy was in a good mood.

Panic loved to spend time with Betsy when she was in a good mood. She would play games like checkers and card-match. Sometimes they'd cut pictures out of old magazines and make up their own games or stories. Once, when the Chevy still ran, Betsy took Panic into El Cajon, and they went shopping at K-Mart on Broadway. Betsy told her to pick out an entire outfit. This was not during school-shopping time, a time the family usually saved for, and Panic knew Betsy didn't have a lot of money, but she couldn't resist. She loved Garanimals clothes. Each article of clothing had a different animal type that, when matched together, made an outfit, like elephant-tagged pants went with an elephant-tagged shirt or a lion-tagged skirt with a lion top. The colors went together, and the patterns were always a perfect match, too. In this way, shopping became more like a game. Plus, it was fun to try on clothes and pretend they could afford them all. Panic ended up with a Zebra-tagged top with black buttons down the front and black capri pants that went together perfectly. She loved the outfit and wore it every day to school for a week until the kids teased her that she didn't change her clothes. They also teased her that she was poor and couldn't afford anything besides one outfit from K-Mart, which Panic learned was a "discount store."

Still, it had been a fun day with her mom, driving around El Cajon in the Chevy. They went to the Jack-in-the-Box on Second Street and got hamburgers in the drive thru. Panic had never had such a fancy meal. And the radio in the car played Andy Gibb as they drove. It had been the best day.

Now, the car sat next to the house hosting tarantula hawks and kangaroo rats. It hadn't run in over a year. Betsy took the bus to the café or sometimes walked. If the family needed to go anywhere, they took the bus. But where would they go? They had no family, besides Aunt Fancy who lived too far away to visit. They could go to the beach, but Betsy always had to work. Maybe they could sell the car, Panic thought as she watched the jet plane get smaller as it moved away from her and toward its destination, descending toward the airport. Maybe they could sell the car and go to Australia and then Panic would see how eucalyptus trees look when they grow straight up in the air.

She wondered if anyone on that airplane was from Australia, then everything changed.

A flash of bright flame and a puff of smoke burst from the plane, and a thunderous noise shook the air. Panic sat forward, eyes fixed on the aircraft. She hoped her vision betrayed her then, like she might be seeing things the way distance can make the horizon look watery. But then the plane took a dive from the sky, and it fell and fell for what seemed like a long time. When it hit the neighborhood below—the same place where PJ had pointed the night before calling it "North Park"—a cloud of black smoke grew like an angry fist. She heard a second sound, like an explosion from far off. Panic, realizing she had been frozen, stood up on the rock. She felt like she needed to do something or tell someone what she had seen. She put her hands on her head and looked around. An expansive horizon surrounded her. Her breath came in short bursts, and she felt her heart thud in her chest. She stumbled backward and slipped from the rock falling, falling in slow motion to the trail below where she had scattered the avena seeds a short while ago.

Righting herself, she shook her head. She did a quick scan of her scrapes and cuts but seemed otherwise okay—nothing broken, everything movable. She climbed the rock again to look again, but this time, her hand throbbed where she had landed on it, and she found it difficult to hold to the fissure the same way she had before. By the time she pulled herself atop the boulder again, the angry smoke had taken on an ominous shape. It rose straight up, the way a eucalyptus might grow in Australia, and it bloomed into a larger cloud at the top. The black of the cloud became a darkness Panic had never seen in the smoke from wildfires brought by the Santa Anas. She moved her hand to her mouth and covered her lips and cheek. Then, something which seemed quite incredible happened; Panic thought she saw the people from her imagination—the ones on the way to the wedding party—flying with their arms out like wings, like the turkey vultures on an updraft, upward in the plume of smoke. Only then did she let out an audible cry.

She scrambled down the rock and ran along the trail toward home. A left turn then a right. She missed where she needed to go. Her feet pounded the dirt, then hardscape, then dirt again. She looked around then doubled back seeing the people flying above her and around her at every turn. The animal trail disappeared into chaparral broom and sage brush. She'd started uphill again, which couldn't be right. Panic stopped running and spun on her heel looking in all directions. She had no idea where she had ended up. When she looked up, she saw them again, saw the people like large birds drifting upward toward heaven. They teetered as they ascended. And Panic ran from them as fast as she could run.

•

On her walk to school that morning, PJ met up with Luis and Manny Gonzáles as she often did. Manny was in her grade, and they walked together a lot. He was tall and slender with shaggy, dark hair— the way the boys wore it in Teen Beat—and his light eyes looked like glass from the bottles they recycled. He had a hint of a mustache along the upper corners of his lips, lips that PJ seemed to notice more. She thought about this and concluded that she must be noticing his lips more because of the faint mustache, though she couldn't explain the distraction beyond that. When he smiled, Manny looked down at the ground and PJ found herself growing warm and light-headed. This was one of the things that she liked best about him, his bashful grin. If she was honest with herself, she thought of touching his mouth. But she could never be so honest with herself. When this happened, she looked at the ground, too.

A few weeks earlier, Manny gave PJ a gift: a bright pink rabbit's foot key chain. PJ had never owned anything like this soft trinket, something so extra and unusual. She had no keys to put on the keychain. They didn't have a family car anymore and they rarely locked their front door. But the small rabbit's foot fit in her hand like it was made to fit, especially when she gripped it tight. There was no harm in having something extra, even if it had no purpose. Manny said its purpose was for good luck. PJ liked that idea, that she could have good luck right in the palm of her hand. She figured Manny must have known she needed that luck too. The pink of the fur was rich and vivid, a color unlike any PJ had seen in nature. It reminded her of the scratchy wool blankets the Gonzáles family had around their home, with stripes of all colors and thickness: white, red, black, and pink—this pink—ever so vivid and eye-catching. She thought of its color as she thumbed the soft rabbit's foot concealed in her pocket and caught the eye of Manny before he looked away again.

"Where's Panic?" Luis asked.

"She has a stomachache," PJ said, and the brothers nodded at each other like they understood it was something else. Boys always thought they knew more about girls than they did, PJ thought, but she kept that to herself.

She walked with them the rest of the way to school. Luis and Panic went to the same school, Madison Avenue Elementary, which was right next to Granite Hills High School. There weren't many other kids who lived up their way—certainly none up Forester Creek, their rural canyon—so the four of them had become friends and knew each other well.

"Adios, hermano," Luis said when they got to Madison Avenue.

"Don't let Mami hear you using Spanish, pendejo," Manny called after his brother. "Not at school anyway."

"¡Todavía no estoy en la escuela!" Luis called back as he jogged off toward the school yard.

"That kid, I swear." Manny turned to look at PJ but quickly looked away again. He blew his bangs out of his face with a pursed mouth. "How's your mom?" he asked as they started to walk again.

"She worked late last night. Took another cocktail shift."

"That's tough," Manny dragged his feet as they walked. "Did you get the math homework done? It seemed endless."

"I did it at school yesterday," PJ shrugged.

"Got time to help me out with mine? I couldn't figure out the last four problems."

"I might," PJ answered. "Can you get together after second period?"

"Nah," Manny said looking fully at PJ then. "We got auto shop safety. I'll see if Mr. Hinkle can walk me through it. It's okay."

"You sure?"

"Yep."

As they neared the parking lot of Granite Hills, PJ saw some of the boys that Manny hung around. They were watching the two of them walk and they started whistling and calling out in Spanish. PJ felt hot on her cheeks.

"Okay, I'll catch you later," Manny said, and he turned and moved toward the other boys.

"Bye," she said without knowing if he heard her. She stuck her hand in her pocket again and ran her thumb along the smooth fur of the rabbit's foot. She felt the tiny balls of its chain all linked together in a loop, the length of its silky fur, the tips of its claws protruding from its fluffy end. For a second, she wondered how the rabbit had died. Then the thought of good luck came to her, and she shook her head. Of course, she needed luck, or anything that might offer an advantage. One day, she would make a move, an actual move to leave this place, and not just her school either, but the valley and everything: her sick mother, the impending fear, the dead-end of their rural road, Forester Creek. A truckload of rabbits' feet would not bring enough luck to help her escape, but this one in her pocket offered a start. Eventually, she'd go the way her dad had gone, to somewhere better than where he left his family. She nodded at this thought and moved through the quad toward her first class. She passed many other students as she walked, generic faces in a sea of people. Even though she had lived in the same house since she was a baby, grew up in this part of the county, she didn't know any of these other kids. Their house was much farther away than the close-in neighborhood around the school. It had been hard to get close to the other students, and she told herself she was fine with that.

First period, she had science with Mr. Manlow. The class that day covered San Diego weather patterns and low pressure offshore. PJ loved learning where the marine layer came from and why they had "June Gloom" in spring with night and morning low clouds, Santa Ana winds in the fall, and dry hot summers. Science might have been her favorite class. She memorized the botanical names of plants, knew everything about the various habitats around San Diego, coastal, Mediterranean, chaparral, sage brush, conifer forests and deserts. She even enjoyed dissecting worms, though she would never let on that she did. Most girls in the class were squeamish about that sort of thing and PJ figured she should pretend to be, too.

The plane crash happened during second period, while PJ had P.E. Students had gathered around Coach Kendall to run laps around the track. A few students still lingered in the locker room hall and around the quad. Echoing laughter still filled the air. Inside classrooms, chairs scraped along hard floors screeching from open doors. When the loud explosion sounded everyone in the halls and along the track froze. The sound was followed by an unmistakable boom. They stared at each other wide-eyed. They all knew the sound of earthquakes as they rolled along in waves throughout the bedrock below their feet. Sometimes an earthquake could be heard from far off long seconds before its arrival; other times a quake might bubble up around them as it shook with a sudden presence. They waited to hear, to feel, to see if the buildings would move, but no other sound came. Like a thunderclap, the explosion came with more urgency than an earthquake, more like a mounting storm but without a single anvil cloud on the horizon. The sound did not come and go, but rather came then ended, an abruptness to its hallow shudder, the way Mrs. White, the music teacher, would grip the tuning fork to silence the horseplay of squirrely teens. And then the sky grew ever more eerily silent. Even the birds seemed afraid to sing lest that terrible hush find them and grip them, maybe turn them inside out.

"What was that?" a tenth grader said to a friend or to anyone. "I bet it's a bomber out at Miramar," came an answer too quick to be true. "It's not an emergency or we would have heard the bell by now." Coach Kendall told everyone to "gather up."

Quickly dismissing the fear PJ felt, she imagined the explosion was merely a sonic boom, that the other students were overreacting. "Just an earthquake," she heard the coach call out. They pulled in toward him and waited a few minutes before Coach told them to continue with their laps. As she ran, PJ picked up bits of conversation from the other students about what the noise could have been.

Over the morning, she learned that the explosion caused more questions before any answers came. Some students claimed they saw what happened; others accused them of lying. "We're at war," PJ heard a senior boy tell a group of freshmen. "We are under attack from the Ayatollah," another reported. PJ even heard, "The San Onofre Nuclear Power Plant blew up!" More guesses seemed to find their way into the students' assumptions. By then, the teachers knew the truth, whispering amongst themselves about the television in the teachers' lounge and the special broadcast. They spoke to each other and not the students. But soon the students pieced together news that a jet had crashed. It had gone down in a neighborhood within a few miles of the school, careening into houses and families, people who stayed home during the day.

PJ thought of Panic.

Finally, the school closed early, and the students were sent home. By then, PJ knew more information about the crash but without any of the details, like which neighborhood the jet careened into. The explosion seemed loud enough to be nearby, she thought. But some of the kids were saying coastal and not inland. Others said they heard the explosion so clearly because it happened right there in El Cajon. All PJ could think about was Panic. Why had she let her stay at home with that fake stomachache?

During her long walk from the high school to her house, as PJ hurried along the sidewalk, she imagined where Panic might be at that moment. She reassured herself that there was no smoke in her neighborhood, no sound of emergency sirens. Knowing Panic, she would have been in the backyard or up the hill exploring some new section of trail, especially if Betsy had started drinking.

PJ passed a telephone pole with a hand-drawn "lost dog" sign on it, featuring a five-dollar reward for a dog described "like Benji," the famous dog from the movies. Aunt Fancy had told her that Benji was not one dog, but many. Sometimes the filmmakers would get Benji into a situation that they could not get him out of, and they'd have to bring in a "backup" Benji. PJ knew what that meant but hoped that Panic couldn't also read between the lines. She got mad at Fancy for telling them about those poor dogs and ruining the Benji movies. As PJ passed the missing dog sign, she wondered if Fancy had made the whole thing up. She touched the lost dog sign with her rabbit's foot. "Good luck, Benji," she said.

She had been clutching the rabbit's foot the entire walk home and noticed its fur had become damp. She stuffed the keychain back into her pocket.

As she walked, PJ thought about Aunt Fancy and her strange ways. Fancy was her dad's sister, a bit younger than him and eccentric. She ran a lodge of sorts in the San Jacinto Mountains north of San Diego near a place called Idyllwild. PJ had gone there a few times with her family and she and her dad would explore the wilderness climbing buttes and bluffs. Panic claimed she didn't remember much about Fancy's place, so

PJ filled her in. She thought Panic would be old enough now to go exploring those dense woods. She wondered, too, if Aunt Fancy would remember them or if she thought about her nieces at all; it had been a very long time. In fact, PJ had a hard time remembering what Fancy looked like. Long hair, auburn maybe. Beyond that PJ could not form an image of her aunt. The struggle to recall her appearance made PJ's heart sink. But then she remembered why she really had that sinking feeling—the plane crash—and PJ doubled her pace. She had to get home and talk to her little sister. Panic might have seen the crash on the news and would be horrifying for the people on board. Or worse, she might have been outside when it happened. She might have seen the crash.

Santa Ana conditions brought miles of visibility. Because of this, PJ was afraid Panic would have seen the crash from their hill out back, especially if she had climbed to the boulder where they'd gone the night before. Knowing Panic, she would have wanted to catch lizards sunning on a rock. That boulder offered a great place to collect and build a small arsenal of lizards to use against Heidi Hill. Maybe, though, it was too early in the day for catching lizards, PJ hoped. Maybe Panic would have stayed around the house, cozy on the couch with Mom, snuggled under the granny-square Afghan watching Mister Rogers' Neighborhood, even though she said the show was for babies. She could imagine Panic's voice saying so, as she stood next to the T.V, changing channels yet stopping to watch the nice man change his sweater or talk to Daniel Tiger. It might be worse if Panic was with Betsy when the newsbreak came. PJ wondered if the news would interrupt whatever program they had been watching, drawing Betsy into the coverage Channel Eight had on the crash. If there was news coverage, Betsy would start drinking early and Panic would be obligated to fetch Betsy another and another until the bad news could be assuaged.

By the time PJ reached their gravel road, the heat of the day pushed the mercury upward. Forester Creek, a dead-end gravel road, wound its way up the side of Shadow Mountain to a water storage tank and pump. The tank provided water for a large portion of El Cajon's residents. It held two million gallons of water, which PJ found fascinating. She had learned about the water tank in her civics class at the beginning of the school year a few weeks earlier. Her teacher, Miss Abernathy, a young woman with startled eyes and plain, brown hair, began the term

teaching local civics before moving on to county civics, then state, feder-
al, and eventually the civic organization of other countries. PJ could not
remember how water storage tanks had anything to do with civics, but
she found it interesting to know something so specific about her own
backyard. She felt like a local celebrity when Miss Abernathy brought up
the water tank and asked if any of the students were familiar with it. Both
PJ and Manny raised their hands and gave each other knowing looks.

Besides Manny, no other high-school-aged kids lived on Forester Creek, a sparsely populated area with houses spread out along a two-
mile stretch, houses which couldn't be more different from each other.
Mrs. Stanislaw's house was first on Forester Creek and by far the nicest.
Her husband was a shift supervisor at the Convair plant where they made
airplanes and jets. They were "well off," as PJ's mom often said with a
sneer. Mrs. Stanislaw sold AVON and sometimes drove her car up and
down their desolate road looking to sell eyeshadow or rouge to a neighbor. She probably had customers up Lotus Lane across La Cresta, too, or
else PJ wondered how she could stay in business with so few customers
on Forester Creek. Not only were there not many women along their
road, but PJ's rural neighbors also did not tend toward vanity; fashion
and beauty were not essential in raising horses or growing avocados. But
Mrs. Stanislaw made sure everyone knew about the newest AVON prod-
ucts, available for women and men alike. She also told PJ that she could
come and use her phone if she ever wanted to "gab with a girlfriend," but
PJ thought that seemed weird—weird that she would ever want to talk
with someone on the phone and weird that Mrs. Stanislaw knew PJ did
not have a phone at home. But then, a lot of the homes along Forester
Creek didn't have phones. PJ wondered if many of the residents there
even knew about the plane crash. This thought made her hurry again.

After the Stanislaw place was the Minkus Farm with its vast
acreage of avocado groves. They never minded when Panic and PJ
helped themselves to a few avocados, though sometimes the girls took
the fruit uninvited. PJ worked on the farm during harvest and sometimes
after school. Mr. Minkus appreciated her help and the work, along with
its pay, always seemed to come when they needed it most. Beyond the
Minkus property lived the Gonzáles family, Manny's family. They had
a large plot of land, bigger than PJ had been able to explore. PJ's dad
once told her that all of it—the entire length of Forester Creek—had

once belonged to the Gonzáles family but, over time, people had found ways to rob them of their land either legally or illegally. Manny's family raised rabbits and chickens and sold wares at the local Swap Meet on the weekends. They made tequila, too, PJ knew because once, Manny's mom had sent a jar home for Betsy with a note that Manny had written in English thanking her for the nice treatment at the café the night before. No matter how PJ tried, Manny would not tell her more about the reason for the gift, even though he had been at the café with his family that night. But since then, it seemed whenever they needed it, Mrs. Gonzáles would send pan dulce home with the girls and sometimes fresh tortillas and tamales.

Farther up the road, past their own house, Mrs. Spencer lived with her three dogs, Roscoe, Chicken Little, and Alfred. Mrs. Spencer's husband had passed away a few years earlier and so she appreciated a little extra help around her house. PJ and Panic were all too happy to oblige. Even though Mrs. Spencer had grandkids that came to visit, she welcomed PJ and Panic whenever they came around, always finding odd jobs for them or asking if they would pick up after the dogs. Then she would send them off with a dollar or two pressed into their palms and sometimes a fresh-baked treat. She seemed to favor Panic for such treats; maybe this was due to Panic's striking wide eyes, which many folks commented were remarkable and wise for such a young girl. Mrs. Spencer called Panic's eyes, "enchanting," said Panic had "stolen her old lady heart." Panic lapped it up for the cookies and lemon bars, and PJ always appreciated making a dollar to pick up after the dogs. Roscoe was Panic's favorite dog, a soft-furred terrier. He always sat quietly next to the young girl when she ate her treat. Maybe the dog was waiting for crumbs to fall, PJ suspected, but Panic said he liked her warmth, even on hot days.

Beyond the Spencer house, there were five or six more homes and rancheros spread out along the gravel road. Where there were horses, there were fences too, like the ranches farther up from the Gonzáles' place. PJ knew of the families up that way, some of them Mexican like Manny's. Before these families lived along the hill, other people had lived there since before history was written. Kumeyaay occupied such places, making use of the perennial streams and native plants like sumac and wild cucumber. Manny told PJ that two of the families, his and one other, had been there since before the Spanish people had come and built their missions. He said his family told stories each year in November of their relatives from long ago. PJ tried to imagine a time so long ago, before the water tank even, but it was hard to put her mind around that span of history. She thought if each of her steps home from school could be years, that might be close to how long ago it had been since before the Kumeyaay learned Spanish.

She tried then, as she walked, to think about her steps as years. Counting each footfall as a period of time along the length of the road. She imagined no fences, no houses, and no road even. By the time she reached her own driveway, she had lost count among the largeness of time. By then, the sun beat down on her with nearly unbearable heat and PJ wiped the sweat from her forehead with her hand. The thick stand of live oaks, which shaded the front of the house, offered a barrier from the sun. Still, she moved quickly through the shade to the front porch and up the steps.

Inside, she found Betsy riveted to the scene on the T.V., which, as PJ thought, showed the local news. As PJ also guessed, the coffee table and floor were littered with empty beer cans.

"Where is she?" PJ asked.

Betsy's head wobbled as it turned to face PJ, which told the girl all she needed to know about the state of their mother.

"Oh my god, PJ, do you know what's happened?" Betsy slurred, ignoring the question. She gestured at the T.V., returning her gaze there once more. She took a long pull from her beer can then shook her head as the scene on the T.V. panned across fire and smoke from the crash.

"Mom, where's Panic?" PJ asked again, and she looked back and forth, between Betsy and the T.V. screen.

The static-shrouded image of a black mushroom cloud bloomed up over the houses of a charred city street; the shape of the smoke took the odd resemblance of a hand reaching westward into the sky. The reporter on the scene offered wicked descriptions of terror saying things like, "There aren't any bodies—only pieces. Just arms, legs, and feet..."

"Turn it off, Mom, please!" PJ said as she tossed her satchel down on the chair. The sound of the weighty books inside the sack hit the chair with a thwack grabbing Betsy's attention. Her head snapped around and she looked directly at PJ, the beer can in her hand tilting before she righted it and then set it on the table.

"It's just so awful, PJ. All those people." She leaned onto the arm of the couch, propped in her usual tragic pose, only now she had a reason for her melancholy. PJ knew Betsy would seize this tragedy and run with it, placating her own grief with whatever alcohol she had in the house and any she might be able to get from work or other sources, sources that PJ could not name.

PJ looked from Betsy back to the newscaster on the T.V. The man's yellow shirt clung to him, damp with sweat, and an orange and brown striped necktie hung loosened from his unbuttoned collar. He spoke into a microphone near his chin. "The heat of the fires and the sun is unbearable for the rescuers, though what is there to rescue? Our eyes are burning with the kerosene and smoke…"

"I think you should turn it off," PJ said again, this time with more pleading to her tone. She moved to stand in front of the T.V., to block her mother's view. "Has Panic been in here watching this with you?" PJ looked around but saw no sign of her sister.

"She's gone out back to her fort, I think," Betsy managed before reaching forward to grab another beer. She cracked it open and took a drink from the can. With froth clinging to the corners of her slack mouth, she started to cry. She had been crying before PJ's arrival; it was obvious. Black tracks of mascara ran down her face and along her cheeks. Her eyes were puffy, with swollen lids framed by dark circles.

PJ had no patience for the state in which she found her mother. She only wanted to make sure her sister was okay. She was not surprised that Panic was outside that morning. Betsy would not have tried to keep her inside. And Panic wouldn't have wanted to be anywhere else while Betsy got drunk. Anymore, Panic preferred to be outdoors in the wild regardless of what Betsy did. Still, PJ tried to imagine how long her sister had tolerated their mother's drunken state before she left. She knew from firsthand experience the challenges of taking care of Betsy under such circumstances. But PJ knew it could be worse. No matter. PJ only wanted her sister and not Betsy. She tried to gauge the type of consoling

Panic would need once she found her sister; for this, she looked to Betsy, examining her state while the woman sat on the couch watching the crash trauma unfold, soothing herself on sips of pity and gluttony. She thought maybe Panic left before their mother got wasted or even before the crash. Was there a chance the young girl had not seen the news? PJ needed to find out.

"I'm going to find her," PJ said, though she doubted Betsy cared. Then, she slipped out the back sliding glass door into the bright fall day and turned toward the hill behind their house.

As she climbed the buff-colored path, a siren wailed in the distance. She watched her feet as she walked and noticed black debris in the tawny gravel, gritty fragments of charcoal from a broken aquarium filter that Panic had found a few weeks earlier. She had scattered the charcoal behind their property telling PJ she wanted to ward off raccoons. PJ shook her head at the memory and tuned her ears to the wild world opening around her, listening for Panic. The siren continued to cry from far off—a lonely squalling through the heat of the day: 101 degrees by the time PJ got home from school that September afternoon. PJ hoped Panic had the sense to bring some water with her, using her scout's canteen. She had found the canteen last summer on another one of her scavenger hunts. But she doubted Panic would have thought about water if she only wanted to flee Betsy.

A breeze moved the hot air thick with the scent of sage and dust. The heat permeated her skin and hair. PJ knew this type of heat, the kind that silenced the land. Even the snakes would not come out in this temperature to sun their cool bodies on the warm granite, lest they whither like the prickly pear after a long summer drought. At least under a rock they could hide from the blazing scorch of the sun. Panic would be hiding too—PJ was sure of it—especially with no lizards to catch in that dire afternoon heat.

The words from the newscaster crept back into her thoughts as she climbed the hill. PJ had an image in her mind of an alleyway filled with limbs of people, though she could not imagine anything more real than dolls' arms and legs. She had an old Barbie who lost an arm and an image formed in her mind of a box full of lost Barbie arms, rigid and plastic with fingers fused together, a generic peach-colored flesh that matched no one's skin tone. She shook away the image and continued climbing farther up the trail. She pushed against her resisting muscles and the repelling inferno of the afternoon temperature. She longed for the gusting winds of the Santa Ana to come and blow the heat away from their hill or to, at least, move her thick hair from her neck as she walked.

When she reached a fork in the trail, she turned back to scan the earth for signs of Panic. PJ saw clouds of beige smoke swirling along the path she'd forged. A tumbleweed rolled down the hillside. Along the silty trail, dust had kicked up in tiny puffs as she trudged, puffs that hung in the air like incomplete magic spells. Nearby, she saw tennis shoe prints, Panic's size. They could have been there from a thousand different adventures into the thicket, but PJ knew her sister well enough, knew where she'd be headed. She tried to imagine Panic, if she knew about the crash, and she followed the tracks toward a place where they talked about building a new fort but had never started the project.

"Panic!" she called out and a memory came to her as she said the name. It began as a simple thought, but one that brought PJ hope on such a low day. She thought of her sister's laughter in her younger years. Panic's giggle, a six-year-old chortle with a pitch that matched the thrasher as it warbled a spring song. And younger still, Panic's baby giggle. Both sounds had the gift of making everything seem light and funny. The memory reassured PJ that she followed the right tracks in the dirt, but it also made her wonder what had been so funny then, in that memory so long ago. Images of their kitchen flashed in her thoughts. They had been making noodles, egg noodles; the buckled shape of the pasta grew vivid in PJ's mind. Panic had taken a few noodles and stuck them to her eyebrows. They laughed about the silliness of it. In all their mirth, PJ forgot that, after she drained the pasta, she had placed the empty pan back on the burner of the stove and left the burner on high. As the girls ate their pasta and continued with their silly game of sticking the curvy noodles to their cheeks like sideburns, to their upper lips like fat mustaches, the pan continued to heat. Eventually, the pan overheated and began to smoke. By the time PJ noticed the smoke, the burning smell was all through the kitchen. She grabbed the hot handle of the pan then and thrust it under running water only to have the water steam up in protest to the quick cooling. As Betsy rushed into the kitchen, the billowing vapor filled the air with plumes of steam and an acrid smell.

The memory halted her. PJ stopped walking and stood still, like a jackrabbit wary of a circling hawk.

She liked to believe her mother did not mean to lose control that day in the kitchen. The smell of smoke and the rising cloud of steam had scared Betsy—that was all. Besides, PJ had been the one who left the burner turned on, the one who forgot about it allowing it to get white-hot on the unattended flame. The threat of fire scared Betsy and, of course, she needed to teach PJ a lesson. PJ had learned it, too. She never forgot to turn off the stove from that day.

In another memory, PJ heard her dad say, "Some people need more space for their anger." Betsy's anger did not mean she loved PJ any less. Their mother wanted her to understand that she could have hurt herself or Panic. It was a lesson PJ had learned, too, ever vigilant and attentive with the stove since she was eleven years old.

As she resumed her walk, climbing the hill, PJ's thoughts returned to Panic. She wondered what Panic might be thinking then as the world filled with updates of death and tragedy. She tried to imagine her sister's experience, having been at home all morning with their mother glued to the news and nursing beers. PJ started up a steeper section of the hill and she remembered why they had not built a fort there. With each step along the trail, a slide of her foot scattered the gravel and mocked her determination. She almost fell, and her heart jumped in her chest, beating out the type of signal that warned of something terrible. In truth, a terrible thing had already happened: a passenger jet had collided with a smaller plane in midair; this much she had pieced together from the newscast report and the kids and teachers at school. The two aircraft had exploded upon impact and then careened into a neighborhood below taking out blocks of homes and killing moms and grandmothers and pets—no telling how many yet. She heard the voice from the T.V. echo in her head, the deadpanned words: "There aren't any bodies—only pieces . . ."

"Panic!" she yelled against the hillside. She cursed herself for encouraging Panic to be a good hider the day before. A bird, too quick to identify, fluttered from a bush and sprang skyward. In her distraction toward the bird, PJ considered the strangeness of yelling the word "Panic" to the world during this surreal tragedy. She tried to reconcile the number she heard: "over a hundred passengers..." She considered counting her steps again.

"Panic!" she yelled again.

Then she saw it: a glint of blue, a swatch of familiarity, Panic's t-shirt! PJ remembered Panic doubled over with the false tummy ache that morning. Through the foliage of the lemonade berry branch, just off the trail, the flash of blue seemed to say, "Come and find me; I knew you'd come." There inside the bush, the very place where they had planned their next fort, she could see the huddled shape of her sister.

Renewing her efforts against the heat and exerting herself over the rocky obstacles that increased in difficulty as she left the main trail, PJ climbed on. She knew this place, though not as well as some of the other places they frequented. Still, the shady area ahead was a haven where small animals could take refuge, to be tucked away from possible attacks or threatening elements.

"Panic!" PJ called out again. The escarpment leveled. The slightest breeze tickled the leaves with the first exhalation of relief parting the stagnation of hot air for something fresh and new.

When PJ reached her, she saw Panic had curled into a ball, holding her knees to her forehead with her arms wrapped around her shins. Nestled into the base of a towering laurel sumac that neighbored the lemonade berry, Panic looked like any other small animal. She merged with the dark chaparral, its leafy arms canopied above and around her. Instead of calling out again, PJ moved the lower boughs of the dark sumac, green and thick, and ducked down, creeping into the safe recess to join her. She sat down burrowing in close to her sister and put her arm around the mouse of a girl. Panic was crying with muffled exhaustion, as if she had been crying for a long while. At this, PJ assumed her sister had seen the crash either from their hill or on T.V.

"I know you saw it, Panic." PJ steadied her voice to her gentlest tone. "I heard about it at school and the first thing I thought of was you sticking your head up out of some bush the moment you heard the bang. Or else you were up on that rock I took you to last night." PJ scooted closer, the gravel of granite pressing into her legs through the denim of her Dittos.

"I wanted to know if I could get that far on my own." The little girl sniffed. "Please don't be mad."

"I'm not mad," PJ gave a shrug. "I just want you to be safe. Nobody knows these hills better than us, right?"

Panic nodded then tucked her head down again.

"Listen," PJ said. "I know there's a lot to understand about life and death. We don't even need to talk about that now. Let's just be glad we're okay. Okay?"

For a moment nothing stirred, and the world seemed to wait for Panic to speak. When she finally did, her voice was shadowy, like the first breath of a breeze after a heatwave.

"PJ." She waited a moment. "I saw the smoke from far away. I saw the angels zipping away just after the fire went out of the sky." Her voice gained urgency. "The angels were zigging and zagging all over the sky. The plane was gone already but the angels kept swooping. I saw it, PJ."

"I know you did," PJ said. Panic lifted her head slightly. She glanced sideways at PJ from between her long, bushy bangs. PJ continued, "I also know that Mom's had the news on all day since then, and she's been drinking. And I'm guessing you don't feel good now, for real."

"The cloud came like a black hand reaching up to the sky," Panic said with terrible awe, and she held her hand up looking at her own fingers. "The cloud was the worst part. The angels were all swooping and soaring, and I thought the hand wanted to grab them back."

PJ looked at Panic's hand too, as if it told the entire story of the crash. Then Panic pulled her hand back in close and she leaned into PJ. PJ leaned closer to her sister taking in her temperature. Even in the heat of that early autumn day, feeling Panic's warmth—along with the cool shade of the sumac that leafed out above them—seemed essential to PJ. Water and air and good food and her sister's warmth.

In a shift, Panic moved one arm, the one closest to PJ, and wrapped it around her sister's back pulling her nearer. The world paused with them, like they needed the moment to collect themselves, to reflect on what had happened, and to prepare for what was to come. PJ wasn't even sure they were still breathing then, nor did she think the birds flew, the ants crawled, the world turned.

The sound of a jackrabbit scampering nearby broke the silence and Panic spoke again. She asked, "Will you tell me about our dad?"

PJ eyes found a lone honeybee drifting lazily around the leaves above them. She watched it dip and glide then fly off before she answered Panic. "Sure," she said as her own tears came, welling along her bottom lashes then spilling down her cheeks. She pressed Panic closer to her. "Well, you already know his name is Chet, or Chester, really. He's tall and funny, like Lenny on Lavern and Shirley."

"Only not dumb," Panic added quickly.

"Goodness, no. Not dumb like Lenny!"

Panic giggled at this, a happy thrasher sound that lifted her mirth like a song, and PJ swallowed hard. She wanted to tell Panic that their dad had come back from Vietnam a changed man, that he flinched when Betsy yelled, went into distress mode when she threw flowerpots and frisbeed vinyl records at him. Instead, PJ stayed quiet listening to the blackbird sing its song, "poke your neighbor." Finally, Panic nudged her to continue, and PJ's words came out strained. "He likes basketball and Bill Walton. He likes to fly airplanes—"

"Was he flying today?" Panic asked.

"No," PJ assured her, though how could she know? "No, today he was helping orphans in Mexico." She smiled at her own invention. She wasn't sure where the story had come from, but this new fiction came easy, so she continued. "Today he is in Ensenada at Sangre de Cristo helping out the holy sisters with all of their many children who have no dads at all."

"And he's building fences?" Panic asked, sounding hopeful.

"Sure, and taking care of the chickens, because you know they have so many chickens that the children can't possibly name them all."

"But Dad has named a few, right?" Her eyes sparkled at PJ. "There's Henrietta, Helen, Beatrice, and of course the rooster. His name is Manuel."

"You think so, huh? Manuel?" And they both laughed.

"Like Manny, but not as handsome," Panic said.

"Oh, you think Manny is handsome?" PJ pushed her sister lightly. "Do you want to tell me about this crush you have."

"Not me. You," Panic said, her eyes alighted with mischief. They both blushed into their laughter.

The sisters stayed there long into the afternoon spinning fantastic tales about their dad and his great adventures in Mexico. The Santa Ana winds had picked up and the smell of the mountains swept by on a trek toward the ocean. Panic and PJ spoke in hushed voices about the invented life of a man they could no longer know. All the while, PJ had an image in her mind of what the world looked like from up there, sitting in the passenger seat of a white and tan Cessna, an airplane so light her dad could move it with his own strength on the ground. She imagined herself looking out the window at the sun-bleached colors of the landscape. Her dad had flown her up there. She remembered the washes, dried riverbeds where the colors streaked like swirling paint before they desiccated to sand. She could not remember what their house looked like—maybe because the oak trees hid it from view, or maybe because she simply couldn't remember—but she had clear recall of the bird's eye view of the hill where she and her sister sat close together beneath the sumac, anchored to the earth. Over and over, she imagined the view of El Cajon— the box—from an airplane. PJ saw inside the box, too; two timid animals tucked away within those walls, near the churning Pacific to the west, the unknown southern highlands of Mexico, and the towering mountains to the east and north. They were like two huddled rabbits, contented in the chaparral that concealed them, unseen in the vast wilderness, anonymous creatures sewn into a blanket of earth, barely on a map.

CHAPTER THREE

As the girls headed down the hill toward home, Panic took in the glow that washed the sky in orange hues turning pink near the horizon. The setting sun caught the smog and dust that had blown west over the Pacific and the entire world glowed in a strange radiance. High veins of cirrus clouds bled crimson across the zenith then faded to the darkness rising from the east. Nightfall would come before they'd reach the back porch, but their conversation had been worth the late return home.

Panic felt a little surprised that the talk about their dad felt okay. Most of their conversation was light. But a few thoughts still bothered her. Her memories of their dad were not as happy as PJ's. She had no clear image of Dad—what he looked like—but she remembered feeling afraid of him. She also felt glad he was gone.

From what she remembered, if she really tried to think back, Chet was a fireball of emotion, hurtling out of control through their lives, igniting everything he touched. Panic was five years old when he left. Maybe she didn't have the clearest recall of what he looked like or how he talked or laughed, but she had a clear memory of the calm that came to their home after he was gone. The difference was striking. Before, there was only chaos, loud noises, yelling, breaking bottles and broken glass. He shoved their mom around, too, like she was in his way. He made Betsy cry. Panic thought he made PJ cry too, but PJ didn't seem

to remember those times, or at least she didn't talk about them. For all
the grief her sister shared about her sorrow since he left, Panic was the
opposite, never sad for his absence. In fact, she sometimes felt afraid he
would come back. That was when the guilt was unbearable.

One memory that stood out clearly from after he left was not
of her dad at all but of Betsy standing alone in the dark kitchen in the
middle of the night. Panic had gotten out of bed, as she sometimes did
back then. She would often go into PJ's room and crawl into bed with
her sister. But on this night, she heard some soft sounds coming from
the kitchen. As she walked down the hall, her bare feet padding along in
the dark, the sounds became more pronounced. Her mom was humming
a song. When Panic got to the kitchen, she peered around the doorway
into the galley and saw Betsy standing, swaying, bathrobe askew, hanging
off one shoulder and dragging on the floor. A wine bottle hung in her
hand and the liquid that remained sloshed around as Betsy swayed and
sang. When she turned around so that Panic could see her face, her eyes
were closed, and her cheeks shined with tears. Panic knew the song, too.
"Yesterday," by The Beatles.

A curious fear gripped Panic then, like she didn't know how to
take care of Betsy the way her mom had taken care of them—her and
PJ. If she had a skinned knee or a bee sting, Betsy hugged her until she
stopped crying, scraped the stinger out with a knife. But this was a type
of crying Panic had not seen before. Even as little as she was, she knew
she did not recognize the emotion Betsy expressed then. Panic wanted to
reach out to her mom and tell her that it was okay. She felt guilty that she
was glad Chet had left. Panic was afraid of him, afraid of his loud voice
and unpredictable moods. She tried to imagine how she might comfort
Betsy, go to her and say that they were better off that he left gone, that
he had only hurt them, but the truth was, she could see how much pain
Chet's leaving had caused her mom. Panic could not deny that fact, seeing Betsy swaying in the moonlight. From that moment, she knew that
when he came back, she would never accept him, never love him for
what he had done to her mom. Or maybe that was how her younger
self remembered it. She was bigger now, her memories cast through the
lens of her now nine-year-old view. She still resented her dad for leaving
but never lost the gratitude that he was gone. He could never hurt them
again. He could never hurt her mom again, she hoped. Let him stay in

Mexico, or wherever he had gone. She didn't need him. Her sister didn't need him. Their mom didn't either.

Their mom. She wondered what condition they would find Betsy in. She had been so light and carefree that morning, laughing about invisible dragons while gluing stamps in a booklet. The residual taste of baking soda, acrid and bitter, returned to her and she became aware of her hunger. Panic wondered what PJ might find in the cupboards to make for dinner. A can of pork-n-beans might be all. And her sandwich from earlier was tucked into the fridge. Lots of government cheese was left; that would help. She knew her sister would give her the lion's share if there wasn't much else. Panic stumbled in the low light along the trail and PJ grabbed her elbow to steady her as they walked.

"I'll make us some beans for dinner," PJ said, reading Panic's thoughts.

"Think mom's still around?" Panic asked. The question meant more than whether their mother was still at home or if she had decided to go to work. Betsy might have passed out already or she was still drinking, maybe even moving on to harder alcohol by then or out looking for something quicker than booze.

"She's probably up but she'll skip dinner." They both knew that when their mom drank, she did not eat. This pattern was reliable. There would be enough pork-n-beans for Panic to have a full belly by the end of the meal. PJ would get a decent fill, too. Betsy would rely on the calories in the booze for sustenance.

By the time they reached the back sliding glass door, darkness washed the land. Coyotes yipped in the distance. An owl issued a call that matched the pitch of the heavy door gliding in its groove as Panic pulled it open. The girls passed through the thick drapery and found the room within shrouded in darkness, the T.V. off. As she and her sister slipped through the room to the kitchen, Panic heard the familiar snores of Betsy, face-up on the couch. By then she could make out the shape of her mom there, too. She thought to pull the Afghan over her before moving into the kitchen.

"You hungry?" PJ whispered.

"Starving," Panic mouthed.

"Let's see what we have," PJ turned on the small light near the stove. This, the dimmest light in the house, permitted PJ to move about the kitchen without causing a bright disruption to Betsy's slumber in the other room. She could see enough by the low light to discern between the rolled oats and the can of Savarin coffee. She moved the coffee aside and found the can of beans tucked into the back corner of the cupboard. PJ pulled a saucepan from the lower cupboard, careful to avoid any clattering. She set the pan atop the stove and then started the burner below the pan, checking the low flame. A hand-crank can opener lived in a permanent spot atop the golden Formica counter near the sink. PJ felt for it, and then clipped the device to the can.

As she cranked the handle, PJ looked out the kitchen window. There was not much to see there. Besides the darkness, the window hosted a view of the slat-board shed in the side yard, one that her dad had built too close to the house. She could barely make out the vertical boards stretching from corner to corner. PJ could not be sure what her father stored within the shed. An infestation of black widows had taken over the interior and no one dared try to investigate its contents since her father left. She remembered they once had yard tools and an old rototiller. Those items would certainly be in there, but, besides the spiders, what else could be hiding in that space, PJ wondered.

As she gazed at the vertical lines through the evening's cloak, she noticed something else. Her reflection gazed back at her. The last time she noticed her reflection in that window, the top of her head only barely crested the mid-frame, but now it exceeded that mark by what seemed to be a considerable measure, maybe a few inches. She found it interesting that she hadn't noticed until now.

"I'm taller," PJ said in a plain voice, abandoning the whisper.

"Yep," her sister said, popping herself atop the opposite counter behind PJ to sit on the Formica. PJ now saw Panic's reflection in the window, too, a smaller version of herself, seemingly perched atop her own shoulder. The illusion took on the effect of an angel or devil, like in the Tom and Jerry cartoons when the red-clad imp showed up encouraging bad behavior or the angel appeared heralding virtue. She laughed at this thought.

"What?"

"Nothing," PJ smiled. "I just thought of something silly."

"Well, come on then."

"You know when Tom and Jerry have the angel and devil show up on their shoulders? I just thought you looked like that in my reflection."

Panic tipped her head. "Am I a devil or an angel?"

"Well, neither." PJ stirred the pot.

"What if I'm both?" Panic asked.

"What would you tell me? I mean, if you were my conscience, how would you . . ." She paused and thought about how to form her words. "What would you want me to do? Pick something that you know I would have a hard time doing."

"You should kiss Manny," Panic blurted and then covered her mouth with her hands.

PJ turned her head to look back over her shoulder at her sister. The small girl fought to hide her glee at what she'd said.

"Oh, you think so, do you?"

Panic nodded.

"Who's talking? Are you the devil or the angel?"

"Both!" Panic said then giggled like a wind chime blown by the Santa Ana.

A grumble came from the living room and PJ froze. Panic also went silent and regained her composure. She slipped quickly off the countertop.

Returning to the whisper, Panic leaned in and chided, "best not cross either." A saying PJ recalled from that cartoon or another. Panic shook her head with a precocious nod that seemed to belong to someone else.

PJ watched her sister for a long moment trying to decide if it had been the devil to encourage such words from her sister. She and Manny were close friends; this was true. But to think about him in a romantic way, the way people fell for each other on T.V. shows like The Love Boat or Fantasy Island, seemed silly. She brought down two bowls from the shelf above the sink and scooped the beans into the bowls making sure that Panic received the larger portion. She might have a devil in her to make her say such crazy things, PJ thought, but her sister still needed to eat enough to satisfy her hunger. PJ could assuage her own hunger in other ways.

They sat at the kitchen table and ate in silence, only sounds of spoons scraping ceramics. The jet crash seemed unreal by then, like something they had watched in a movie, part of a story they had only heard about, but in the back of her thoughts, PJ remembered the horrified expression of the news reporter as he described the scene from earlier that day. Panic's question about their dad also replayed in PJ's thoughts, "Was he up there?" She glanced across the table at her sister dragging her finger inside the empty bowl then licking the sauce she scraped. Had her dad been flying? The news said a smaller aircraft had collided with the jet. A smaller aircraft like the one her dad used to fly. PJ thought about turning on the T.V. but would not dare disturb her mom on the couch. Instead, she gazed at Panic amused by her little sister's playfulness.

Noticing PJ's attentive gaze, Panic touched a bit of sauce to her own cheeks. "Look, I'm blushing. Manny, oh, Manny—" Suddenly Panic's brown eyes grew large and terrified as she looked to a place behind PJ. She shook her head slightly, and reached out her small, sticky hand.

Then the world erupted in pain. Time slowed and raced at once.

PJ did not know a shoe had hit her until the second or third blow. It connected at the arch of her temple, that place where worried people rub with absent-minded circles. Its force knocked her to the floor. As the shoe hit her again—this time in the shoulder, the next in the arm—she became afraid. Each thump arrived with an urgent power, colliding with her body. Every blow sent a searing shock of agony through PJ's shoulders, spine, skull. She moved her arms around her head to stave off the blows.

Drunk with booze and rage, Betsy beat PJ with the shoe, an espadrille sandal with a thick sole, the strap looped around the back of her hand. She came at PJ with a raw volume of howling screams; shrieks exploding in a cacophony of chaos that matched her pounding. When she connected with PJ's head, the sound of sharp clangs rang out in PJ's ears with a deep, resonating thrum, but Betsy's voice was all shrill and high. She bellowed in mangled grievances, base noises and grunts that held no shape of words. None of it made sense.

By then, PJ reached through the pain to connect with something concrete, cohesive. She wanted to make some sense of this attack. Before the assault, PJ had been looking at Panic. . . Panic! Where was she now?

From the floor, PJ turned her face upward so she could see Betsy. Tiny details zoomed at her: the smell of booze and sweat, greying auburn hair flying wildly, broken capillaries in the whites of Betsy's eyes—whites that had picked up quite a bit of yellow in recent weeks. PJ saw the shoe then, that espadrille, its tawny leather straps and jute-wrapped wedge held aloft, suspended in the moment. She noticed its gold buckle, hoped that buckle would not pierce her skin. And PJ wondered at the shoe. Somehow, in all the chaos as it exploded and re-exploded around her, she wondered why Betsy came at her with a shoe—this particular shoe—and how she could fix this situation that had suddenly gone so wrong. Then, PJ heard something beyond her own terror and pain, beyond her mom's drunken screaming and the explosion of internal and external noise. A single word sounded from the din like the rasping of saw-teeth as they cut wood.

"Shoe," Betsy grunted from the melee. PJ heard the word.

In that brief moment, between catching and losing her breath, PJ was granted a possible reason for her mom's assault. The shoe was not only her weapon of choice this time, it was the key. The shoe could offer some clue for Betsy's fit of rage and could also mean that PJ might learn what it was she had done to warrant this punishment. She needed a reason. Even in that instance, PJ desperately sought a reason. Without a reason this sort of thing could happen at any time, a more frightening possibility than the events that were unfolding. Being beaten for something that she had done—deserving the thrashing—meant that she was not simply hitting her because Betsy needed an outlet for her own anguish. Perhaps PJ had found the shoes while cleaning up and not put them away. Maybe one was missing. It could have been any number of things, but at least PJ could center on a reason; Betsy had said, "shoe" and that was something better than another meaningless eruption of anger that had slipped the bonds of her alcohol barrier.

Then a smaller voice spoke. Panic's soft but clear words rose from across the room. PJ heard her say, "It is your shoe, Mama."

A new horror took PJ; Panic might also be in danger. Peering out from beneath her shelter of folded arms, she saw Panic fox-holed between the dining room chair and wall, an earnest plea shaping her wide eyes.

Stay quiet, PJ thought before another strike to her mouth dizzied her. PJ felt the skin of her lower lip throb as the room swam into grey, tasted the tin of blood. Then another blow hit below her left eye and the room splintered then swirled into blank space.

•

Panic had slipped beyond terror and felt instead a strange calm as Betsy moved away from PJ's motionless form. Her mom lumbered out of the room making some commotion as she went. Panic heard the bedroom door down the hall slam shut, then she sprang to action. She rushed to her sister's side and scooped her hand under PJ's neck.

"PJ." she said with urgency. "PJ, wake up."

Thankfully, PJ stirred. She murmured and groaned. Her mouth bled and her temple had already started to turn a deep pink color.

"Can you talk?" Panic asked. She pressed her fingers to PJ's neck like she had seen on T.V. shows, to check for a pulse, only Panic did not know what to feel and instead she felt PJ's larynx. It vibrated as PJ moaned.

"Just breathe, okay?" Panic said. "Just stay there and breathe." She got up and ran to the sink filling a coffee cup with tap water. When she returned, PJ had rolled over on her side. She moaned as Panic knelt next to her and asked if she could sit up and sip some water.

"No," PJ said plainly, and Panic was relieved for the clear answer.

"Are you hurt much? Do you need a doctor?" When Panic said this, she felt her own throat catch, constricting like she might cry. But she needed to be brave for PJ.

"No." PJ said.

Panic thought maybe she should go to Mrs. Stanislaw down the street and ask to use her phone to call an ambulance, or else see if she might come over to check on PJ. The swelling on PJ's temple and along her cheek continued to rise. The cut on her lip oozed red.

"Should I get help?"

"No." PJ said again, and Panic wondered if that might be all she could say. But PJ pushed herself up and managed through strained lips, "Help me?"

Panic got under her sister's arm and helped the bigger girl up. They stumbled together into the hallway and then PJ's bedroom where, to Panic's relief, she was able to help PJ into bed. She pulled down the blankets from under PJ's body, which was more difficult than she thought it would be. She pulled off PJ's shoes before pulling up the blankets up to her chest.

As soon as PJ had settled, Panic ran to the hall closet and found a few old towels. She went to the kitchen. One towel she wet under the running faucet and the other she laid flat on the countertop. She went to the ice box and grabbed the trays of ice cubes; grateful they had been refilled the last time they were used. She cracked the ice trays into the flat towel and then twisted the towel making an ice sack. It was not perfect, but it would do. She returned to the bedroom and used the wet towel to wipe her sister's cuts, cleaning the blood on her face and mouth. Next, Panic put the towel filled with ice on PJ's temple and cheek and she held it there.

With nothing left to do but hold steady, Panic started to cry. But the sounds of her crying roused the older sister and PJ brought her hand up and absently patted Panic's arm. So, Panic held her breath. She could cry at another time. Right now, PJ needed her to be strong. She sat steadily holding the ice to PJ's face and holding her breath to keep from crying and holding the emotions and thoughts in her tiny mind to keep the feelings away. Her eyes came to the spines of the magazines in the corner, a stack of National Geographics that PJ had brought home from school. How silly, Panic thought, that she would carry those heavy things so far across town and up their street. She glanced back at PJ and the fear rushed in, pain and sadness, and emotions that moved through her like a wave, so she looked back to the spines of the magazines, their black words against the yellow of National Geographic. PJ had arranged them in order from January to July. Such a clever thing to do, Panic marveled.

"January," Panic read. Then, "Northeast, Moscow, Zulu, The Hudson . . ." Zulu, she thought. They were in Africa, somewhere in Africa. Africa is a continent filled with countries. She glanced at PJ, saw the red on the towel, how the melting ice carried the color through the fabric, spider-webbing it out in diffused proof of pain. "The Hudson." Was that a river? She thought she knew. Then, "Crocodiles, Milford Track, Flight." How smart of National Geographic to print their topics along the spine. And all that just in January! She read the next, and the next, saw topics like eagles and Spain and the continental shelf. Sometimes PJ stirred. Sometimes she cried, cried in her sleep like some horrible dream held her captive and she could not wriggle free. When she cried, Panic leaned forward and whispered in her ear, "you're okay. It's okay, PJ. I'm here." And she patted her sister's hand and held the ice on PJ's face until her own hand started to buzz with the immobility of her care. So, she got up, and got some new towels. Refilled the empty ice trays and replaced them in the freezer, scolding herself for not thinking to do so earlier. She returned to PJ's bedside with fresh towels and a damp washcloth that she folded up and placed on PJ's brow. Panic stayed there long into the night. When she started to feel scared or shaky or even tired, she reminded herself that she had to be strong, that she had an important job to do, to take care of PJ. It was her turn to be the big sister. PJ continued to cry off and on, and Panic whispered small words to her about how she was okay, how she would be okay, about how she wasn't alone—all the things she thought she might need to hear if she was the one in the bed. And she herself did not cry, not really. Not out loud, anyway.

She thought of the angels then, the ones above the plane crash. Angels that even then might be circling still ever higher on their way toward heaven.

•

When PJ woke a familiar mouse of a girl smiled down at her from the moon and stars of PJ's oblivion. Panic's cheeks were wet with tears. Her small, cool hands gently touched PJ's forehead and stroked the hair around her sister's face. A wet rag, blood-stained and heavy, moved in and out of PJ's vision. The poster of Leif Garrett blurred into view on the wall by her bed. She was in her own room. She remembered she had been in the kitchen before but couldn't remember why. It seemed important to remember; she had been there earlier eating dinner with Panic. The harder PJ tried to remember, the quicker the pain arrived. What happened? She looked at Panic. If words were spoken then, PJ would never recall them. Instead of hearing, she sank backward once again into the darkness of sleep, a slumber that held her tight and removed her again from the searing ache of consciousness.

PJ slept without dreams.

The next morning, Betsy's profile loomed in PJ's fuzzy vision, replacing the careful, caring expression of Panic. Her mom glanced toward her, a moon's face swimming into focus, and PJ could see that Betsy's eyes were red and swollen, and also full of remorse. The same broken capillaries still lined the whites of her eyes, and dark circles pooled beneath them. Unlike Panic, she did not look at PJ for long, did not examine her, but instead she looked away to a place on the wall or at some far-off memory in her mind. She blinked and it seemed an audible sound emitted from Betsy's eyes, a moist click almost imperceptible, but PJ heard it. A more pronounced sound came from Betsy's parched mouth, framed by her chapped lips which parted as her tongue smacked within the thick roof of her mouth, such a thirsty sound. Her cheeks displayed broken blood vessels too, red and veiny like evil spiders had taken up residence there across her blotchy skin. Her eyes flitted to PJ's then quickly looked to her own hands, wringing them as if she could squeeze the betrayal out of them, as if they caused her such misery she needed to push the malice out. She kneaded them into submission. PJ watched Betsy grip her fingers, a new wince twisting her face, the wrinkles near her eyes and brow creasing ever deeper in her contemplated anguish. Or at least that's the way PJ saw her then or remembered seeing her. Her mom's glance shifted again nervously traveling the room, then away.

When Betsy's voice came, the sound seemed to ring in PJ's ears. Until she heard Betsy's voice, PJ didn't know how necessary the silence had become. At once, she longed for calm, as the vibration of noise—even such subtle, fluttering sounds as the dry leaves of words from her mom's lips—caused her great dizziness and nausea. And yet, PJ also longed to hear her talk, explain, soothe. She wanted her mom's comfort.

"PJ," Betsy started. "I didn't know who I was," she said with a croaky voice, gravelly like the road to their house under the march of her thick waitress shoes. Her gaze stayed fixed on her hands as she wrung them. She had started to rock back and forth. Then she held her hands still for a moment, but because the shaking of her fingers became immediate, she called the wringing back. "PJ," she said again, though she stopped with her daughter's name this time.

PJ made no attempt to respond. Couldn't. Instead, she felt remorseful. Strangely, PJ was the one who burned with guilt at that moment; she couldn't stop herself. She wanted to make it okay for her mom. She didn't enjoy seeing Betsy agonize over what had happened. PJ wanted only for Betsy to love her, to comfort her, to crawl into that tiny bed, wrap her in her arms—shaking or not—even as much as that would have hurt her already-aching body. She longed to hear her mom tell her that she was safe and that she would always protect her from the evils of the world, even if that evil was Betsy herself.

A new emotion had also begun to bud and sprout from deep within PJ that she couldn't quite discern or name, one she had never felt before. It grew from within her like a vine climbing up from somewhere deep in her soul. PJ started to feel embarrassed. She felt embarrassed for making her mom suffer, like PJ had been the one to inflict the pain on Betsy, like PJ had been the one who delivered this anguish. PJ longed to end Betsy's suffering and knew she could if only she could get up. Yet, she felt weak and sick and small. Or maybe she was embarrassed that she hadn't been strong enough to take the beating that Betsy had needed to vent after watching the plane crash coverage on the news all day, the cans collecting with her tears near the couch.

"Mom . . ." PJ managed, though it came out more as a groan and PJ felt frail and useless.

Betsy's troubled eyes connected with PJ's and rested there before she stood. She rocked on her heels for a moment, her hands trembling again before she started clutching them again.

Afraid Betsy would leave, PJ attempted to speak again, "Mom." She didn't know if she could speak but felt more afraid to not try.

Betsy wrapped her arms around her own torso. She continued to rock, forward and backward, in a motion that reminded PJ of a teeter-totter—so far forward, then so far back. PJ thought Betsy might tip over. Even through her swollen eyelids, she could see Betsy's skin held a yellow hue—the same color PJ noticed in Betsy's eyes. She wore a terry-cloth bathrobe that was stained down the front with old coffee and other, sloppier drinks. Her auburn hair gave way to thick straws of grey, wiry like a witch's, or like the witches PJ had seen in the production of Macbeth, the high school play from last spring. Three witches around a trash-bin cauldron, their appearance merely a caricature of sorcery without the threat of anything truly frightening. PJ could have been one of those witches, worrying over a fat pot of frogs and newts. Panic could have been a witch, too. And Betsy was certainly a witch, casting spells that made PJ feel the guilt for this crime. Instead of casting spells, Betsy rocked and bobbed, silently assessing the mess she had made, perhaps even calculating when she could get her hands on another bottle.

The trauma came back to PJ like a wave, an unavoidable surge of terror. The image of the shoe, the third first blow, came at her, only this time it existed in her thoughts where it didn't inflict its damage in the physical realm but instead wreaked havoc in PJ's psyche. It came into her mind as if she were struck again and again. Contrary to her visions, her mom stood quite fixed then, continuing with her swaying motion, no weaponized shoe in her hand. Yet, PJ flinched as if smacked; she flinched again as if hit by her temple, which is where the first blow landed. She recalled with such clarity she felt the imagined blow and she winced. Then, as if Betsy had hit her again, as if she struck PJ again and again with the shoe, PJ called out in agony at the memory.

Betsy froze in place, the bobbing and swaying coming to a halt. Her mouth hung agape. For PJ, the entire room collapsed into the memory of the day before, the trauma of it swallowing her. Even though she lay safely in that bed, she squeezed her eyes shut and brought her arms up around her head again, despite the part of her rational thinking which knew that she was only reliving yesterday's terror and memories. The abuse became real and threatening all over again. Each sound replayed in PJ's mind, but at a higher volume; each sensation of pain reenacted, but with more intensity. A physical reaction accompanied the memory as it came, so real that she writhed in her bed, her arms shielding her head and face.

Betsy's expression turned from shock to horror, warping her face as PJ screamed in pain. Then PJ cried with such a terrible moaning and wailing. She lamented for her suffering and for her mom's suffering, too. To the latter, she cried more, feeling she had betrayed herself for taking pity on her mom and feeling she had betrayed Betsy for taking pity on herself. After all, hadn't Betsy been the one to bring this on? Yet, PJ wailed on and on, sobbing long into sleeping, until the flashback of her terror faded and intermingled into a restless state of unease. Replaced by vivid dreams of the hill in her backyard and its great expanse of chaparral, her sleep was filled with chittering birds, bounding rabbits scattering for safety, and the recurring vision of a coyote with a squirrel hanging limp in its jaws.

The next time she woke, Panic was there, that sweet little mouse, with her cool hands and soft, brown eyes.

"I didn't know you could cry in your sleep," Panic said. "Well, I don't mean just you. I mean anyone. But I mean, you were sleeping, and you were crying at the same time, PJ. It was terrible." She leaned over and touched her sister's face and hair like she had earlier, careful to avoid the swollen cheek, the fat lip. Then she sighed and her eyes filled with tears. "It was terrible," she repeated, only quieter the second time, and PJ knew she meant something different. "Are you very hurt?" she asked, though barely forming the words. PJ knew her question referred to more than the cuts and bruises.

"I'm tough as nails." PJ said trying to sound as strong as she could, for her sister's sake. But her words were limp, falling out of her like loose pages from an old book. PJ hesitated then asked, "What about you?"

"Well, I tried to stay brave." Her younger sister's eyes glossed over, and she looked down at the bed. "I got the ice. I remembered to make more. Do you need ice now? I've made extra."

"No." PJ moved and ached.

"Why does she . . . pick on you?"

"I remind her." PJ forced clarity to the words but knew they came out depleted. She knew that she reminded Betsy of their dad because Betsy told her. She would say things like, "You have your father's temper," or "You're just like him, wit and all!" Even though she knew their mom meant it in a bad way, PJ took a bit of pride in her likeness to their dad. It helped her to feel closer to him.

She tried to sit up but couldn't and waited for her breath to catch. PJ didn't want Panic to worry so she forced a smile and felt the cracked skin of her swollen lip weep. To soothe Panic, she managed, "She doesn't know what she's doing." Her words felt stronger, though still shallow. "If she knew, I know she wouldn't. I just know it." PJ tried to reassure Panic by resting her hand on top of Panic's smaller hand, but her own hand lay limp until Panic picked it up and started stroking her big sister's fingers.

"What do you remind her of?" Panic asked.

"Not what, but who." There was a long silence. "Dad," she said. The room moved into focus for PJ. Faded yellow curtains hung on tension rods jammed into the window frame that faced south. The curtains were parted enough so that she could see the dark leaves of live oaks beyond the front porch. Their shadows blocked the sunlight completely, casting a mottled greyness back toward their house and draping their box-shaped home in a certain gloomy hue even during the brightest time of the day.

"But are you hurt, hurt? Like, will you be okay?" Panic asked.

"Don't you worry, Panic. I'm tough, too. Like Dad." PJ noticed Panic's shoulders hunch when she mentioned dad. The younger sister curled into herself with a bend, like a wilting flower. Then PJ tried to lean forward and prop herself up on her elbow again, though her head screamed and spun as she moved. She wasn't sure her shoulder would support the effort if she leaned. She needed to talk less, to try less, so she let Panic take care of her.

As PJ regained her awareness, Panic regained confidence that her sister would be okay. She enjoyed playing nursemaid, taking care of PJ.

"Can I bring you a cheese sandwich?" Panic tilted forward eager to help, eager for PJ to eat. She adjusted the pillows, then kneaded the blankets with fisted paws. PJ's eyelashes fluttered in quick blinks as Panic worked and the bridge of PJ's nose crinkled above its small, round tip. "Am I hurting you?" Panic asked.

"No." PJ managed.

PJ's eyes were a deep golden brown, usually so full of wonder, even when she was worried, but now her eyes seemed vacant. Panic thought her sister was beautiful, even then. Her best wish was to look like her sister when she grew up. She already came up to PJ's shoulders when they stood next to each other. Panic hoped in the next couple of years, they would be the same height and maybe share clothes by then, too. Already, Panic borrowed her t-shirts to sleep in and sometimes to wear to school. Maybe soon they could even share shoes—

The thought of shoes made Panic's stomach lurch, so she pushed it away.

"A sandwich sounds good," PJ said. Her speech sounded more labored now that she was upright and Panic worried about her ribs. "I think water would help, too," PJ said.

Before too long, Panic returned with a sandwich wrapped in a dishcloth and a chipped mug of water. While PJ ate, Panic stayed close.

"By the way, where is she?"

Panic knew she meant Mom. "She's sleeping still. Has been all night and morning since—"

"No, she was in here for a bit," PJ said. This news surprised Panic and PJ must have seen it on her face because she went on. "Yeah, she was in here. She cried a little, too."

"What did she say?" Panic asked.

"I think she meant to apologize."

"God, PJ, it's not okay." Even in her sweet, nine-year-old voice, the urgency rang through. "She can't do that. It's not okay, and it's getting worse." Panic looked at the bruises on PJ's face, the place along her cheek and temple where the skin had turned purple and green. "You should see yourself."

"Bring me a mirror," PJ said.

"Um, maybe not."

"I'm sure it looks worse than it is," PJ said. She paused for a beat before speaking again. "As long as she keeps her hands off you, it'll be okay. Besides, what can I do about it?"

"I've been thinking about that," Panic said. "Let's leave. Let's not wait."

"You don't know what you're saying, Panic."

"I do," she insisted, and she folded her arms across her chest. Running away was all she thought about since their mom beat PJ with the shoe.

PJ raised her eyebrows at Panic. They had talked about this before. Now, Panic nodded with assurance at her big sister.

"I'm sorry you had to see that," PJ said with her short breaths.

Panic looked to the stack of National Geographic magazines. She glanced toward the image of Leif Garret on the wall, then her eyes found her hands. "The plane crash?" Panic said. "I've been watching the news and a lot of people saw it. It was such a clear day with the winds and—"

"You know what I mean."

Panic looked to the window. "I know. But I am glad I was here."

Now it was PJ's turn to worry.

It seemed only a matter of time before Betsy took out her rage out on Panic, too, instead of PJ, and what then? But running away was something PJ thought would come when they were both much older, maybe when they could drive or when PJ could get a job. Even so, if they did get away, what about their mom? Betsy wouldn't do well on her own. Still, PJ thought again about Betsy possibly hurting Panic, or worse, hurting both of them like this. She could not allow that to happen. And besides, their dad never came back so there must be something better out there. It couldn't be all bad.

The long walks they had taken in the chaparral were always about preparing for the biggest walk of all. The walk when they would leave everything behind and find their way to something better . . . but they were still kids. Panic could do a lot for a nine-year-old, but PJ knew she was still a kid. She didn't like to hike more than two hours, less when it was hot. She only wanted to come home after school and watch T.V. However, the glint of hope she saw then in Panic's eyes said that maybe she was ready, that they could go. Maybe it was time to leave.

"I've thought about it too," PJ admitted.

"The plane crash?"

"No. About running away."

They sat looking at each other for a long moment. Panic's eyes locked with PJ's and PJ was determined to keep her sister's gaze. With all of the factors to consider, it seemed feasible that they could go, escape Betsy and the uncertainty of her unstable moods and excessive drinking.

Panic finally broke the silence. "But where would we go? I mean, we're kids. And school and . . . and, Mom. What about Mom?"

"What about her?" PJ said. "But maybe we are too much for her, you know?"

"I know." Panic said.

PJ had thought a lot about how much of a burden they were for Betsy, raising them on her own, mostly isolated in their rural valley, with only work friends and café customers in her life. They had no extended family, no church fellowship on Sunday, like Manny's family. Only Aunt Fancy in the mountains to the north, her dad's sister. Betsy's lack of community extended to her daughters, and they all suffered from isolation. They had nobody to reach out to, no one to visit on the holidays or birthdays, and no one to ask for help. They needed help, though; PJ was certain they did.

"What about taking the bus?" Panic asked. They took the bus to the grocery store sometimes with Betsy. Sometimes got rides from their neighbor, Mrs. Stanislaw, to, but where would they go? Mexico? "What about Mexico?"

"Do you know any Spanish?" PJ asked. The girls had learned a few words from Manny and Luis, but they only remembered a few words, and most of those were words for food. That could be helpful.

"Listen," PJ said. "I have a responsibility to you, Panic. This outweighs my need to escape. As terrible as Mom can be, I have to make sure you're safe."

She assumed Panic hadn't thought about that. If they left, could PJ find them food to eat? At least at their home they had cheese and beans, shelter and school. Betsy's restaurant tips provided some basic needs, basic needs and security. But how secure were they? Maybe, PJ wondered, maybe they could try to find their dad. Sometimes PJ wondered if he had gone to Aunt Fancy's house in the mountains. But Fancy would have likely forced him back home to his responsibilities. Maybe he had gone to Mexico. This was something PJ hadn't thought of until their talk under the sumac after the plane crash. Still, it didn't seem likely they'd find someone who didn't want to be found, especially in another country. Besides, where would they start? Most people they knew didn't even have phones. It was hopeless.

"But how can we stay?" Panic asked. Her eyes glossed with tears. "That's what I kept asking myself while she was hitting you."

"I wonder too," PJ said, and she took Panic's hand, squeezing with a light grip. "I'm not sure where we could go, though."

"Into our backyard, PJ. Into the hills." Panic stood up now. She grew excited. "Like camping. Lots of kids at school go camping all the time." Panic lit up like this was the best idea since their valley had been settled. "Or take a bus to Auntie Fancy's." She said this, even though the only thing Panic knew about Aunt Fancy was that she lived in the mountains near Los Angeles.

Fancy might turn them back, but it was an idea, PJ considered. She remembered their mom saying that Fancy was prone to take in strays, and their dad agreed and laughed, then talked about her many dogs. She would take in the girls, too, no doubt. And PJ could help run the lodge and maybe learn the business. Fancy might welcome the help.

But why had they not heard from Fancy since their dad left?

"It's been a long time since we heard from our aunt," PJ admitted.

"Do you know why we haven't heard from her all these years?" Panic asked.

"I think Fancy and Mom had a fight; I can't remember. I remember Idyllwild though."

"Ida, what?" Panic asked.

"Idyllwild." PJ laughed, though her ribs hurt with the effort. "It's the name of the place where Fancy's lodge is." She went on. "Fancy's lodge is surrounded by sugar pines and crisp air, and it's on the edge of this beautiful meadow." PJ described an image of a sturdy cabin in a picturesque forest. She said the old log cabin had a wide porch.

Panic almost remembered going there, but she couldn't be sure if she really remembered or if she only remembered because of the way PJ described it so vividly. PJ said their family went for visits when she was little, before Dad had gone off to Vietnam. Before he came back different. PJ also remembered that their mom didn't like Fancy, said she called her 'hippie' like it was a dirty word. PJ admitted there was some truth to the title. Fancy kept outlaws at her place, out of the way of the law, mostly marijuana growers and draft dodgers. But PJ assured Panic that Aunt Fancy was always hospitable and kind; she was the type of woman who kept a fresh pot of coffee on all day in case visitors dropped by. PJ said, "Dad used to say all people should be as welcoming as Fancy."

"Is she pretty?" Panic asked.

"Well, Fancy wears an apron all the time, which makes mom fuming mad. I never understood why."

"Maybe because aprons are for waiting tables, not wearing around the house," Panic said.

"Aunt Fancy's aprons are not like restaurant aprons," PJ said. "Hers are bright colored and made of mismatched fabric. I always like them: cherry fabric and gingham check. She'd keep a kitchen towel tucked in the strap so she could wipe her hands or a quick spill, always ready to take care of whatever might happen."

"I like that," Panic said.

"Me too."

The more the sisters talked about it, the more Aunt Fancy's place made sense. What started as a bud of interest began to sprout like one the bean plants at school; but by the time Panic heard more of what PJ had to say, the sprout had grown wild tendrils of desire, compelling Panic to go. That was where they would go.

"I got about nine dollars saved," Panic said sweetening the idea to go to Idyllwild. "I know you got some too, and that would make up the bus fare to get to the mountains."

"We'd have to find out if the bus goes that far."

"It does," Panic announced, sounding proud of herself. "Leroy Mason at school said his whole family took the bus up to the mountains in Los Angeles from Santa Fe Station downtown here. I called him a liar, but he told the whole trip."

"How would we get to Santa Fe Station?" PJ asked.

"The 63 bus from Greenfield Drive. We can take it to the transfer over at Washington."

"You've thought this all out." PJ eyed her.

Panic pursed her lips and leaned back in her chair. She folded her arms across her chest, and she smiled at PJ and nodded her head, so certain.

"Well, I do have some money. Plus, there are the bottles collected out front, the unbroken ones, anyway."

Panic knew that PJ had been in the habit of squirreling away resources for times when their mother's binges would go on and things like shopping for groceries would come to a halt. They'd become resourceful with top ramen and canned goods, and they also knew Mr. Minkus never minded when they pilfered avocados. They found out long ago that avocados could sustain a kid for quite some time.

The more they talked about leaving, the more Panic believed the plans they made were real, solid plans that would lead to an escape. There were details to work out like how they might contact Aunt Fancy. Panic and PJ had no phone at their house. They thought about using the neighbor's phone, Mrs. Stanislaw's, to call their aunt, but that ran the risk of alerting the nosey neighbor to their predicament. Mrs. Stanislaw was a busybody, was what Betsy always said. She might know something was up and tell Betsy or call the cops. Kids that ran away went to jail; they'd heard. Besides, the call was long distance and would cost money. Neither Panic nor PJ knew how to make a long-distance phone call, besides. Asking for help would bring questions, and PJ was in no shape to talk to grown-ups. There would be questions about her bruises and about their mom. No, they couldn't ask for help. They'd have to do it all on their own. And so, they decided it would be best to show up in Idyllwild and explain everything to Fancy in person, without asking anyone for anything ahead of time, if they could help it. They could certainly help it, with Panic's bravery and PJ's logic. At least, Panic hoped they could.

CHAPTER FOUR

After three days PJ felt stronger. Her cuts had started to heal, and her bruises had turned from a grey blue to light green. She was able to walk around and help gather things they would need for their trip.

In the early morning hours of a Saturday, with one duffle bag of personal items, a change of clothes, and a grand total of $33.72 between them, the girls set out. They tiptoed down the hall, crossed the entryway, and quietly shut the door behind them, hearts thumping and palms moist with fear. The night before, their mom had drunk herself to unconsciousness, as she had all the nights since the assault with the shoe. PJ and Panic both knew that her bottles would soon run dry and then she would be on a different type of bender. And so, it was time to go.

The plan was to walk to the bus stop and pay the fare for the city metro line that would take them to the exchange station on the other side of El Cajon. There, they would buy a transfer to the Santa Fe Station in Downtown San Diego. They'd been on the city line enough times to know the routine and the cost, thirty-five cents. PJ would have to ask about the cost of the transfer, but she figured they had enough cash. Once downtown, they could buy two fares to Idyllwild on the Greyhound. Panic found out from Leroy Mason that his entire family had gone to Idyllwild for less than twenty dollars. There were three people in

Leroy's family, so the sisters figured their thirty-three dollars would be plenty, with money for food along the way.

Panic brought along her stuffed elephant and a pencil drawing of her mom folded up into small squares. She clutched the elephant in her hand but stuffed the drawing in her pocket. PJ brought her lucky rabbit's foot keychain and a quartzite rock she had found in the yard. She wanted something from their land, a connection. The rock's color was translucent white with gold and silver veins.

They had decided to set out in the early morning as the sun came up because they knew their mom would still be sleeping or passed out. Whatever her state, she wouldn't notice them gone for quite a while. The girls figured their mom might assume they were at school, even though it was Saturday, but the ruse would give them a good head start.

"What did you pack for clothes?" PJ asked her little sister.

"Like you said. Two pairs of underpants. One extra pants. Two more shirts. The green one has long sleeves." She was wearing her Star Wars t-shirt and a light jacket with a hood, which was really all she needed in the early autumn chill of Southern California. The mountains might be cold this time of year, but they decided they needed to travel light rather than weigh themselves down with the extra items. PJ had also brought two pairs of underpants, a jacket and two shirts. But she only brought the jeans she had on. Her sweatpants would not fit in the duffle. She was glad she hadn't tried to cram them in either. The bag was heavy enough already. Besides, the sweatpants were stained and had a small rip in the knee. PJ rather enjoyed the thought of leaving them behind, something used up and unnecessary. She wore her dad's sweatshirt, as always.

They walked through the oak woodland shade crunching fallen acorns and stiff oak leaves under their feet. The sound made a grinding, shuffling rhythm as they trudged along reminding PJ of the impossibility of their trek, each step marked by a shushing of resistance. She could not remember the last time she had been away from home. Was it that time when their dad had come home from Vietnam for good? Betsy had made a big effort to get them all clean and shiny and she'd packed a picnic, which had only happened that one time, as far as PJ remembered.

They'd driven down to the army base in Chula Vista to pick him up and when they got there, Chet just sat on the curb and wouldn't be moved until his superior officer came out and told him he had to go with his family. His sullen demeanor was so surprising and off-putting that they'd driven home and not eaten the picnic at all. In fact, PJ thought maybe the food had all gone bad because she never saw the picnic basket again. She remembered hearing her mom talk to Fancy then about Chet's condition. They called it "shell shock." Betsy said he had seen some things while he was fighting in the jungle, things that people should not see. It wasn't until PJ's mom started hitting her that PJ thought she knew what that meant (seeing things you should not see) by the look of horror on her little sister's face when she saw Betsy's violence.

PJ looked at Panic as they walked along beneath the trees. Sunlight broke through the canopy and fell along Panic's cheeks. She looked so small to PJ then. Small, but confident and carefree, not all like a kid setting out away from home.

"I packed three jam sandwiches each," Panic announced, as if she could feel her sister assessing her age. She gave PJ a sidelong glance as they approached the gravel road, Forester Creek, which led to the main road, Greenfield Drive. "I also found some saltines in the top of the cupboard, but they were a little crushed. Doesn't matter, though. It all goes to the same place. Right?"

"Right," PJ answered. She appreciated her sister's optimism, and she gave her a quick smile. Still, in the pit of her stomach, PJ was terrified. She had taken her young sister away from home, away from food and shelter. Their mother had never hit Panic, so she wasn't the one in any real peril. Why hadn't this occurred to PJ before? But it had. She thought this through. Their mom was so out of control when she was drunk that if PJ wasn't around to absorb her violent outbursts, the rage would find its way to Panic soon enough. This thought was more terrifying than being on the open road without the security of home, without walls or food, with unknown variables facing them at every corner. PJ felt scared to take her sister away from their home, but the truth was that she was more scared to leave her behind. And if they'd stayed, it was only a matter of time before they both became victims of their mother's temper.

"The crackers are great, nice thought. Thanks Panic." She mussed her sister's hair as they walked coming alongside the road and falling into stride together. "How long do you think the walk to the bus stop will be?" She asked Panic knowing that her sister liked to calculate such things, but Panic didn't get a chance to answer. With a crunch of gravel, a large, green station wagon with wood-panel sides came around the bend in the road up ahead. The girls were directly in line with the driver's side of the car as it approached. Within seconds it would be along them and pass them, PJ hoped.

"It's Mrs. Stanislaw," PJ said, her mouth suddenly dry. "If she stops, let me talk."

The car slowed as it got closer and then came to stop right alongside the sisters. Mrs. Stanislaw rolled down her window as she eyed the large duffle and then PJ's bruises. Her face animated with exaggeration as she explored PJ's fading contusions, her eyes traveling from her temple and cheek to her chin. Then she looked to Panic and winked.

"Morning girls. Awfully early to be out and about already," she said with a sticky voice.

PJ noticed right away that Mrs. Stanislaw had no eyebrows, like she hadn't drawn them on yet. Her hair was all bundled up in pink, foam rollers piled atop her head. She wore a plaid headscarf tied protectively around the hair rollers to keep any from jumping free, and her skin was pock-marked and rough looking. This was not the way Mrs. Stanislaw normally looked. She seemed to take a great deal of pride in her appearance. Her makeup was usually impeccable, because she represented AVON and sold their cosmetic line to the women in their neighborhood——well, most of the women. Betsy would "never buy such crap," she often said.

"Josephine's going for a sleepover at her friend's house," PJ explained, not looking directly at Mrs. Stanislaw but instead, scanning the trees and chaparral beyond the car's dust trail, before settling on Panic's scowl. She could tell her sister was annoyed by the use of her real name, Josephine.

"Kinda early for a sleepover, kiddos. Where's your ma?"

"She's still in bed. Worked late." PJ rolled onto her tiptoes then rocked back down on her heels. She glanced at the woman then. Mrs. Stanislaw's eyes rested on PJ's bruised cheek.

"What happened?" Mrs. Stanislaw asked. "Did you get into a fight at school?"

"No Ma'am." PJ looked long at Mrs. Stanislaw then, through the rolled down window, the trapezoidal frame making her look tiny. Her lips were chapped, and her cheeks were sunburnt, but the missing eyebrows gave her a surprised expression. Mrs. Stanislaw pulled out a cigarette and lit it. PJ heard the crank of the emergency brake as it was set, though the engine continued to idle; she took this to mean that Mrs. Stanislaw wanted to know more about the bruises.

"I fell down the back hill. Josephine . . . eh, Panic and I were chasing jackrabbits, and my toe clipped a boulder. We were close to that ridge where those poor puppies were found, you know the ones, and I just went over." PJ hoped the mention of the dead puppies would change the subject. Nobody wanted to talk about the puppies found in the hills that summer.

The AVON lady took another, longer drag of her cigarette as she looked over PJ's face and then she examined Panic, too.

"It isn't proper, girls." Mrs. Stanislaw scolded then blew a cloud of smoke out her nose with the rest of her breath. "Traipsing around in the hills like that, and nearly Thirteen years old now."

"I'm Fourteen."

"Fourteen!" her eyes widened at PJ. "You're nearly old enough to sell makeup. Wanna be my colleague? It's good money." Mrs. Stanislaw's enthusiasm gave PJ a new feeling of discomfort.

"No, Ma'am. I don't even wear makeup."

"Uh huh. And what about you, Sugar? You help your sister when she fell? Was your mama around?" Her eyes found Panic.

Panic looked down and kicked at a rock submerged in the surface of the dirt road. PJ knew she wouldn't answer, following orders like a good soldier.

"She's not feeling too well, Mrs. Stanislaw." PJ offered.

"Oh?" the woman leaned out of the window and looked to where Panic toed the rock in the gravel road. "That so, huh? Thought you said she was on her way to a sleepover?"

The girls looked at each other and PJ thought fast. "I just mean shy, Mrs. Stanislaw. She's been feeling real shy around grownups, is all."

The smooth skin where the woman's eyebrows should have been vaulted upward pushing into astonished ridges. Mrs. Stanislaw puffed on her cigarette then let out a large exhalation of smoke. "What aren't you girls telling me, huh?" She leaned back into the car, but she kept her eyes trained on PJ.

"Ma'am?" PJ asked.

Taking another long drag of her cigarette she blew the smoke out the window and the cloud billowed up from the roof of the car catching a slight breeze before moving away in a cloud of escape. Mrs. Stanislaw tapped her red fingernails on the hard arch of the steering wheel. She turned her head to look over her shoulder, and then she looked at herself in the rearview mirror adjusting the frame of the mirror with her hand. The tip of her ring finger blotted the corner of her mouth, her cigarette an extension of that same hand.

"Alright then," she said, looking forward over the steering wheel, and patting it with her palm. "You feeling alright about your daddy?"

"Ma'am?" PJ asked, not knowing what the woman meant by the question. "Our dad hasn't been home for two years now."

"Not home, hu? Well, ain't that a shame," said Mrs. Stanislaw with a shake of her head.

PJ thought it was cruel that Mrs. Stanislaw had asked about their dad. Everyone on their road knew their dad had been gone for the past two years. She couldn't imagine why Mrs. Stanislaw would ask such a question.

"I guess that settles it," Mrs. Stanislaw said to no one. "You girls come on around here and get inside. I'm taking you home. If you are off to a sleepover, your mama will tell me that for myself and then I'll be the one to give you a ride. How's that?"

Neither girl moved. PJ's heart pounded in her ears. She felt her sister press into her side.

Mrs. Stanislaw's head turned back toward them; her invisible eyebrows raised again. "I ain't asking," she said with a tone of finality as she flicked her hot cigarette into the dry brush behind them. Then she leaned across the seat to the passenger side and wrenched the door handle, popping open the passenger door. PJ and Panic shuffled around the station wagon and climbed into the front seat with Mrs. Stanislaw. It was a wide bench seat and PJ tossed the duffle bag over into the backseat before shutting the door. The car smelled like cigarettes and vinyl, and something else that PJ found familiar but couldn't quite place. Was it sweet? Old syrup? Mrs. Stanislaw released the emergency brake, and the car began to move forward along the gravel road in the direction from where the girls had come.

"You know, if something happened to you girls, I just couldn't forgive myself. It wouldn't be neighborly, would it?" Mrs. Stanislaw asked. The girls remained silent. "Oh, come on now. The worst thing that can happen is you get a ride to your sleepover, right?" The lady goaded, but silence still held the sisters. "Unless there is no sleepover." Now Mrs. Stanislaw slowed the car, looking over at the two of them. "You wanna tell me what's going up there at that house of yours, PJ?"

"Ma'am," was all PJ could manage. She had been thinking of how her mother would react to being woken up under these circumstances, and with Mrs. Stanislaw at her doorstep, uninvited, unexpected, and with her two escapee daughters in tow. Sure, Betsy could be cordial enough on the spur of the moment, but as soon as Mrs. Stanislaw left, then the questions would start, questions that her mother never intended to hear answers to, nor would she care. And if she started drinking, it would get bad fast. On the other hand, if she didn't have any booze, it would be worse. Their mom's violent outbursts would be better if she had her elixir. PJ frantically tried to recall whether there was alcohol in the house. She didn't care about responding to Mrs. Stanislaw at all. Instead, she tried to remember if her mom's vodka stash under the bathroom sink had already been depleted, or if there was still that old whiskey in the garage, or the fifth she had in the kitchen. She tried to recall if the jar of tequila had been drunk. But PJ couldn't think straight. Even the whereabouts of the beer, in its neat six-packs, seemed to evade her memory. Did she recall a pile of crushed cans on the living room floor? She felt horrified imagining that their house was dry, that her mom would be met by Mrs. Stanislaw and a barrage of questions with hardly a drink to quell her after.

"Here we are," said Mrs. Stanislaw, though the girls could see plain enough their own house under the dark oak trees as they pulled into the drive. The house looked so eerie from where PJ saw it then, shaded and quiet, the shadows of the trees muting the beige, cracked stucco, russet trim ashy where the paint had oxidized in the many years of neglect. A lone screen hung on a dirty window; other windows advertised glazed, dirty glass but without screens. One window had a crack that ran down the length of its pane, a remnant of a fight her parents waged over why her dad was too afraid to go to work in the slaughterhouse down the street. PJ recalled the ketchup bottle hitting the window during that fight, saw the spray of red in her mind; it stained the curtains where the glass Heinz bottle had shattered. PJ remembered her father crying as he described scenes he'd seen in Vietnam. As the ketchup and shards of glass dripped from the window to the floor, PJ and Panic huddled in the corner. It wasn't long after that when her dad left, the crack in the window's pane evidence that he had also escaped after a fight. But PJ and Panic hadn't escaped after all. They were right back where they started.

"I'll give you another chance to tell me what's going on in there, PJ." Mrs. Stanislaw said, and PJ noticed that the car was still idling and that the emergency brake was not set.

"Mrs. Stanislaw, thanks for the ride, but if it's all the same to you, I think Panic and I will just go inside now. She doesn't need a ride because . . . there is no sleepover, okay? That's all. We're just gonna go in. Okay?" PJ spoke these words carefully, without too much inflection. Then, she reached over and pulled the door handle and stepped out into the cool shade of the oak trees. As Panic got out of the car, PJ opened the back door and retrieved their duffle bag. "We appreciate your help," she said to Mrs. Stanislaw with finality, then shut the door. She and Panic walked hand-in-hand up their front steps without looking back. PJ only let go of her sister's hand to open the front door. Once PJ's hand was on the cold brass of the doorknob, she heard Mrs. Stanislaw's car idle stop as the engine shut down. She heard the ratchet of the emergency brake being set. As she turned around, PJ heard Mrs. Stanislaw's car door open, saw Mrs. Stanislaw rise from the car followed by the familiar sound of crunching acorns and brittle leaves under heavy feet as the woman with the pink hair rollers came around the car.

"I think I'll just check in with your mama, if it's all the same to you, PJ," Mrs. Stanislaw said as she stepped toward the girls on the porch.

PJ grabbed Panic's hand again. That's when they heard Betsy's voice from deep within the house.

"Everything's fine in here, Laurie," their mom yelled, her voice reverberating through the door. "Thanks for bringing my girls home, now get the hell off my property!" The voice was loud and forceful, but clear, sober even. PJ squeezed Jo's hand and looked blankly back at Mrs. Stanislaw. Mrs. Stanislaw froze in her stride when she heard their mother's voice. Dappled sunlight broke through the trees and danced along her headscarf and shoulders.

"Betsy?" Mrs. Stanislaw called out. "Betsy, we haven't seen you at the café in a few days when Ed and I stopped down for our nightcap. Are you okay, hon?" And though Mrs. Stanislaw sounded convincing, like she really did care about their mother, her eyes swept the scene of the house, from the piles of garbage bags near the over-flowing garbage cans to the deteriorating boxes of broken bottles that the grocery store would not recycle because they were broken.

During this exchange, PJ calculated exactly how she would usher her sister through the house, out the back sliding glass door, and up the hill; how quickly they would move to that safe place under the laurel sumac and chamise where she had found Panic after the plane crash. They could stay there all day, maybe all weekend if they had to—Panic would get her camping wish after all. The cheese sandwiches and crackers would go to good use. The tension would pass. She gave Panic a reassuring look, trying to convey the plan with her eyes.

"No business of yours, Laurie. Now get on out of here before I call the sheriff and have you arrested for trespassing." Their mother's words came again from inside the house, though this time with less volume and less threat. "Girls, get on inside now."

"Calling the sheriff for no reason is not very neighborly," Mrs. Stanislaw remarked, though only loud enough for PJ and Panic to hear.

As PJ pushed the front door open, she heard the car door shut and Mrs. Stanislaw's station wagon engine start. With an anxious feeling, PJ shut the front door behind her. There in the dark hallway stood the outline of their mother facing down the two girls. PJ's heart pounded so hard her throat nearly shut with the pressure of its beating. Panic grabbed PJ's hand once more. Her mother's figure outlined by the frame of light in the hallway towered over them, and PJ could feel Panic squeeze her hand painfully tight.

"What's this?" her mom asked, eyes moving between them and the duffle bag.

"Panic was going to sleep over at Ida's," PJ said, thinking quickly and telling the story she'd too late thought to tell Mrs. Stanislaw. PJ's hands shook even though she clutched the handle of the duffle bag with one and the small, warm hand of her sister with the other. She gathered herself and added, "Only, then we figured we should check with you first."

"Well, you figured right," her mother said scrutinizing her older daughter, eyeing the cut on her cheek with strange bewilderment. Was she surprised that PJ was still so obviously injured or was she alarmed that the girls had been out when clearly PJ was so badly hurt, she should be resting? No, it was more likely she was mortified that someone outside the house had seen PJ in that state of abuse and would think ill of her. Surely the car's idle had been heard from inside the house; this was likely why she was even out of bed in the first place.

But always the quick thinker, PJ thought it would be better if she explained right away. "We got a ride from Mrs. Stanislaw back here. We didn't ask for a ride, but she insisted. Said she wouldn't feel right if something happened to us out there."

"That so?" The tension in her mother's voice crept toward menace. Her sad dark eyes bore in on PJ with uneasy misgivings.

PJ did not respond. Instead, she positioned herself in front of Panic, releasing her hand, she put her arm in front of Panic, pulling her behind her. The gesture seemed to soften their mother. She let out a sigh and along with it went her anger replaced with a look of exhaustion. Her shoulders slumped and her head bowed slightly. She sagged forward frowning with a tired lilt. "I'm drained, girls," she said. "But let me make you some eggs and toast. We got eggs, PJ?" She raised her head and looked at her daughter.

PJ was stunned by the question. It felt like a trap. She didn't want to trust the shift. She thought that maybe her mother waited for her to say or do the wrong thing—to reveal that they were going to run away to Aunt Fancy's house or try to find their dad—so that she could explode into another blind fit of rage and tear into PJ with fury and madness. PJ felt her heart thump, constricting her throat so she could not form words. Silence held them. It was Panic who finally broke the spell.

"I think there's only two eggs, Mama," Panic said, moving a half step around PJ and toward Betsy. "But there's flour. We could make pancakes."

Their mom's eyes found Panic and filled with relief. Her lashes fluttered. She even smiled. "I'll make pancakes, little JoJo." She added the last bit with a warm tone, then continued with an afterthought, "We haven't had syrup in some time, but I can melt down some brown sugar and margarine. What do you say, PJ? Want some pancakes this morning?"

Her words came at PJ like a peace offering. Whether they were intended to erase the bruises and cuts, PJ couldn't tell, but in all actuality, they could not fix what had been done. Still, PJ figured it was a start. But how long would it be before it would all happen again? She glanced down at Panic who was smiling back at her. Panic might believe that pancakes could fix it all, but PJ knew better. Still, PJ figured if it gave her sister a little reassurance that all would be well, maybe PJ could go along with the pancake charade.

She finally set the duffle on the ground. "Sure. Pancakes would be great," PJ said.

Her mother straightened up and she tipped her head sideways looking at her girls. Then she gestured for them to all move into the kitchen.

Standing near her mom in the small kitchen, PJ could smell the old beer on the woman, stale and pungent remains of the gluttony from the previous night or nights. It made her stomach quiver. The thought of the hideout up the hill seemed to call to her, beckoning with some comfortable resolve that she could get there if she needed to, run and hide away the same way the brush rabbit tucked away from the red-tail hawk. She would not rule that place out as an escape plan for later, but for right now, the breakfast seemed to offer solace to Panic. And PJ wanted her sister to have comfort, even an empty gesture. PJ wanted this for Panic.

And Panic wanted pancakes! She hurried around the kitchen gathering items: flour: mixing bowl, wooden spoon. When she could not reach the high cupboards, she opened the lower ones and used the interior shelf as a stepping stool.

"Careful, JoJo," Betsy said, standing behind the younger girl and offering a hand on her back to steady her.

"I got it," Panic said. She brought down a box of baking soda and the brown sugar.

"How are you feeling, PJ?" her mother asked as she emptied the last of the brown sugar into the saucepan and began to stir.

"Okay, I guess." PJ would not look at her. "I didn't go to school this week," she added, thinking that her mom would want to know.

"Well, I bet your teacher will let you do some make-up work, right?"

"Right," PJ said plainly.

"Mama?" Panic interrupted. "Where did you learn to make brown sugar syrup?"

"Oh, here and there, JoJo," she answered and leaned into the younger girl giving her a playful bump with her hip. PJ tried to soften at this, but she kept on alert, noticing the wooden spoon in Betsy's hand. She knew the worst could still come and that not expecting the inevitable was like polishing a time bomb. Listening to the rhythmic sound of the spoon swirling the sugar as it melted in the pan, PJ wanted to run. Instead, she took three mismatched forks from the drawer and set them on the table.

As the pancake batter steamed away forming tiny bubbles on its oblong and misshaped surfaces, Panic told their mom all about her friend, Leroy, from school, how he and his family had gone on a trip to the mountains. PJ noticed that Panic was careful to omit the information about the bus depot and how much the trip cost. She also said nothing about Idyllwild where Aunt Fancy lived. By the time they sat to eat their short stacks, Panic had moved on to talk about her most recent art project at school. She giggled describing tissue paper and starch as she swirled her fork in the gritty brown sugar syrup. PJ snuck glances at her mom as Panic spoke and she noticed Betsy's tired eyes and sagging face. Her mom would sometimes glance back at her and then look away as if she didn't want PJ to fully see her. At least, that's how PJ remembered it.

There was quite a mess at the kitchen table by the time the knock came on the door. The now cluttered tabletop hosted coffee cups and paper plates soaked with brown sugar syrup and soggy bits of pancake crusts, with crumpled up paper towels strewn about the fray. Some pancakes had been burnt, but they were still eaten—mostly. Not much was wasted in their house. The pan of brown sugar syrup sat empty in the middle of the table, resting atop a red gingham potholder. Its walls were sticky with residual drips of sweet liquid running down its sides and the red mitt absorbed the brown pools collecting along its base. They had all been laughing at something Panic said, though PJ's laughter was superficial, when the bang, bang, bang erupted like a shotgun with a stuttered thumping on their door. The laughter stopped immediately. The three of them looked at each other as if they had been caught in some illegal act.

"I'll get that," Betsy said through tight lips as she stood from the table.

In the hallway, the girls could hear their mom greet the male voices at the door. She said, "Well, I'm sure that's not necessary officer, but certainly. Please come in." Then she returned to the kitchen with two uniformed police officers following close behind. Her eyes went to PJ.

Panic had never seen policemen so closeup. The first man removed his hat and looked around the room. He had pale skin and a shaved head. A badge sat on the left side of his chest glistened. His taupe-colored shirt and a dark brown necktie tacked to his shirt with a gold bar seemed too tight for him. Panic stared at the gold bar on the officer's tie. She assumed this was to hold the tie in place, though she wondered why it mattered if a cop's tie flapped around. It was easier to look at his tie than his face, which was so drawn with concern that she wanted to look away. His eyes seemed troubled, but his mouth attempted a smile.

"Hello, ladies," he spoke in a deep voice. "My name is Deputy Lang. This is my partner, Deputy Randolph."

Deputy Randolph came slower into the room, looking around. He kept his hat on, moved his head from side to side scanning the kitchen to take in everything. He was older, had a round stomach that stuck out over his belt. Large hands big enough to crush rocks hung at his sides; the hand closest to his gun looked ready to grab the pistol at any moment. Panic had never seen a gun in real life. She looked away from it, back to the policeman's face. Randolph's eyebrows were grey, but his mustache was dark brown and nearly covered his mouth. His eyes rested on the ketchup stain on the kitchen curtains before he scanned the mess atop the table.

Deputy Lang was near the table now, and he crouched down so that he was at eye level with Panic. "Hi there, sweetie," he said to Panic, but she held her breath. She had the overwhelming urge to run to PJ, grab her by the hand and pull her away, but she was fixed to her chair with fear. Panic's stomach fluttered, and, coupled with the fullness and sweetness of the pancakes she'd eaten, she felt sick.

Standing in the doorway, her mother stared at Panic from across the kitchen, her aged face a mask of distress, arms folded tightly across her body.

Deputy Lang turned to PJ and addressed her directly. "Honey, we are here to talk with you about what happened. Can you tell me what happened to you? Why you have these marks on your face and on your arms?" He tipped his head as a gesture to the large cut on her cheek.

PJ didn't answer. She looked at her mom and then she looked at Panic, who fought to stay brave. But she knew her fear betrayed her, and the tears had begun to form in her eyes. She shook her head ever so slightly at PJ.

In that moment, Panic understood so many things. If her sister told the officer about the shoe, about what her mother had done, or about the other times her mother had hurt PJ, these police officers would take their mom away. She felt her breath catch in her lungs. She remembered the principal at PJ's school had told her this would happen when he asked about her last round of bruises, which she swore to him had happened when she tripped on the stairs. PJ told her the principal said the sister would be taken away from Betsy. Nobody wanted that. Sure, they had tried to run away, to get away from Betsy, but they didn't want their mom arrested. Betsy didn't know what she did when she hit PJ. It wasn't her acting out; it was the booze. Panic knew their mom in a different way. Their mom was really the person who made syrup from brown sugar and margarine and who missed their dad and who sang sad songs about far away love. And besides, PJ was okay now; wasn't she? They just needed to stay out of Mama's way. That's what running away would do: it would keep PJ out of Betsy's way. Panic took in a deep breath. She had to say something.

"Mister cop," Panic said. Tears streamed down her face. "Sir. PJ just fell down the hill out back. It's just out back. I could show you where. Honest, I can." Her voice was tiny and earnest.

Now it was PJ's turn to shake her head. She started slowly at first, but as she looked at Betsy standing against the wall with her mouth hanging open and her eyes glassy, PJ's head shook with more vigor. "No," PJ choked. "No, Panic that isn't what happened." She took a step toward Panic. "Sir, my mom drinks too much. She doesn't know what she does when she drinks. See?" And she gestured to Betsy standing at the wall now openly weeping. "This time, she hit me—" and the words caught in her throat as she tried to force them out. Soon, the image of the shoe slamming down on her came back to her and she could no longer speak.

"It's okay, honey," said Deputy Lang. "We'll get it all worked out. Don't you worry. And don't worry about your mom. We can help her too. I promise."

•

By the time they put Betsy into the patrol car, there were two other cars in the front yard under the shade of the oaks. The first was Mrs. Stanislaw's green station wagon with wood panels. She had come back, now made up with her colorful AVON face and drawn-in eyebrows, to watch the drama unfold. Her rollers were gone, and her hair was perfectly coifed. She waved at the mustachioed sheriff and called out, "I'm so glad you came right away." The second car was a plain Ford, "unmarked," as they were called on the new T.V. show, CHiPs, the highway patrol drama that Panic liked to watch sometimes after school. The unmarked car arrived with a man and a woman who talked with PJ and Panic about their Aunt Fancy and how they could get in touch with her up in Idyllwild. They said they would have more questions for them but would ask down at the sheriff's station where they promised to have hoagies and cokes. Fritos too, if they wanted them. Panic was thrilled about that, but she could tell that PJ was scared for them, maybe also for their mom. The woman tried to reassure them that their mom would be okay, but Panic wasn't easily convinced. It was finally decided that PJ could talk to her mom in the patrol car before it drove off, and Panic was relieved to go with her, holding her hand like when she was much younger.

"You be good, okay. Take good care of JoJo. I'll see you in a little bit, PJ. Just a little bit, now," her mom said to PJ through the opened backdoor of the car. She was not in handcuffs so Panic thought maybe she hadn't been arrested like PJ said.

"I'm sorry," PJ said.

Silence fell around them. Panic wanted to say something, too, but she examined the inside of the police car instead. Black seats, a barrier of mesh and glass that separated the backseat from the front, a dashboard filled with fantastic lights and gadgets. Panic heard the wind shifting the leaves in the trees above her, creaking the branches that canopied their yard.

Betsy looked at Panic briefly, offered a smile, then returned her focus to PJ. She said, "Now you listen. I know what I do when I do it, PJ. You hear?" Her words were stern but strained with emotion, like they pained her to say. There was something else too, there in her tone, like a hidden animal, frightened and backed into a trap. The hint of fear warped her tone. "I know what I do when I do it, and I mean it, too. You don't know how hard it's been. You don't. Only I really . . ." She sat back against the dark upholstery, pressing her lips together in a tight line, and gave her voice back to the silence, to the rustle of leaves.

"It's okay," PJ said, looking at Panic now instead of at their mom. She squeezed Panic's hand. Panic, who could not look at either of them earlier, now could not take her eyes off of PJ.

"I think the booze makes it okay. I don't want to hurt you; I really don't. Maybe if they lock me up, you'll finally get peace. Maybe it's a service they do, these uniformed men and that lady, and that damned Mrs. Avon busybody." She said "busybody" with a sneer but then laughed. "If they have to lock me up to keep me from hurting you, well then, they've done us both a service, I'd say."

It was a horrifying idea, that their mom might go away. As much as Panic feared Betsy, she was more afraid their mom might leave one day and never return. She could not imagine life without her. Even trying to run away, planning to escape the valley, had always been more of a dream than a goal. What a puzzle. Even though they had tried to leave, Panic knew that Betsy would always be there, up Forester Creek. Their attempt had been half-hearted. Plus, Panic wanted to believe her mom could stop hitting PJ, maybe even stop drinking, that she could change. But this had been their story for such a long time that it was difficult to imagine any other version. Maybe Panic would help her to imagine another way.

The leaves of the trees fell silent, like the world around them held its breath long enough for the faintest whisper to be heard then.

"Mom," PJ said, now looking at Betsy's tired, swollen face. "I wonder . . . it's just that. . ." She paused then asked, "What was it about the shoe that made you so mad at me?"

Panic's heart sank. She thought of the shoe, how she had learned to say "espadrille" when Betsy showed her the shoes, tucked away in their special box in the closet. The word was all she could say for several minutes, the joy of the ess and pee rolling off her tongue. But she'd been trying to push away the word since the incident. The week before, because of her boredom, or sheer curiosity, Panic had gone into their mom's room. She had opened her closet and tried on some of Betsy's clothes: a pretty dress, a fur-collared jacket, and those shoes, the thick-soled espadrille sandals. She thought she'd been careful to put everything away but when the shoe became the weapon of PJ's attack, Panic had the disturbing thought that the punishment belonged to her. The beating should have been for Panic, she knew, if she gave herself space to think about it further. The guilt that came with her gratitude and relief that PJ had taken their mom's abuse that day, weighed on her. So, when PJ asked what about the shoes had made their mom so mad, Panic knew exactly what it was. Maybe their mom had figured it out, too. Her response was overblown, but Panic knew why. The shoes had been a gift from Chet, their dad. And Panic had left them out, near the foot of Betsy's bed, exactly where she might trip over them. She clearly remembered kicking them off during her dress-up session, and, as their mom hit PJ with the shoe over and over, Panic was sure the brutal attack was misdirected.

Betsy looked at Panic now; her face washed in defeat. Then, back to PJ. Their mother's face hardened. This time the control of her emotions played out plainly as she turned to stone then turned away. She faced forward, leaned back into the seat, and did not look at either girl when she answered, "Nothing. You ought to know that. There was nothing about the shoe. I might have hit you with a bat, if that's what I'd grabbed."

Betsy face stayed expressionless.

Panic and her sister stood still examining her for a moment longer. PJ's hand loosened around Panic's. Finally, the female officer guided the sisters away from the car and shut the door. Then the patrol car pulled away from the oak trees, crunching gravel and acorns under the tires as it went. The car took their mom away, down the road.

CHAPTER FIVE

The sisters rode with the female deputy to the sheriff's station. Her shiny name badge said Deputy Friedman, but she told the girls to call her Lila. Besides her outfit, Lila Friedman didn't look like a cop. Panic thought she could have been an actress or a roller derby star. A tall woman, taller than their mom, Lila had blond hair pinned up into an intricate bun on her head. Panic couldn't imagine Lila as anything but a police officer, but she tried. She thought of Lila dancing or hiking or even playing hide-and-seek, but nothing seemed practical. The one thing Panic thought did not fit about Lila was her long hair. It didn't seem right for a sheriff's deputy to have long hair, Panic thought, even if it was tied up. What if a bad guy grabbed it? What if it got caught on a hook when she was chasing a burglar?

"Have you ever chased a burglar?" Panic asked from the backseat.

"Sure have," Lila said. "Are you girls hungry?"

"No ma'am," answered PJ. "We just finished breakfast." Then she shifted her tone and asked," Are we being arrested?"

"No," Lila chuckled. "Probably your mom isn't even being arrested. We just need to make sure everyone is safe, right?"

Panic could see Lila's eyes through the rearview mirror. She watched the girls. They had been cordoned off into the back seat behind a mesh partition but, besides that, the car seemed like a regular sedan with a broad backseat and thick seatbelts, which Lila had insisted the girls click across their laps. The car had a police radio and occasionally a static voice came on and spoke a series of numbers and letters that made no sense. Panic found the sound abrupt and nearly jumped the first time the voice crackled through the radio.

Lila had offered to let PJ sit up front, but PJ opted to stay with Panic in the backseat. Panic was glad about that choice, to stay together. The backseat was roomie and she felt comfortable next to PJ, as comfortable as she could under the circumstances. She looked over at her sister who seemed to examine the inside of the car. PJ's gaze moved around the dashboard, from the radio to the glovebox, to the mirror where Lila's eyes glanced at them. Panic followed her sister, looking around. She touched the window handle. She felt the upholstery of the seat and the seatback in front of her and ran her fingers along the headrest trim.

Then, Panic had an idea. "Can I open the window? Would that be okay?" She asked.

"Sure. This car is different than the squad cars. It's not for transporting bad guys."

The words 'bad guys' resonated with Panic. She wondered about all the different kinds of 'bad guys' Lila had encountered: car thieves, murderers, mobsters. PJ once told her about one of the high school kids arrested for selling marijuana at school. Panic thought of that kid as a 'bad guy.' PJ said the guy had been taken away in a police car, in the back seat, with the windows up.

Their mom had been taken away in the back seat of a police car. Was she a bad guy?

Panic rolled the window down, the crank turning round and round in her hand. The smell of sage hit her nose as soon as the window gave. Even before the warm air came rushing in, Panic could smell the smoky oil of the bristly leaves, the sweet nectar of the pollen from the black sage. She loved the name of it, black sage, even though it grew purple blossoms, purple and stout like a last stand or a defiant wish. She smelled the plants before seeing them, but once she saw them, they took her breath. A wave of amethyst-colored spires stood at attention as if to salute them in their carriage as they passed. Panic couldn't help but smile at the wall of black sage, smile at the comfort it brought her. She craned her neck as they passed the purple blossoms along the roadside, and in that quick instant, she spotted fat bumblebees frolicking amidst the stems and blooms. They rose and dove above the plants' tall spires.

"I noticed a packed bag in the hall at your house," Lila said, interrupting Panic's contemplation. "Taking a family trip?"

Panic started to speak but PJ pressed her foot into her sister's leg and Panic let out a tiny mew. It wasn't a kick, really. Panic thought of PJ's kick as code to keep her mouth shut. They didn't know how much Lila could be trusted. Sure, she was pretty and nice, and she'd let Panic roll down the window, but she was a cop. If there was a chance their mom could be arrested, PJ should be the one to do the talking. Panic thought of that phrase on cops shows, anything you say can be used against you. She gestured for PJ to answer Lila.

"We just got back from visiting our aunt," PJ lied.

"Oh?"

"She lives in Idyllwild," PJ said, and so Panic joined in the fabrication of the story.

"She has a hotel up there where all sorts of people stay," Panic added with enthusiasm. PJ shot her a look then turned away and looked out the window.

"What's her name?" Lila Freidman asked, moving her head a little closer to the rearview mirror to direct her question to Panic.

How tricky, Panic thought, and she looked at PJ to shush her, but PJ answered, still facing the window. "Her name is Fancy. Fancy McCormack."

Panic tried to give PJ a look to show she didn't understand why PJ would speak up, tell the truth to this woman they did not know, but PJ would not turn back to see Panic's face.

Lila saw this exchange from the rearview mirror, or at least Panic caught the woman's eyes staring at hers from that small rectangle of glass. And so, Panic turned away, too.

Looking out the window at nothing in particular, Panic pretended to watch the oaks as they passed. In the distance, the blond hills of Dehesa marked a low point in the valley walls to the south. Birds circled on an updraft too far away for Panic to know which type, though likely turkey vultures. She thought about the figures in the smoke after the plane crash, how they circled upward toward heaven. She'd walked that area a hundred times, it seemed. She knew the grasses by their names because PJ had taught her the names: avena, wild rye, clumps of sedges and fescue. She knew the bright red monkey flower, which was really called California fuchsia, a willowherb, with its long tubes of red flowers that bloomed for a long season in the mild Southern California climate. Panic loved the monkey flowers, the special relationship with the tiny hummingbirds who carried kisses between the blossoms where petals could not reach. The monkey flowers and hummingbirds evolved together, PJ had told her; the longer the tiny bird's beak grew over thousands of years, the longer the flower's tube grew, or vice versa. Who really knew which influenced the other more? It was a chicken-egg scenario, PJ joked. Which came first: the chicken or the egg? PJ also taught her to pollinate the monkey flowers, touching the tiny stigma, the tip of the pistil, with her pinky. Once covered in pollen, her finger would act as the forehead of the hummingbird, taking the pollen to the next flower, to the next plant. After contact, the white mouth of the stigma would close faster than a Venus Fly Trap. Mr. Newman had a Venus Fly Trap in his classroom. There was a character named Venus Fly Trap on one of the T.V. shows she sometimes watched, but he looked nothing like the other-worldly plant in Room 12. He was a cool, tall black man with a smooth voice. But neither the Venus Fly Trap from the T.V. show nor the one from the classroom gave her such sweet satisfaction as pollinating those fuchsias with her pinky, just like the hummingbirds had for so long.

Lila finally broke the silence. "When we get to the station, you'll go with me to the briefing room." Panic looked at the back of Lila's head as the woman spoke, careful to avoid her gaze in the mirror. She didn't want to give her that satisfaction after noticing she was being watched.

"The briefing room," Lila continued, "is the room where we usually meet to talk about things that are happening. It's our meeting room."

Panic noticed the redundancy. Grownups did that a lot, she knew; they repeated things when they didn't know what else to say or else wanted you to talk.

"I'm sure you girls have heard about the PSA crash, right?" "I saw it from our hill," Panic said, though Lila seemed to not hear her.

"We had a big meeting in the briefing room just this morning to talk about some of the fallout from that event."

Panic thought the word 'event' didn't seem like the appropriate word. Neither did 'fallout.' She turned and looked at her sister. PJ continued to stare out the window. Not fair that PJ chose to sit in the back with Panic but then ignored her.

When they pulled into the sheriff's station parking lot, Panic felt restless. She had never been to the sheriff's station before though the building was not new to her. They'd passed it by on many of their trips to Alpha-Beta, the grocery store along the number 63 bus route. The rock façade made the building stand out like something from The Flintstone's cartoon. Covered in large, granite rocks, the station only appeared to be constructed from individually stacked boulders; the rocks were just for looks. The rest of the station was a normal, rectangular building. Through the center of an arch of cobblestone, a ramp and a staircase led to the entrance. An oversized, bronze sheriff badge nearly six feet tall hung on the wall next to the glass doors. Lila escorted Panic and PJ through the doors where they were greeted by a cheerful red-haired woman in a green sweater seated behind a reception desk.

"Who's this?" the woman asked beaming at the girls as they came through the doors.

"This is Josephine and Paula," Lila answered.

"My name is PJ," PJ corrected.

"Well, that's lovely," The lady said and smiled wider. "Josephine, do you have a cute nickname also?"

"Sure do. PJ gave it to me on account of how quick I am when there's trouble."

"Well, what is it?" the lady asked, as she stood and came around the desk with a small glass dish in her hand. She was a tiny woman, Panic noticed, and she liked that she was almost as tall as her. She wore a green skirt that matched her green sweater and Panic thought she looked like an elf or maybe a leprechaun. The dish in her hand was filled with star-light mints wrapped in pink cellophane. She held the candy out and Panic took a piece then looked at PJ. PJ nodded before she eagerly unwrapped the candy and plopped it in her mouth.

"We call her Panic," PJ answered for her and Panic grimaced at her forgetfulness.

"That's clever," the woman said and offered the candy dish to PJ.

Panic wondered if the woman had heard what PJ said. People almost always had a reaction to Panic's name. But often, like in the car, when she told Lila she'd seen the plane crash, she wasn't heard. Grownups didn't really care about what kids said.

The woman made her way back around the desk then said, "I'll buzz you through."

Glass doors to the left separated the reception area from a bus-tling room beyond filled with busy people and metal desks cluttered with papers and notebooks. The people—mostly men—moved about the room or else sat at typewriters stabbing pointed fingers at keys. They flipped through documents while cradling phones between their shoul-der and ear. Through the smoky air, Panic could see that the walls were lined with dark, wood paneling, which made the entire space feel like a cave.

The buzzer sounded with a monotone trill and then the deputy pushed the doors open and gestured the girls through. Bustling sounds of working, typing, talking, phones ringing, filled the silence of the re-ception area. Across the room, through the thick cigarette smoke, Panic could see her mom sitting at one of the desks with the deputy who had called himself Randolph. Panic broke into a run toward their mother.

Lila reached out to grab her but missed. "Darn it," she said to PJ, though PJ thought she hadn't really tried to keep Panic back.

"She's just upset," PJ explained. "This is hard for her, to see Mom arrested."

"Your mom's not arrested." Lila frowned. "She's probably going to be released and go home with you in a little bit, so maybe you can comfort your sister, huh?" Her words sounded like a question but when PJ played it over as they moved across the room, she thought of Lila's words more as a demand. Comfort your sister, how ironic, PJ thought, thinking back to the shoe, but she pushed it away. If Panic needed PJ to comfort her, then she would.

When they approached the desk where their mom was, PJ stood still. Her arms hung at her sides. She focused on a streak of grey in Betsy's hair. Their mom reached out and put her arms around PJ with forced affection.

"How are you doing with all of this?" She asked.

PJ didn't answer. Instead, she looked at her feet.

Deputy Randolph dragged a chair over from a nearby desk. "Have a seat, kiddo," he said. PJ sat. His thick, dark mustache reminded PJ of Tim Conway working with Mrs. Wiggins on the Carol Burnette Show. Deputy Randolph continued, "We are having a lady come in from Social Services to talk with you and your mom about your fight."

PJ looked at her mom then, but her mom looked away. Fight? PJ thought. Betsy reached toward Panic and rubbed her arm.

"She's a very nice woman." Deputy Randolph continued. "She comes in all the time to talk to kids and parents. I'm sure we can all agree that things will be better at your house if you and your mom can get along, right?" He paused and raised his eyebrows at PJ, but PJ was unmoved. With a sigh, Randolph said, "Well, let's have Deputy Friedman grab us some hot cocoa."

"Yum!" Panic said and she spun in place on her heel.

At that moment, a severe looking woman with grey hair that matched her grey suit, walked up to the desk, and extended her hand to PJ's mom.

"Betsy McCormack? My name is Eugenia Perón, but please call me Mrs. Perón." They shook hands. Mrs. Perón glanced at the girls but did not greet them. "We'll be meeting in the briefing room just as soon as they are finished up in there."

A voice from across the room called out, "All yours, Mrs. Perón."

"Well, then," Mrs. Perón said through a pinched smile. "If you'll please follow me, Mrs. McCormack."

Betsy looked at Deputy Randolph and he gestured for her to follow Mrs. Perón. Betsy stood and followed the severe woman. PJ and Panic fell in behind their mom, but Deputy Randolph held them back.

"Let's let your mom have a turn with Mrs. Perón first," Deputy Randolph said.

PJ noticed that no officers went with them as they wove their way through a field of desks. They disappeared through a doorway into a room out of view.

Panic took the chair where her mom had been sitting, as Lila returned with two hot cocoas. As they blew on their cocoa to cool it, they overheard a red-haired deputy sitting at the desk across the aisle talking to a co-worker about the plane crash.

"… I couldn't make out bodies by then because everything was so burned up, but I could smell it, you know. I could smell the charred flesh, like a backyard barbeque. The wreckage of the jet was all around me and it smelled like a goddamned tailgate party."

Lila cleared her throat with an exaggerated sound and the red-haired deputy looked at her. She gestured to the girls sitting close by. The man swiveled his chair and looked from Lila to Panic and PJ and then sat upright.

"Sorry Friedman," he said. "Didn't know we were PG rated."

Panic shifted in her chair and came to sit forward on the edge of her seat. She looked directly at the cop and said, "I saw it too, the plane crash. It was awful."

For a moment, nobody spoke. The room seemed to hold its collective breath. The deputy who had been talking about the crash was a young man. His gold name tag said he was Sampson, in his mid-twenties with a clean-shaven face, freckled, and short sideburns of red hair. He held Panic in his gaze. For a moment, his eyes glossed over then teared up. Then he asked Panic something remarkable that PJ herself wanted to answer. "Didn't it make you want to run away?"

"Yes," Panic answered without a split second's lapse. "But instead, I couldn't move. Instead, I was stuck, you know?"

"I know," he said. Sampson bent forward resting his elbows on his knees and leveling his face with Panic's.

"But then I fell over. At first there were these angels flying all around. And the smoke was so tall." Panic went on like she had when she told PJ about seeing the crash. "I saw an arm of black smoke reach up to the sky. A great dark hand was trying to catch them. I saw the angels swimming in the air and the hand was grabbing at them." She mimicked the hand in the air. "I knew they all died. I knew it right away, before I even saw it on T.V." Then she sat back and took a sip from her cocoa as if she'd just reported on Heidi Hill, the tattletale.

PJ looked at her sister then to Sampson who was visibly shaken by Panic's account. Tears spilled down his cheeks as his mouth hung open.

"If that ain't something," Sampson said at last.

"What about you?" the small girl asked like she was talking with a fellow classmate about how well they liked a chapter book.

Sampson shook his head and sat back blowing out a long breath and wiping his palms on his knees. Then he stared at Panic as if she had magically struck him dumb by what she shared.

Lila Friedman broke the spell. "PJ, I think we should go see if your mom is ready for us. Why don't you girls follow me?"

The girls stood to follow Lila, but not before Panic placed her small hand on the male deputy's leg, looked directly into his face, and said, "You should've run away. You still can."

"Come on," PJ said, and she grabbed Panic and pulled her along.

As they made their way across the station, PJ pushed her sister in front of her. "What the heck was that about?" She asked Panic.

"What?" Panic responded and hurried her step.

When they got to the door where they'd seen their mother enter, Lila indicated they should wait and then she disappeared through the door. The sisters stood facing each other, staring one another down. There was no menace in this act. They simply had no other place to look. They sometimes did this to see who would look away first, laugh, or crack a smile, stick out a tongue. But before long, Lila returned and ushered them into the room.

PJ noticed that the large room housed rows of long tables and chairs all facing a central podium at the front, with a T.V. mounted in the corner on a shelf. PJ and her sister made their way to a small circle of chairs in the back corner of the room and sat where Mrs. Perón and Betsy were already seated. Betsy looked agitated and uncomfortable. Mrs. Perón crossed her feet, and then placed a notebook on her lap. The girls looked from their mom to Mrs. Perón awkwardly awaiting instructions.

"Please have a seat," Mrs. Perón said.

PJ sat and decided she did not like Mrs. Perón. She wondered who this woman was and what kind of authority she had to remove them from their abandoned cocoa and the warm smiles from Lila Freidman and the red-haired cop. Even the thick mustache concealing the weird grin of Deputy Randolph had been a better option than being in this cold room with this cold woman.

Now that they were seated, PJ had a chance to get a better look at Eugenia Perón. Her grey hair was actually more silver, but the color must have turned prematurely because the woman had a youngish face, not like a grey-haired old lady. Her skin was smooth and tan, and her eyes, though cool and unexpressive, had a youthful charm to them, like she might at any moment burst out laughing at them and tell them the jig was up and that they were all on Candid Camera. But somewhere below her surface appearance, on a deeper level, Mrs. Perón personified seriousness. She was all business and she started by clearing her throat and tapping her pen's clicker on the notebook on her lap to bring out its ballpoint tip for writing.

"Before we begin, I need to let you know by law that I am a government employee who must conduct myself by certain rules. Although I am your advocate, I will report any abuses as necessary. This means that anything you tell me about sexual misconduct or abusive behaviors that lead to harm or jeopardize the health and wellbeing of these children—" She stopped and looked at PJ. "Or vice-versa—can be used as evidence for conviction. The same rules apply if abuse has already occurred." Mrs. Perón's eyes moved over PJ's fading bruises.

It seemed odd that Mrs. Perón would state this up front. It was almost as if she didn't want Betsy to confess to hitting PJ with a shoe. Perhaps such a confession would lead to more work for this woman, a woman who maybe didn't like her job so much, based on the way she talked with such pithy words and upright superiority. PJ wasn't sure why, but she hated her; she hated Eugenia Perón from that moment.

"One more thing I should mention," Mrs. Perón said. "Running away from home is against the law for minor children. And taking younger siblings away from home can sometimes be construed as kidnapping." She narrowed her eyes at PJ before she continued. "Now then," Mrs. Perón said. "Tell me about the . . . fight." And her tone seemed to emphasize the word 'fight' as if she were referring to two teenagers who had had a squabble over a boy. She even paused for a millisecond before 'fight' like the she needed to find the right word for the act.

The air grew thick in the cold room. Betsy looked from PJ to Panic and then back to PJ. Then she took a deep breath. "It was stupid, really. My daughter took my shoes and we argued. I had been drinking and she didn't want me to go out to the bus stop because I might get hurt. So, she took the shoes, and we grabbed each other's arms. There was a tussle . . ." The word "tussle" angered PJ further but Betsy continued. She spun a complete fabrication of the events that had taken place that night.

PJ listened to her mother's words as the story grew from her throat, from somewhere deep inside a sad place in her heart. What had really happened was that PJ had been sitting at the kitchen table laughing with her sister and eating pork n' beans when her mom had come at her, hammering on her with a single shoe, a thick espadrille sandal, a shoe PJ would never forget. PJ had no idea why her mother had attacked her with the shoe; she still did not know why. Betsy just snapped and started hitting her. Maybe it had something to do with the PSA crash. Betsy had been engrossed in the news coverage all day. Her mom had been so upset watching the news reports, sipping on whatever she could find to soothe her feelings. But it was weird, so sudden and unexpected. During any of the past times there was a reason her mom had hit her. PJ had sassed her mom or done something dumb, like left clothes on the laundry line. During those times, her mom needed to teach her a lesson. But the day of the PSA crash was unwarranted. Plus, Betsy didn't seem upset at all when Panic told her later that she had seen the crash. Even when PJ asked her in the front yard about the shoe, Betsy had not given her a clear answer. Yet, now, there she was, telling Mrs. Perón that PJ tried to take the shoes to. . .to keep her from leaving? From walking to the bus stop? PJ was baffled by this, but then she realized she hadn't been paying attention. When she picked up what her mom was saying next, she almost fell out of her chair.

"And she scratched me here, and here," Betsy said, pulling up the sleeves of her shirt to reveal deep scratch marks on her arms. Mrs. Perón looked at the scratches and jotted something down in the notebook. Betsy continued, "Then, she just sort of went crazy on me. She started yelling about her dad. You might see in the notes that I told Officer Randolph about their father."

"Yes, I saw that."

"Well, I was just so drunk and I—" she choked. Then Betsy started to cry. Through sobs she managed, "I didn't mean to hurt her, but I guess I sort of went into self-defense mode."

PJ could not believe what she was hearing. Her mom's version of things was so completely different than what had happened. Yet, the way Betsy told the story to Mrs. Perón almost made PJ wonder if there was some truth to this story. It certainly gave her pause. One of the things PJ could not reconcile was the shoe. She wondered if this was part of an earlier conversation and that her mom had remembered something about it during her drunken haze.

"I see," said Mrs. Perón, not showing any emotional reaction and jotting something else in her notebook. "And you, young lady?"

She turned to PJ and looked directly at her for the first time. PJ saw gold flecks in the blue irises of Mrs. Perón's eyes. She stared at Mrs. Perón. She studied the subtle lines around her eyes and at the corners of her mouth, guessing the woman to be about 35 years old. Her mom was only 33 and she figured Mrs. Perón was a little older, because of the grey hair, though not older by much. Mrs. Perón had a soft chin and neck that mocked her rigid demeanor. Her forehead had a few horizontal lines that indicated she might be a worrier. PJ wondered why she had gone into this kind of work, this 'social work.' What even was social work? It sounded like someone who organized events for the spirit club at school.

Mrs. Perón cleared her throat.

"I was afraid my mom would go to the bus stop," PJ said, resigned and parroting what she'd heard Betsy say. "I guess I got scared."

Mrs. Perón frowned and the horizontal lines on her forehead deepened. Now PJ understood why they were there. Mrs. Perón seemed to know that PJ was lying, and she tipped her head to the side and harrumphed. "So, you say you wanted to keep your mom from leaving while intoxicated?"

PJ looked at Panic where the small girl sat bent forward in her chair looking between them all, her mouth hanging open.

"She was headed out and I wanted to stop her from leaving." This time PJ said it with more confidence, almost daring Mrs. Perón to contradict her.

"How old are you, Paula?"

"It's PJ."

"It will be Paula for this interview," Mrs. Perón said.

"Well, then I'm sure you won't mind if I call you Eugenia?" PJ crossed her arms over her chest.

"Oh, I see," Mrs. Perón said with her eyebrows raised toward Betsy. "I'm sure this teenage attitude is part of the problem in your home, is it?"

Betsy shrugged but did not say anything.

"Fine, PJ," Mrs. Perón said. "Are you 14 years old?"

"Yes."

"And do you attend Granite Hill High School and are you in your freshman year?" She was looking at her notes, reading from a sheet of paper with a handwritten scrawl. "That is 9th grade, correct?"

"All of that is correct." PJ unfolded her arms.

"And how about you?" Mrs. Perón now spoke to Panic and Panic sat upright.

"I'm just fine, Mrs. P.," Panic blurted. "Er, Perón. Sorry ma'am."

"It's okay, Josephine," Mrs. Perón said, and she smiled. PJ found her grin more disconcerting than her cold, rigid face. The smile turned the wrinkles at the corners of her mouth in outward arrow shapes giving her an eerie clownish grin.

"Her name's Panic," PJ said, but her sister shook her head.

"It's okay, PJ. Mrs. Perón can call me Josephine. Just for now, okay?" And she reached over and placed her hand on PJ's knee. Mrs. Perón's eyes followed the little girl's hand in the act, and she quickly jotted something down on her notepad.

"Now, Josephine, can you please tell me what happened on the day that your mom and sister had such a terrible fight?"

"Yes, ma'am," Panic said. "Well, first, that jet crashed. It was terrible. There was smoke and a huge bang like the end of the world. I was on the hill looking at the islands like PJ had shown me the night before. When the planes hit, I saw the smoke and everything. Even angels."

"Dear, that is not what I am talking about. I mean, tell me about the fight that your mom and your sister had that night, the reason for Paula's . . .PJ's bruises." Again, the woman's eyes swept PJ's bruises, though her gaze was fleeting.

"Oh, sure, only it wasn't like my mom said and it wasn't like PJ said." When Panic said this, both PJ and Betsy shared a glance. They had been caught in their lie and they would need to figure a way out of it quick. Panic went on, "PJ made my dinner and we sat together and made jokes. Then Mama came out of nowhere and started hitting PJ with the shoe." She stopped and her eyes welled with tears and Mrs. Perón wrote something down. "It was scary. At first, I said, Mama, Mama, stop. Please stop. But then, when I knew she couldn't hear me, I sat in the corner and covered my ears." Panic recreated the act of covering her ears. Tears now flowed down her cheeks. "I wanted to help but I was so scared."

Mrs. Perón looked from Panic to Betsy and PJ, and then back to Panic.

The door opened, and Lila came in with two hot cocoa mugs. When Lila surveyed the group of them and saw the tears on Panic's face, she stopped short.

"Sorry, thought the girls might still like these. They left them at my desk." she said.

She held the cocoa mugs in one hand with both handles, like waitresses with steins of beer, like Betsy did when she served them hot cocoa at the café.

"Should I come back?" she asked. "These are cold anyway. I can make new ones."

Panic was sniffling. PJ shifted in her chair and Betsy leaned back and sighed.

"No," Mrs. Perón said. "Instead, would you mind taking Josephine out for a bit? Maybe she can enjoy her cocoa at your desk? I need to talk with these ladies about some private matters." Mrs. Perón's tone shifted when she said, "private matters."

"No problem, Mrs. Perón." Lila answered. PJ noticed that even Lila called the social worker 'Mrs. Perón.' "I'll leave your cocoa here, PJ." And she set the second cup of cocoa on Panic's chair once the little girl stood to join her. Then, Panic and Lila left the room, with Panic wiping her eyes and Lila gently guiding her by her shoulder.

Once the door shut, Mrs. Perón turned to PJ. "What kind of games are you running with that child?" She asked PJ.

"Ma'am?" PJ was flummoxed.

"I see how afraid she is. Have you ever struck her or harmed her in any way?"

"No, ma'am. Panic is my baby sister and I—"

"Have you threatened her to respond, forced her to lie? I've seen her type of behavior before. Both you and your mother have corroborated this story, yet Josephine seems compelled to tell another version. Perhaps this is a version you coerced her into telling."

"Oh, now," Betsy said shaking her head.

"Let me finish, please, Mrs. McCormack." Mrs. Perón snapped the pen's clicker with her thumb. "Your family is in a bad way, and I intend to help. I will mandate visits to your home once per week and I will interview everyone in the home at that time. Do you understand me?"

"I don't think I have a choice, do I?" Betsy asked.

"Actually, you don't," Mrs. Perón smirked.

Betsy's face remained emotionless. PJ did not understand what was going on, but she knew enough to keep quiet.

"I understand." Betsy did not blink or look away.

"And as for you," Mrs. Perón turned back to PJ. "I am going to pay close attention to you, young lady. If I think you are manipulating that child or abusing her, there will be juvenile hall for you. I think your generation likes to call it 'Juvie,' but it is not a cool place, young lady. No cigarette smoking, no Bad News Bears or T.V.; I can tell you. You just keep that in mind."

PJ did not answer. She couldn't believe what she was hearing. It seemed that what her mother had done to her had been turned around to appear like PJ either brought it on herself or else had inflicted the abuse on Panic, maybe even put Panic up to the lie. PJ loved Panic more than anything in the whole world, more than she could ever love Betsy and even more than she loved their dad. Panic was innocent and pure and sweet, like white sugar poured straight form the bag into the sugar bowl before the ants found it, or the coffee drips formed nasty brown lumps. How could they think she would ever hurt Panic? Then, PJ wondered if maybe she had been harming her sister. Was it fair to convince her sister to run away? Fair to have Panic choose a side? After all, Panic was only nine years old. She couldn't survive on the streets, even if they were on their way to their aunt's house. It was a stupid idea and PJ knew it.

She looked at her mom who seemed to age ten years in the last ten minutes. Betsy's shoulders sagged and her jaw hung slack. A look of defeat shadowed her face. PJ imagined her mom's worry: that these visits from Mrs. Perón would interfere with her drinking. PJ's mind always went to her mom's drinking. From the yellow in the whites of Betsy's eyes to the sallow, sagging skin on her face and neck—a stark contrast to Mrs. Perón's smooth skin—PJ knew Betsy was sick, but not the kind of sick for a doctor. At first, PJ had been certain that Mrs. Perón was older than her mom, yet, at that moment, she could not be sure. Betsy looked so sad, so sad and old, slumped in her chair looking at the floor, not looking up at PJ. Not even looking at Mrs. Perón. PJ noticed the floor, then too, a cold linoleum with a mosaic of large, multicolored squares— all sorts of muted browns and yellows, probably intended to subdue, to keep people calm, but PJ found herself wanting to pry the squares up with her fingernails. Her eyes found a seam where the corner of the tile curled up. She saw her fingers work the corner, even at the expense of her fingernails. She'd pry up every tile, put the brown colors together in a pile and all the yellow colors together in a different pile. Even the varied shades of brown: darker browns with each other and tans in their own group. She did not find the floor pattern soothing.

"I am going to release you," Mrs. Perón said, checking something off from her clipboard. "I will get a more in-depth interview with both of you when I come out to your house." She quickly added, "before the week is out."

Then, Mrs. Perón stood and left the room without another word.

Betsy and PJ stayed in their chairs. PJ waited for her mom to get up first, but Betsy stayed and stared at the door where Mrs. Perón had exited. Large, dish-shaped lamps hung from the ceiling in rows. PJ thought they looked like UFOs all flying in formation, coming to take over the world. Each lamp had a light bulb dutifully glowing in its center. A few lamps, PJ noticed, had burnt out bulbs.

When Betsy spoke, her voice sounded strained. "I'll need some help getting the house cleaned up."

"Yeah, sure." PJ said, and she bit the inside of her lip.

"PJ," her mom said, looking at her then. "Thank you."

It wasn't an apology, but it was something and PJ managed to say, "Yeah." Her version of "you're welcome."

They got up and walked across the linoleum floor back into the bustling sheriff station. The two girls went back to Lila Friedman's desk where the young deputy sat typing on a fillable form. PJ asked about the location of the restrooms and was given directions to proceed down a dim hallway. Once she found the bathroom for "women" PJ went inside. She did not need to use the restroom, but she did need to be away from Betsy.

The room was stark white, with porcelain, white sinks hung along the wall and two thin mirrors like eyes to another dimension. PJ washed her hands and then looked up examining her face. She noticed that a new crop of acne had sprouted along her forehead, and she smoothed her bangs over to cover the pimples. The bruise along her temple still showed a thin green tint. Freckles she'd always hated seemed more conspicuous along her cheeks, a result of the ever-radiant sun of early autumn. She placed her finger along her lips to feel how chapped they were.

She thought of Manny Gonzáles, imagined his smooth, bronzed skin, seemingly without blemishes. She wondered how he could look so perfect but decided that it must be a trick of the way she imagined him. She wished Manny were there then. She had a brave notion that she might like to kiss him. Then, she thought of Betsy. PJ was glad that her mother wasn't arrested. She was terrified of her mom's rage, but she was also terrified that Betsy would go away to jail or prison. Once, Betsy had been so drunk, she'd forgotten how to get home and got on a bus that went to Chula Vista. According to Betsy, when she got there, she found a pub that would serve her in the early morning hours and there she stayed until the blackout consumed her. It was four days before she made it home and, during that time, PJ and Panic were sick with fear she might never return. As much as they feared her, it was worse to imagine she might never return. When Betsy finally made it home, she was so casual about the entire ordeal. She called it an adventure and gave the spotty details to her girls. But PJ knew that something like this could happen again at any time. And what if Betsy didn't make it back next time? Or what if she decided she liked the place where she got lost? This terrified her. Even though PJ longed to run away, to escape El Cajon, she was more frightened that her mom would escape and leave the girls alone in their dark house to an unknown fate.

PJ pushed the fear away and left the bathroom. When she re-turned to where she'd left her family, Betsy was nowhere in sight. She found Panic sitting at Lila Friedman's desk sipping cocoa and talking in an animated tone.

". . . and the cloud of smoke looked like a giant hand, and it was reaching up and grabbing the angels and they were all swooping and crashing. I'm sorry. Not crashing. Not like the planes were crashing, I mean." Panic made wild motions with her hand in the air showing flying and swooping, her fingers swiveled and dove. Then she clapped once and shook her head. "Then they were gone."

Lila noticed that PJ had joined them. She smiled at her and said, "Panic has been telling me quite a story about the PSA crash."

"PJ!" Panic shouted and jumped out of her chair. "I got a badge!" She showed PJ a plastic badge pinned to her shirt.

"You can keep that, too," Lila said, as Betsy returned—from where, PJ could not tell. Lila asked Betsy, "Do you need a ride?"

"Well, obviously." Betsy seemed agitated.

"I'll have to see if I can get one of our volunteers to run you home. We are swamped here since the crash. There was some looting in the neighborhood where the planes went down. It's terrible, folks taking advantage, and all. Our precinct has been helping out. Tough work."

"I'm sure it is," Betsy said, placing her hand on Panic's shoulder. "I do not envy the job of you and the fire department. Do they have any idea what caused the crash?"

"Not at this point," Lila's voice lowered. "They think the tower at Lindbergh Field gave bad instructions or missed a warning signal, some new alert system. Nobody knew how it worked." She winced when she said this, like it hurt to say.

"How terrible," Betsy said, still her mouth remained set in a firm line.

PJ had the impression that the two women forgot the girls were standing there, even though their mom still held Panic's shoulder.

"So," PJ started. "Can we go?" She'd had enough of the police, and she'd had enough of grown-ups to last her a lifetime.

"You know," Betsy said. "If I had the right amount of fare, we could just make the 24 bus. That bus comes down Main about every thirty minutes and I think we'd have time to get the next one." She gave Lila a withered look. "But I was brought here without my purse, see."

"Oh, sure." Lila said. "Let me see if I can help."

PJ rolled her eyes. She knew her mom wasn't about to take the bus. She knew that whatever amount of money the lady deputy gave her mom would go toward buying a bottle. No matter. It would get them through the aftermath of this visit, settle her mom down after all this turmoil. It would mean a long walk back to their neighborhood, they might not even get there until late in the afternoon or even nightfall, but Betsy could be pacified.

"I have a five," Lila said, and she handed Betsy five dollars. "Please take it and get the girls a little snack up at the Bi-Lo. Actually, Kaelin's Market is closer. You can get change for the bus and the 24 stops right there, too."

"Oh, I couldn't," Betsy said, though she reached for the money as she said it.

"It's nothing."

"Thank you," Betsy smiled and took the five. "The sheriff's department is better because of people like you, Deputy Freidman. Thank you for looking after my girls, too."

Lila turned to PJ and took her in for a long moment then said, "If you need anything, you can always call here. You have a phone book? The Yellow Pages?"

"Ma'am, we don't have a phone at our house."

"Well, you go to a neighbor's house. You can go up to . . . what's her name? Mrs. Stanislaw's house, you hear me? Not that you'll need to." And then she gave a curt grimace to Betsy.

As the family made their way out of the sheriff's station, the receptionist with the starlight mints candies asked the girls if they would like to take a candy for the road. Panic accepted and then, so did PJ, but only so she could give hers to Panic later.

PJ thoughts were still heavy. She wondered if she might be manipulating her little sister. She thought of all the talks they'd had and of all the times PJ thought she might have been preparing Panic to run away or to protect herself if their mom decided to turn on Panic and start hitting her too. Maybe, in all her preparations to keep Panic safe all PJ really accomplished was instilling fear in her sister. Maybe what was really happening was PJ taking all her own fear, pain, and insecurities and imprinting them on Panic, making her little sister feel scared too. Panic had nothing to fear. She had never been hit by their mom. She had good friends at school. She got good grades and did really well at everything she tried, even when she missed as many days as she had since the beginning of the school year. And on top of it all, Panic barely remembered their dad, so she probably had a different kind of grief that was more nostalgia than pain. Panic seemed to only remember their dad through the lens of PJ. He was more a storybook character to Panic, or so PJ thought. If PJ never brought him up at all, maybe Panic wouldn't even experience the sadness of his absence. Instead, Panic could have the nostalgia of him, without the pain of abandonment.

"I know what you're thinking, PJ," Betsy said.

PJ looked at her mom as they walked along the street. For a second, she wondered if her mom had been able to read her thoughts.

"You think I'm going take this money and buy booze and make us all walk home, right?"

"Well . . ."

"Well, I'm not. We're gonna catch the 24, like I said. I'll get you girls a candy bar, too. Kaelin's got 'em for twenty-five cents. The bus will only be thirty-five cents each and only seventy cents total, cause Panic'll be free of charge."

"How do you figure Panic will be free?" PJ asked.

"Cause she's under ten years old. It's a rule. I never pay for her. I never paid for you when you were younger than ten either."

This was information that PJ did not know, and she made a mental note. Even though she was concerned that her behavior might be influencing her sister, one thing was certain: she needed to protect Panic. If that meant having to take her away someday, then knowing the bus was free to get to Santa Fe Station—at least for Panic—would give them a little more money for resources and for other necessary things. Why had she not noticed that her mom never paid for Panic before?

"That will leave just enough for a six-pack, way I see it," Betsy said, looking pleased with herself. She took Panic's hand in hers as they walked along the sidewalk down Main Street.

CHAPTER SIX

The bus let them off near Greenfield and East Madison, only a short walk to their rural neighborhood. Panic felt tired. She was hungry but kept it to herself. The small amount of candy she ate only made her feel worse. Somewhere along their bus ride, Betsy had opened a beer can and started sneaking sips, and, by the time they walked up their long dirt road, she was already on her third can.

"You know they'll take you girls, don't you?" Betsy said as they walked.

Panic looked at PJ. Neither girl responded, knew better to talk.

"That's right," Betsy continued. "They'll take me away and lock me up, which wouldn't be so bad." She took a slurping pull from her beer car. "They eat well in prisons for ladies, I hear. But I'd be worried about the two of you." She caught eyes with Panic before she continued. "They'd surely split you girls up, no family to ship you to. I don't want to imagine where you might be if that happened. Yes, sirree."

Panic had never imagined such a fate. Couldn't. Betsy stopped talking as they walked along the hot, dusty road, so Panic only had her thoughts. She knew that PJ had the same thoughts—they had to stay together, no matter what. And, as terrible as Betsy could be, neither girl wanted to think about not having their mom around. Panic was often gripped by a deep fear when Betsy did not come home after work, when she wasn't in her bedroom or on the couch in the morning. What if she left like their dad? The fear became so visceral for Panic that she pushed it away and, instead, turned her attention to the whispering oak leaves overhead, to the crackling gravel below their feet, to the depth of blue above and around them.

When they passed Mrs. Stanislaw's house, no one looked toward the pristine ranchero framed by silver dollar eucalyptus trees standing like sentinels along its sides. Panic sensed the eyes of Mrs. Stanislaw peering out through the drapes from the front window, still she dared not look. Instead, she noticed her worn tennis shoes, dirty and old. By the time they got home, the late afternoon sun had stretched the shadows of the oaks across their yard in long lines of shade.

"I gotta rest my eyes," Betsy said as she crossed the threshold into the cool house and lumbered off down the hall toward her bedroom. This statement was familiar. She'd said it a hundred times, maybe a thousand. Their mom would go to her bedroom for a few hours—or maybe until the next day if the remaining beers went with her. She wouldn't go to work that night. Plus, Panic and PJ would be on their own for dinner, not that they'd had lunch.

PJ's stomach growled. Panic could hear it.

"Why does she need to rest her eyes all the time?" Panic asked.

"It's got nothing to do with her eyes."

They made their way into the kitchen and PJ started going through the cupboards while Panic cleaned up the table from that morning's pancake breakfast. It seemed like a week had gone by since they sat there laughing that morning.

PJ said, "I don't want to cut into our food stash." She meant the food they packed for their escape. So, she explored the kitchen seeking ingredients for something—anything—that she could make for a late lunch or early dinner. After their pancake feast, the cupboards were nearly empty, save a box of Italian style breadcrumbs and some dried onion soup mix. PJ said she could make meatloaf if they had any ground beef. Even without ketchup, she could pull it off, but meat was a key ingredient. Panic loved PJ's humor. She asked if Panic would eat plain onion soup, but the thought of warm onions turned Panic's stomach and she feigned a gag. It was such a hot day that any kind of soup sounded terrible, no matter their hunger. The prospects in the refrigerator were worse. In the center of the middle shelf stood a can of beans that was capped by a square of tinfoil held on by a red rubber band. The can had been there for longer than a week. The only reason anyone hadn't thrown it out yet was because the mayonnaise jar would become the last remaining item in the fridge. Having only one item left in the refrigerator seemed too depressing to any of them. Plus, Panic was a little afraid to touch it, afraid that any movement would stir up its stench.

Panic sat at the kitchen table.

"We're gonna have to eat some of our supplies," PJ finally said.

"Okay," she said, biting her fingernail.

"Okay?" PJ asked, "If we dip into our stash, we'll have to give up our plans, at least for now."

Panic knew their resources were too thin anyway. And now they had to worry about visits from Mrs. Perón, whether their mom would go to jail, maybe being arrested themselves for trying to run away, and possibly getting split up. That's what happened to kids when their parents weren't around; PJ had told her. A sick feeling grew in the pit of Panic's gut that said her mom could get in big trouble, maybe even go to jail for real. Plus, they both knew they needed a better plan than simply walking into the chaparral or taking a bus to see an aunt they hadn't seen in years.

"So, let's have sandwiches and then we can go outside and build some more on the fort before it gets dark. I know where we can get some particle board and plywood trimmings."

"Where?" Panic asked.

"I've got my sources."

"Okay." Panic brightened. Working on their fort was one of Panic's favorite things to do. Her sister always knew how to cheer her up.

•

They ate their dry sandwiches, sipping tap water and sitting outside along the side-yard retaining wall. A tarantula hawk dragged the carcass of a dead tarantula across the dirt. Its orange wings glinted in the sun. A horny toad basked on a rock nearby. Their yard, like many of the yards in their neighborhood, was unfenced and mostly wild. In fact, to call the area where they lived an actual neighborhood implied a certain organization to the place. Everyone used that familiar convention, but Forest Creek wasn't like a neighborhood at all.

Their closest neighbors were the Gonzáles family, but with a section of the avocado farm, which belonged to the Minkus family, in between. Even though Manny's family was technically farther away, PJ thought of them as their next-door neighbors.

PJ loved to listen to Manny tell stories about his family. He told her about his visits to his abuela's house in Mexico, where the tortillas were so thin they melted in your mouth. Once he told her about how his Tio Mike had hitchhiked all the way to Washington D.C. to ask President Jimmy Carter if he would pardon all the draft dodgers. Of course, he hadn't gone alone, but the story was about his antics more than the act of pardoning those who evaded service during Vietnam. PJ's dad didn't like draft dodgers; he called such men "Conchies" and thought they were cowards. But Tio Mike didn't seem like a conchie. His blundering adventures were so funny that PJ didn't mind listening to Manny tell them again and again.

"The particle board's over at Manny's," PJ said to Panic as they finished their sandwiches.

"Ah, jeeze, PJ," Panic groaned and gave an exaggerated eye roll.

"What?"

"If we go over there, you're gonna end up talking to him forever. I don't wanna get stuck there. You said we could work on the fort." Panic kicked the dirt and pouted.

"Do you want the boards or not?"

Panic stared at PJ for a solid ten-count. Neither dared a blink. "Fine," Panic said, folding her arms.

"We won't stay but a minute. Only long enough to get the boards," PJ reassured her. "Besides, today is Swap Meet day so they'll be tired. I bet they're still unloading. He'll be too busy to hang around with a bunch of girls."

"How do you know he'll give you the boards?" Panic asked.

"He already told me."

Panic's arms stayed firmly locked around her chest, crossed tight. She stuck out her lower lip and narrowed her eyes at PJ.

"Fine," PJ said. "He didn't tell me I could have the boards. But I know he has scraps from the new rabbit cages they are building, and I know he won't need them or want them."

"That sounds like a lot of talk to me." Panic said raising her eyebrows.

"Listen. If you want to count to one hundred once we get there, I'll be done before you get to ninety."

"Promise?"

"Cross my heart," PJ said, and she drew an 'X' on the middle of her chest with her fingertip.

•

As PJ expected, Manny was in the driveway with his dad unloading items from their morning at the Swap Meet. They were pulling crates out of a pickup truck when the girls arrived. The screen door screeched and then slapped with a clack as Luis came out of the house. He saw Panic and PJ and bounded toward them with a happy grin on his face.

"Hola, Panic," Luis said.

"Hola, Luis," Panic responded but quickly added, "We're not staying."

Luis's grin faded.

"But I do need your help," Panic added, squinting at Luis because the sun was behind him. "I need you to help me count to one hundred."

"Que?"

"I don't know why. Just one hundred, Luis. I need to count. Can you help?"

"You can't count to one hundred?"

"Don't be silly. Of course I can. But I thought we could count together, being as I can only stay for a little bit. Can you count with me?" She spread her arms as if posing a grand question.

"In English or Espanol?"

Panic looked at PJ and PJ laughed and then shrugged. This earned her another eye roll from her little sister.

"I guess whichever you think is faster," Panic said.

"Si. My mom has fresas. Let's go inside," Luis offered and then the two younger kids walked together toward the house with Luis carrying on about Atari and gesticulating wildly with his hands.

By now, Manny had stopped unloading crates and had come over to PJ.

"Hi," he said. He hooked his thumbs into his belt loops.

"Hi," PJ said. She felt a little lightheaded looking at Manny sweaty in the afternoon sun. "Can I ask you a favor?" PJ said pushing away her timidity. Manny's face and arms were slick with moisture and his shirt clung to his chest. She could see the contour of his muscles and she felt flushed even though she knew the afternoon heat was breaking.

"Sure," he said, wiping his palm across his brow and dragging his fingers back through his dark hair. "I'm about done working with my dad. We had such a great day at the Swap Meet. What do you need?"

"Hmm?" PJ asked, coming back from a thought that hadn't fully formed.

"The favor you were going to ask?"

"Oh, right." PJ looked away at the trees on the hillside. "Well, you said you built some new rabbit cages?"

"Hutches. Yeah?"

"Oh, well, I wondered if you had any scrap wood left over and what you were going to do with it."

"You want it? Sure." Manny said. He turned to his dad and asked, "Papi, can I give PJ some of that wood by the garage?"

His dad grinned and waved at PJ, then gave a thumbs-up. "You tell your mom we said hello," Mr. Gonzáles.

"I will, sir." PJ nodded. "Thank you."

Manny touched PJ's arm and PJ felt her stomach turn in a way that reminded her of her younger going high on the swing set.

"You need it for something special? We got lots." Manny took a few steps toward their garage and waved for her to follow. They went around the side of the garage to find, stacked against the house, an assortment of lumber. More than scraps. Two-by-fours and whole sheets of plywood were arranged in neat piles along with pressure-treated posts and other lengths of cut wood.

"That's a lot of rabbit hutches," PJ said, trying to make a joke.

"Well, we have a lot of rabbits."

"How many?" PJ asked and she turned to watch him bend to a pile of assorted cuts of lumber.

"Well, right now we only have about forty. But soon, we'll have a lot more. Our population is exploding. We have about twenty does expecting right now." He stood upright with a few boards in his arms.

"Does? Like deer?"

"Yeah. The males are called 'bucks' and the females are called 'does.' The babies are called 'kits' which means kitten." Manny smiled at her when he said this. Then he returned to his work stacking the wood he gathered near PJ's feet.

"So, with twenty does expecting, how many babies will you have?" PJ made small talk trying to distract herself from noticing Manny's beautiful eyes and taut muscles. But as she thought more about the rabbits, she became genuinely interested.

"Oh, that's the crazy part." Manny stood and placed his hands on his hips. His eyes seemed to sparkle in the sunlight. "Each doe can have a dozen kits, so we are expecting to go from forty rabbits to two hundred and forty for inventory! It could start any day now."

PJ admired Manny's smooth skin. His light eyes gave her a fluttering sensation each time he looked at her.

"Wow, that's a lot of rabbits." She said and she wanted to fan herself with her hand.

"Sure is. Which is why we need all the new hutches."

Then, Manny tipped his head sideways in a gesture indicating PJ should follow him. He moved around the back of the garage. She followed Manny around the corner and saw two rows of wooden hutches standing on stilts. They were boxy and plain, with slanted roofs, and no windows. Manny made his way to the closest hutch and slid a latch off a nail attached to a small door. The door opened like a drawbridge; it even had short chains along its sides so the door wouldn't flap all the way down. Manny reached inside and pulled out a white rabbit with pink eyes. Its whiskered face peered around cautiously, and it jumped against Manny's chest, but Manny held tight to the animal as he secured the door.

"Oh, she's so cute!" PJ said reaching her hand out to stroke the rabbit along its back. Its white fur was the softest thing that PJ had ever felt, even softer than her own rabbit's foot. "She's lovely. What's her name?"

"Oh, this is a buck." Manny grinned and held the rabbit up to his face examining it. "I don't think he has a name. I mean, we never name them. Luis sometimes still wants to but it's better if we don't."

He passed the rabbit to PJ, and she took it in her arms. She could feel the rabbit squirm a little but then it settled into the crook of her arm and wiggled its nose up at her. Its pink eyes looked so intelligent to PJ that she was tempted to speak to the animal. Then, with a quick thrust, the buck jolted and kicked into PJ's abdomen with great force. Manny grabbed the rabbit before it sprang from PJ's arms. He held it by its ears and stuffed it back into the hutch.

"They aren't pets," Manny said.

"Oh." PJ nodded like she understood. Then she looked around the backyard and took in the wild mustard and chaparral broom. Like her yard, the Gonzáles' yard was open with no fences. The chaparral, wild and beautiful, came right up to their house. Manny's yard had sage brush, lemonade berry, and sumac. Beyond that were mature bushes of manzanita with smooth, spindly stalks that bent upward hosting dark green leaves and tiny, red berries. These looked like apples, which is why the plant was called tiny apple, 'manzanita' in Spanish. The chaparral broom looked exactly like kitchen brooms and worked as well as any broom, too. PJ could see where some of the vegetation had been cleared to make way for the rabbit hutches; new clearings were always apparent to her. Then she counted the hutches: twenty total. This struck her as odd that the numbers didn't seem to quite add up. There was extra lumber, but hardly enough for many more hutches.

"Hey, Manny?" She watched him lock the hutch. "How many rabbits are in each hutch?"

"Right now, two each for the does. One each for the bucks."

"But then, how will they all fit when the kittens come?" PJ asked, a tightening feeling constricting her throat.

Manny glanced at her from over his shoulder.

"Kits, Mija." He sighed as he turned to face her. "What I mean by 'two-hundred and forty for inventory' is the total we can sell. All the does won't have their kits at the same time. Two hundred forty is the number my dad uses to estimate our revenue; you know, inventory. We still need the space, though. After the bucks are harvested, the does will need to be spread—"

"Harvested?" PJ's voice was louder than she intended, and her hands had clenched into fists. She wanted to deny what she thought he meant by the word 'harvested.'

"Well, yeah. I mean, we sell them at the Swap Meet. I thought you knew."

PJ contemplated what this new information meant. Her heart thumped in her chest. Her eyes scanned the backyard again considering any other possible idea and replace the one that had begun to form, but the next thing Manny said solidified what she already knew to be true.

He said, "Where do you think your rabbit's foot keychain came from?"

A thick, sour paste seeped into PJ's throat. She thought she might be sick. PJ examined Manny's impassive expression, high cheekbones, golden eyes. His mouth hung open slightly in an almost dazed expression. She imagined him pulling the buck from its hutch and wringing its neck.

Suddenly her terror was replaced by something else: at once she felt stupid, embarrassed. It hadn't occurred to her that Manny's family butchered the rabbits. Of course, they did. She'd never considered the reason why they raised rabbits. But why hadn't she? She had one of their feet, carried it in her pocket, and she counted it as lucky and good. This new information seemed far too morbid for her to wrap her head around.

"I gotta go," PJ said and then turned toward the front of the house.

"But the wood!" Manny yelled after her.

"I don't think we need it anymore," PJ yelled without turning back. As she passed the front of the house, she called out for Panic but did not stop to wait for her sister to catch up to her.

Panic sat on a cluster of boulders with Luis. She clutched a brown paper bag in one hand and a frozen, red paleta in the other, the popsicle waving in the air as she laughed with Luis. PJ yelled out, "Let's go," and she heard Panic say goodbye. Luis said something in Spanish. Then the younger girl hurried to catch up with her big sister presently stomping away from the yard.

"What gives? Where's the wood?" Panic asked, catching her breath as she fell into stride next to PJ, taking two steps for each of her sister's single steps. "Slow down."

PJ did not slow down, and Panic struggled to keep up. The heat of the afternoon had waned, and the evening was coming faster now. Her face, where the bruise remained, throbbed with each step but PJ persisted. To keep up, Panic took two steps for each of PJ's. The two girls hurried along the gravel road back toward their house.

"PJ, where is the wood?" Panic asked again, but her sister did not answer.

"What happened? Did he kiss you?" Panic huffed her words. "Luis said that Manny wanted to kiss you. And that's why he took you around the back of the house. But I didn't believe him."

This stopped PJ in her tracks. She turned to Panic and searched her face, her red mouth stained with the strawberries from the paleta. She couldn't decide if what Panic said about Manny was true but also, she was unsure how much to tell her about the rabbits. PJ loved her good luck charm, her lucky rabbit's foot, her special extra trinket, but to think back on that sweet whiskered face of the bunny in her arms—that buck that would be dead within a few days, his feet dyed a bright shade of some unnatural color and then hung up to dry, sold at the Swap Meet for a few dollars to some jerk who would dangle it from his belt loop on his way to a bar or auto shop—made her head spin. Her eyes searched Panic's for some guidance or comfort, something to help her make sense of the world in that moment. In all that had happened within that long day, PJ needed to make sense of something.

Panic hoisted up her left hand in which she clutched the small, brown paper bag. "I got pan dulce," she said. Mrs. Gonzáles's sweet bread was better than the panaderia on Main Street. Panic repeated herself and shook the bag at PJ, "Pan dulce, PJ."

Only then did PJ cry.

CHAPTER SEVEN

That night the rabbits came to PJ in her sleep, so veiled in lucid slumber she could not tell reality from dream. They hopped about within her vision, dashing here and there, as she tried to catch them. She dreamt she could hear them screaming like she'd once heard from a rabbit in the eucalyptus tree out back, caught by a mother owl. The dream shifted to the howling wind and then to the screaming rabbit pinned to the branch by the talon of the mother bird. A new pitch rose, frantic. PJ ran to the back porch and looked up the hill at the spindly eucalyptus—tall, towering above the oaks, so out of place in their valley. The tree's long arms stretched above the oaks; its silvery leaves churned in the wind.

In the branches near the tree's center was a hollow where an owl pair had nested for a few seasons. The largest branch extended from the hallow and the mother owl perched there against the thrashing silvered leaves. She was a great horned and the larger of the pair. In her talons, she held the squirming rabbit to the branch. The rabbit screamed in protest, a sound like a human infant in distress, but it also wailed in concert with the screech of the mother owl calling to her young. Then PJ saw the juveniles; two clumsy babies, still thick with down, emerged from the hallow in the tree, and lumbered along the branch, their heads bobbing in an almost comical fashion. Timidly, they hopped along the scratched bark to where their mother held the prize. The rabbit screamed louder still. They closed in on the trapped creature and then silence won out, an absence of sound that was at once worse than the screaming, a silence that shot PJ bolt upright in bed.

Waking from the dream, PJ breathed hard. Her heart raced. She sat looking around the dim corners of the room, surprised that there were no rabbits or owls there.

Once awake, PJ could not sleep again. The first light of dawn described the room around her; the white teeth of Leif Garret came into full view from the poster near her bed. She turned and stared at the pile of magazines, National Geographic, that she'd brought home for her civics project. Their yellow spines laddered up the stack atop her old chair in the corner. PJ thought about reading some to ease herself back into sleep. Instead, she got out of bed and crept down the hall to her sister's room.

With a firm grip, she shook Panic by the arm and whispered, "Wake up."

Panic pushed PJ off with a brush of her hand, such a sound sleeper. She didn't have the same haunting things to keep her awake, and for that PJ was glad. She envied her little sister and wished her all the peace that ignorance could provide. Then she remembered the pan dulce.

"Panic, there's sweet bread for breakfast," she tempted.

"No." A muffled voice came from somewhere deep within her slumber, buried beneath her pillow.

"I'll eat them all," PJ threatened. "I will."

"Fine." The pillow came off Panic's head and she turned to PJ, propping herself up on her elbow. Only one of her eyes opened, the size of a coin slot. Her hair stuck to the side of her face. "What time is it? What do you want?"

"Don't be crabby. I have a mission for us. Top secret, but very important."

"I don't want to go on a mission." She paused and yawned, then lay back down on her pillow before declaring, "I want to sleep."

In an act of desperation, PJ decided to be direct.

"I need to save the rabbits, Jo." That would do it, PJ was certain. She had used her real name, and she only did that when something needed her absolute attention.

Panic continued to lie on her pillow, but now she opened both of her eyes and looked directly at PJ. She scanned PJ's face, an expression of scrutiny developing on hers.

"I have a bad feeling about this."

"No," PJ reassured her and pulled her arms to sit her upright. "You're still sleeping, is all. You need to wake up and hear me out." Once she was upright, PJ produced the pink, soft rabbit's foot and placed it in her hand, closing her fingers around the small keychain, and holding her own hands around Panic's as she held the rabbit's foot.

"PJ, I can't take this. This is your special thing."

"I'm not giving it to you. Jeeze." She let go of her sister's hands and sat back looking at her in the dim light. She looked young then, younger than PJ thought of her, like when she was a baby and PJ would peer into her crib and think about her getting big enough to run around. She remembered her eyes all glossy and wide, and her little sounds like gurgling gibberish mixed with giggles and clucking. There was crying too, the kind of wailing that made PJ's ears hurt, but she didn't remember those sounds the same way, not the way she remembered Panic's baby noises, her chirping and cooing. When she made those sounds, PJ couldn't wait for them to be friends, for her to grow up and be big and daring. And here they were, PJ, all grown up and trying to get her sister to grow up too, and Panic, still a baby, but her body expanding like the stars in the universe, growing light-years per second before PJ's eyes, so much and so fast that she could only see it when she sat back and looked for it—the change. From those baby eyes to the present, her eyes were still so full of wonder, so round and delighted and half asleep but willing to go along with whatever PJ wanted, those eyes following her on her whims wherever they led.

"Why'd you give it to me, then?" Panic held the rabbit's foot up to examine it in the dark.

"I want you to feel it."

"Did you wake me up to feel your rabbit's foot? That's stupid, PJ."

The big sister laughed at this. Panic didn't laugh but PJ put her finger to her own lips to quiet them both before she explained. "Manny's family has rabbits in the back of their house. I held one today. A dad-rabbit."

"Luís told me about them."

"Did he also tell you that's where this came from?" PJ nodded toward Panic's hand clutching the soft lump of fur and claw. She could see the pink even through the low light.

"The mom-rabbits, and all their babies, they use them to make these." PJ waited a few seconds for her to think about what she had said. "I'm not talking about amputation either. They kill them. All of them."

Even through the dark, it was unmistakable that Panic's eyes grew wide. PJ could also see the outline of her hand, her grip tightening.

Then PJ delivered the words she knew would recruit her sister: "I have a plan to save them, Panic, and I hope you want to save them too." Panic nodded before PJ was even done talking, good kid. PJ sized her up then, like she was trying to decide if she could cut it. She tipped her head this way and that and then said, "That's good. We have to go now, before the sun is up."

"Okay," Panic said, already pulling the covers off her bare legs to get out of bed.

•

Minutes later, they were dressed and headed out the front door, slipping into the darkness of the trees like thieves. A perceptible dawn was upon the mountains to the east as the peaks gathered the coming light beyond the horizon. The pale daylight had already hidden a few stars but there was still plenty of time. Many stars above them still shone, bringing more than enough hope to see them through. For PJ, it was hope that they could free the rabbits, all of them. She whispered plans so low that she thought Panic might miss them, but Panic kept rapt attention, never more than a few feet from her as they moved.

Along the gravel, the sounds of their crunching feet betrayed their stealth. Much quieter, they discussed the plan. They would approach the Gonzáles place from the north by cutting through the avocado grove at the Minkus Farm. Then they'd take the game trail into Manny's backyard. Manny and his dad had cleared away a large swath of chaparral the week before and PJ had not yet committed it to memory but knew it well enough to place the hutches. Plus, once they arrived in the Gonzáles backyard, the light would be adequate, and their eyes would adjust enough so that they could find the hutches and release the rabbits into the brush. Panic would take the row on the left nearest the house, because she was the smallest and harder to spot, and PJ would work on the hutches farthest from the house. Once they'd released the rabbits, they would meet again at the game trail, return to the avocado grove, grab as much fruit as they could carry, and then have pan dulce and avocados or breakfast at home. Easy.

Panic whispered, "How do you know the rabbits will be okay in the chaparral?"

PJ didn't, but she couldn't tell her sister that. "There are jackrabbits and brush rabbits out there that do just fine, Panic. Just fine. You're not getting scared, are you?"

"No, it's just that—"

"Good," PJ almost spoke out loud to stop her. "I'd hate to have to turn back now. Plus, think about all those poor bunnies that we might leave there to that horrible fate. Do you know about fate, Panic?"

She didn't answer but PJ thought she nodded.

They walked along for quite some time, well into the avocados before they spoke again.

"I don't understand the latch system on the cages," Panic whispered, and PJ could hear her stress.

"Turn the lever. The door drops downward, like a castle draw-bridge. It's easy." PJ wasn't whispering anymore like Panic, but she kept her voice low. She wanted to assuage the alarm she heard in her sister's voice so she made her own voice as soft as she could. PJ even tried to smile at her in the dark. "Once you do one, you'll see. They're all the same. Drop the door down and reach in. The rabbits are so sweet and so soft. They love being held." PJ thought about the one that had kicked her and nearly bucked itself out of her arms. She hoped the rabbits would be mellower at night. "Just pluck them out and put them on the ground." She felt confident in that last bit of instruction, and she believed herself too, as much needing to hear those words as Panic did. Reach in and grab the rabbits. They'll want to be freed. They'll want to be grabbed. It will be okay, was what she told myself. But as they made their way out of the avocado grove and into the low chaparral, PJ swallowed hard, unsure that she could go through with it.

A waning quarter moon hung in the western sky lighting their path. But by then, the dusky dawn at their backs also climbed up the sky. PJ knew they needed to hurry.

Soon, the chaparral opened to the area where the Gonzáles men had been working, clearing the land. She could see the hutches, rows of tiny prisons lined up against the backdrop of the ranchero. Boxes on stilts arose from the dark earth. PJ imagined the silent longing of the rabbits within, wishing for freedom, hoping to escape their fate. Her heart pounded as she turned to her sister and placed her finger to her lips in silence. She widened her eyes to emphasize the gravity of their situation; but Panic's eyes were also wide, flashing about, on high alert. Once they locked stares, PJ tipped her head toward the hutches closest to the house and pointed her finger toward the row she wanted Panic to work. Panic moved with precision and stealth over the ground between PJ and hutches, to the rabbits she would free. Once there and working on the first cage door, PJ moved into place on her own row of hutches.

She stepped up to the box and exhaled slowly. Turning the level, she lowered the door and placed her hand inside finding soft fur. She scooped her hand underneath the weight of the rabbit and pulled it free from the door. Then she bent and placed the rabbit on the ground. She reached into the same cage to feel for possible others. No more, so she

figured she must have the row with the bucks, one per cage. She moved
to the next cage and repeated this action, opening, scooping, lowering.

She didn't run into a problem until the fifth or sixth hutch. Once
she placed her hand into the hutch, the rabbit hopped away from her.
She tried to scoop it from beneath, but it moved away, backing into the
farthest corner. PJ forced both of her arms through the small opening,
an awkward but manageable fit, and tried to catch the rabbit between
her hands. Then she felt a pain so sudden and alarming that she almost
cried out. A searing ache shot up from the meaty place between her palm
and thumb that made her jerk both of her arms out of the hutch and
flail about, swinging her arms in a silent and wild frenzy through the air.
When she looked at her hand she could see in the dim light where the
rabbit had bitten her. A small trail of blood ran down her skin. PJ looked
at the hutch and saw the small face of the rabbit peering out at her, its
pink eyes nearly black in the low light against the ghostly white of its fur.
Glancing at Panic PJ saw the younger girl continue to work with dili-
gence, unimpeded and perhaps unaware of PJ's injury. She looked back
at the open door of the hutch and the rabbit's face was gone. Fearing that
it had jumped from a great height and injured itself, she looked around
for it on the ground and that's when she noticed most the rabbits—if not
all the rabbits—were still close by where they had been set down. They
were not making their way off into the chaparral to find their freedom.

PJ's eyes scanned the sky assessing its growing light, then
scanned the ground again dotted with the white shapes of rabbits in sed-
entary positions, with an occasional hop here or there. She looked along
the row of hutches opened and quickly estimated half a dozen that remained unopen. By then, Panic was next to her with a rabbit in her arms.

"Can I keep one?" She whispered, and PJ almost jumped at the
sound of her words.

After hushing her sister, PJ took the rabbit from her hands and
placed it on the ground with the others. Then, without words, she pointed to her unopened hutches and pointed back to Panic then back to the
hutches. Panic got her meaning and hung her head, but moved toward
the hutches that contained the other bucks and began removing rabbits. Meanwhile, PJ bent low and started herding the rabbits toward the
chaparral as best she could, which was not easy because they did not

seem easily encouraged. Plus, her hand was throbbing at the bite injury. Finally, she resorted to picking up the rabbits, one by one, and hurrying them off into the cover of the nearby brush. Back and forth she worked with Panic joining her once the other hutches were vacant. She tried to keep her breathing quiet but had worked up quite a pant, lifting rabbits, carrying them across the uneven and dimly lit terrain, all the while wary of being bitten or scratched—or worse, discovered by the Gonzáles family. A few rabbits thumped their mighty back legs against her efforts and PJ wondered if they were even worth saving, but in the end, all rabbits were evacuated from the yard, safely tucked away under the cover over a thick toyon berry or laurel sumac. Satisfied, the girls headed back toward the avocado grove.

As they walked, PJ's heart calmed, though she was aware of the new light growing around them. She could hardly believe they'd pulled off the caper, and for a second, she wished she could tell Manny about it. A snapping twig nearby caused her heart to quicken again, but it ended up being nothing, probably another animal out in the chaparral. Before long, they were back in the avocado grove.

PJ felt safe among the avocado trees, concealed beneath their dark canopy. She knew this farm well. She'd helped with harvesting, from time to time, to earn extra money and also receive free avocados. She knew Mr. Minkus kept picker poles at the ends of every other row of trees. These were used for plucking the fruit from the upper most branches. Each long pole had a metal basket fixed to the ends with a claw extension for snagging fruit. PJ also knew that the best avocados were at the tops of the trees where the sunlight had a chance to ripen them from all sides.

She grabbed a picker pole and found a tree that was heavy with fruit. The trunk had dimples all around it where it had been struck. Some folks believed that hitting the tree's trunk with something study, like a broom handle or a baseball bat, would help it to produce more fruit. PJ thought this was barbaric and always wondered if the harvest would change if Mr. Minkus decided one year to not beat his tress. There was no denying his farm produced an abundance of fruit, so maybe there was something to it. Still, the idea of beating the trees made PJ feel sad, like their limbs hung lower in a defeated sort of way because they had been hit.

PJ put her hand on the bark and said in a low voice, "Thank you." Then she heard Panic groan. PJ often spoke to trees and bushes, but Panic thought it was weird. PJ shot her an angry look but then smiled wide. She felt impressed with what they had done, that Panic had been such a great help. All the fear she was feeling after the rabbits had gone had faded out of her like the stars in the sunrise.

The sky through the branches was now a pale grey and would soon be blue. The growing light gave way to heavy shapes of avocados hanging among the broad, waxy leaves of the tree. The fruits were typically hard to spot but PJ had developed a knack for finding them. She reached the picker pole up into the canopy, hooked its claws around a fat avocado, gave it a quick twist and yank, and then pulled the avocado into the basket. PJ grabbed onto another, and it fell into the basket before she lowered the catch.

Panic scooped the fruit out of the basket and gave each a smell. This made PJ laugh and she pulled her hand up to her mouth to cover the sound.

"What's that?" Panic asked noticing PJ's hand.

She showed her the trail of blood on her palm where the rabbit had bitten her. PJ explained that she probably startled the rabbit but told her sister the wound wasn't deep.

"But what if it gets infected?" She leaned in close to PJ's hand, squinting in the low light.

"Then I suppose I'll die," PJ said, taking back her hand to thread the pole back up through the tree's canopy, eyeing another couple of large avocados.

"Seriously, PJ. Don't."

"I'm kidding. I'll wash it as soon as we get home, okay?" She glanced at Panic before snagging the next avocado and giving it a pull. "I'll even get out some of mom's iodine if it will make you feel better."

"It will."

By the time they were done collecting avocados, they each had five folded into the fronts of their shirts, a trick their mom had shown them so they could carry more by making their shirt into a pouch. Panic called it "the kangaroo hold" and she had perfected it, once holding four loose bottles of Mello Yello soda in her shirt without so much as even clanking the glass. Compared to that, hauling avocados was easy.

As they approached their front yard the sun popped up over the mountains. The dark oak trees would keep the house dark for at least another hour, and she wondered if Panic would want to sleep a little while longer. It was a school day, but they had time before they had to leave. She hoped she wouldn't try to stay home again like she had the day of the plane crash.

"Do you want to try to sleep a bit before school?"

"Nah, I'm wide awake now." She yawned as they trudged, not hiding her exhaustion.

"You can get another half hour of sleep if you want." They moved beneath the branches of the oaks, acorns popping under the weight of their feet.

"I'm okay. Really." Panic stopped walking short of the front step and she looked at PJ. "I want to make sure you'll wash that bite, PJ. And I want to make sure you'll save me some pan dulce."

PJ smiled and nodded. "Yes ma'am."

"PJ. Before we go in, can I ask you something?" She hoisted the hem of her shirt adjusting the weight of her avocados. "Do you think we did a good thing with those rabbits? I mean, I keep thinking about it and they didn't seem to want to be free. I don't think they're smart about the chaparral like jackrabbits and brush bunnies."

Of course, PJ had been thinking about this, too, that the rabbits didn't seem to want to be free. The one thing that kept coming back into her thoughts, though, was that ornery buck that had bitten her. Panic was the one to finally free him. The more PJ thought about him, the more she respected him. PJ felt awed by the spirit of that animal, how he might have felt in that dark box before her strange hands came in to get him. If he knew the sound of his brothers being carried off to slaughter, if they'd screamed the same way the rabbit had in her dream. If he was smart, she couldn't blame him for biting her. She couldn't fault him for not knowing how to be free either. It might take him some time, but he'd figure it out. After all, there were jackrabbits and cottontails and brush rabbits all over their part of the valley. He'd learn; they all would. And at least they'd given the rabbits a choice. In that box he had no choice. Probably the only thing he ever did of his own free will was bite PJ.

"Yeah," PJ said. "I think that we did a real good thing for those rabbits. We gave them a choice."

"Okay," Panic said, and her voice cracked. Then they went up the steps to their door.

•

Later that morning, Panic rushed around the house late for school. With a half-pan dulce in her mouth as she pulled on a light sweater and slipped her feet into her shoes. PJ was already at the door waiting.

"C'mon." PJ said.

Panic tried to respond but her words were muffled through the pan dulce. She grabbed her bookbag and slung it over her shoulder. To her surprise, their mom called out from down the hall, "Have a good day." Panic looked at PJ who had the same expression on her face as Panic, bewilderment. Both girls stifled laughs.

Out the door they went, running to the spot where they usually met Manny and Luis. PJ said the boys would not have waited for them and she was right. Panic hated walking into the classroom without Luis, but it had been worth it, she told herself, to free those rabbits. She remembered their soft, white fur nestled into her before she sat each down, how she longed to keep one for her own. She wanted to imagine them hopping around in among the sagebrush but the image was hard to form. Maybe it was because Panic knew about the wild chaparral and the animals who lived there. Most matched the tawny muted colors of the world. Plus, the rule in their wild was "eat or be eaten." She became afraid for the rabbits but shook her head at the thought. Rabbits were very smart and great diggers. Besides, she saw wild rabbits in the brush all the time.

When they got to the high school parking lot, they went their separate ways. PJ told Panic to hurry, that she had not yet missed the bell. So, Panic ran the rest of way to her school and down the hall into her classroom. Scanning the room, she was surprised that Luis was not there at all. She hoped he wasn't sick as she took her seat and the bell sounded.

•

After school that day, as she headed to the meeting place to walk Panic home, Manny caught up with PJ. He came up behind her, so she didn't see him approach. She heard his hard footsteps and had the feeling in her gut that it was him long before he spoke. Otherwise, she might have been too stunned to act after his response.

"What the hell!" He started, and he grabbed her by the shoulder and spun her around to face him.

PJ's heart was already thumping in her ears and her mind had gone blank. Earlier, she had thought about what she might say to him, had even rehearsed various responses in her mind.

"My family's money. My family's livelihood. Luís's lunches and shoes. Man, screw you."

PJ feigned ignorance. "What are you talking about?" She stared at him feeling the moisture gather on her palms. Then, something shifted within her fear, and she became defensive. She snapped into a defensive reaction without thinking. PJ yelled, "Don't come at me all crazy! You got some nerve."

"Oh, I see how it is, puta. I see."

"Puta? I've never even kissed a boy!" She yelled in her fit of rage, then immediately longed to snatch back the words, her anger at once replaced with embarrassment. Now, on top of feeling doubt, anger, she also felt self-conscious, shameful. But 'Puta' was a term that the boys at school called girls who had many boyfriends or had a reputation for being easy, or even if a girl was stuck up. PJ wasn't sure how that word fit her, especially coming from Manny.

"Is that a rabbit bite you got there?" Manny pushed her hand. He sneered then spit on the ground. "Hope he got you good, too, you thief. You fucking crook."

"Manny, stop it." PJ thought she would appeal to his sensibilities. "What is this? What are we fighting about?"

His eyes squinted and he cocked his head, scrutinizing her.

"Listen, all I know is if you were thinking you set those rabbits free, into some magical life out in those hills, all you really did was put them in their graves." He leaned toward her and hissed. "You fucked up so royally."

That was when Panic walked up, eyes wide, looking between the two of them. PJ shot her a glance hoping to convey she should keep her mouth shut. Manny eyes volleyed between her and PJ.

"Oh, what? You got your little sister in on this? Man, you are messed up!" He spit again before he delivered his final blow. "All we found this morning was clumps of white fur and blood." He shook his head, his words dark with menace. "All of them. That's all we found. You think on that when you look at that rabbit's foot keychain I gave you. Think on that when you eat my mama's sweet bread." He poked his finger at PJ's hand, just missing the bite mark, and added, "Blood and fur." Then he stomped off.

"They were going to die anyway!" PJ yelled after him. She knew the statement would incriminate her, but some pride inside her forced her to respond. By then, Panic was gawking at PJ with her accusing expression, mouth fully opened. PJ lowered her voice and said to her sister, with a more sympathetic tone, "They were going to die anyway."

Then Panic also turned and ran away from PJ, and she was left to walk home alone, dejected and confused with her thoughts and doubts.

When PJ rounded the bend at her house, she saw an unfamiliar car in the driveway. PJ quickened her pace thinking the Gonzáles family had come to press charges. Instead, when she pulled open the door and tore inside ready to defend herself and plead her case, she found Betsy and Panic sitting in the living room with Mrs. Perón, the rigid social worker from the sheriff's department the day before.

"Oh," PJ said as she came to an abrupt stop in the middle of the living room. She looked from Mrs. Perón's impassive face to her mom then to Panic, who sat tucked into a ball on the loveseat peering out over her knees. Panic did not look at PJ but scowled the same way she had when she'd fled the school.

The room seemed too formal with Mrs. Perón there, balanced on the edge of the couch cushion. She wore a cream pantsuit that flared at the bottoms of the legs, but not enough to conceal her plain, leather Earth Shoes. An ugly choice, PJ thought, for such a proper suit. Still the brown leather of the shoes matched the macramé belt Mrs. Perón had stylishly tied around her waist, which lent a certain casual elegance to her overall look. Mrs. Perón sat upright and stiff. In her hand, she gripped an orange Tupperware cup.

Betsy blew cigarette smoke from pursed lips and crushed her Salem into the smooth, glass disk in front of her on the coffee table. "Mrs. Perón's here for her check-up with us, PJ."

"Check in," Mrs. Perón corrected her.

PJ eyes had gone to the smoldering ashtray atop the coffee table. She felt embarrassed about the table, a make-shift thing built from stacked milk crates covered with an old sheet. The stained corners of the sheet were tucked out of view. Several cigarette burns dotted the sheet across the top of the table. PJ thought of the Blue-Chip Stamps Betsy was saving for a new coffee table. The visitor made PJ wish she had been helping her mom collect the stamps. The couch and loveseat set were fancier. A few years back, Betsy had come into some money and splurged on a nice set, a matching couch and loveseat in harvest gold with brown stripes. The center cushion of the couch, the very one Mrs. Perón now sat upon, also had a large cigarette burn in the upholstery, but it had been flipped over long ago concealing it from judging eyes.

"Please join us, Paula," Mrs. Perón said, and PJ winced to hear her real name. She moved to the loveseat and sat next to Panic. She gave Panic a quick glance, but her little sister's eyes stayed on Mrs. Perón, ever peering over her knobby knees, scabs and all.

"Paula, we've been going over a few things," Mrs. Perón informed PJ, stating her line like she was a T.V. actor on a soap opera. She spoke with a kind of authority to bring PJ up to speed. "There's not an adequate amount of food in the house, for instance." She reached down and picked up a clipboard from the coffee table that PJ hadn't noticed until then. Mrs. Perón set the Tupperware cup down and began making notes on the papers on the clipboard. "Mrs. McCormack, I see that you," she paused looking at her clipboard then back to their mother. "You have been employed at the Best Spot Café for . . . three years. Is that correct?"

"Yes," Betsy answered wringing her hands. PJ could see their slight tremor, the way her fingers shook like oak leaves shuddering in the breeze. She kept looking from Mrs. Perón to Panic, who was still ignoring PJ and brooding.

"And you go grocery shopping regularly, then?"

"I would have gone yesterday but we were at the sheriff's station, and then I had to work." PJ noticed how Betsy avoided answering the question. She could have said she went with the five dollars Lila Friedman had given her, but then she might have to confess to the six-pack purchase. Betsy looked at her daughters, first Panic then PJ. When her eyes met PJ's, she held her gaze for a few seconds before looking back at Mrs. Perón. It was as if she was daring PJ to say otherwise, but PJ wouldn't. She knew she wouldn't.

"Uh huh." Mrs. Perón jotted notes down on the clipboard without looking at Betsy. "And what is your hourly wage?"

"Well, ma'am, no disrespect, but I think that's personal information."

"Mrs. McCormack, your personal information is my business. The D.A. is involved. I'll need to convince him that you are fit to care for these children. Now, please, what is your hourly wage?"

Betsy was already in her waitress outfit, likely preparing to leave for her evening shift when Mrs. Perón arrived. They weren't even expecting to see Mrs. Perón for a whole week, but there she was, looking as stern as she had the day before. Betsy smoothed her skirt and PJ thought this might be more to still her hands rather than to flatten the fabric's wrinkles.

"Minimum wage, ma'am. Two dollars and sixty-five cents an hour is what I make on my paycheck. I have tips, too. Most shifts I can bring home an extra fifteen or twenty dollars. Sometimes, when I double and work the bar at night, I can bring home another twenty or so."

"Would you say that's pretty good money, Mrs. McCormack?" Mrs. Perón looked at Betsy with her eyebrows arched.

"I'm not sure I understand."

"Do you think you make enough to see to your welfare and the welfare of your daughters? To have ends meet?"

Panic snuck a glance at PJ out of the corner of her eye and then turned, scooting on her bottom, to pivot her body away from her sister.

"Well, sure. But I—"

"And who cares for the children when you work late?" Her eyes returned to her clipboard.

"Well, PJ's old enough, isn't she?" She looked again at PJ as if asking her daughter if she was old enough to care for her little sister.

Mrs. Perón looked at PJ, too. Her gaze drew a line from the top of PJ's head down to her midsection and knees and then back up to her face. She felt like the rat in Mr. William's science room, when the kids tapped on the glass and Mr. Williams reminded them for what he called "the umpteenth time" to knock it off.

"That's fine," Mrs. Perón said, and she scribbled something before looking at PJ again and then at Panic, but now with a softer gaze. "And how have the children adjusted with the grief these past years?"

PJ wasn't sure she understood Mrs. Perón's word choice, so she looked to her mom for an explanation, but something was off in her mom then.

The color in Betsy's face drained. In fact, everything seemed to drain from her at that moment. Before this question, Betsy leaned forward, her eyes intent, her expression focused, as if she were concentrating on everything that Mrs. Perón asked, as if Mrs. Perón's words mattered beyond anything else. One second, she was poised and attentive; the next second, all expression vanished to nothing. The color of her skin seeped away from her pallor and left her peaked and drawn, as white as a ghost.

"Mrs. McCormack?" The shrewd woman pressed in toward their mother. "The children's adjustment to their father's death?"

Now Betsy's shoulders fell from her ears collapsing around her as if she could no longer bear to hold them up, as if the weight of her arms pulled her posture toward the earth. PJ thought Betsy might lie down. Her eyes sank into their hollow sockets; any spark of their liveliness vanished. But it was Betsy's stare, then so vacant and suddenly distant, so at once empty, that made PJ want to cry with the grief she did not yet know she deserved. The air grew still.

PJ found her voice then, an urgency prodding her explanation. "Ma'am, our dad is gone away. He left a few years back when things were too much. He'll come back someday when it's easier on him." But even as PJ said it, she saw by her mother's slumping form how wrong she'd been in her assumptions. And then, like the flashing of a montage in a dream, images flickered by PJ's thoughts in fleeting spurts, and she knew at once what had happened. All those many years when Betsy spoke of their dad leaving, she meant that he had left in the most permanent way one can go.

But how? Was it his heart? PJ knew he had a condition that was discovered after he'd left the army. This was the reason Chet had never earned his pilot's license. But then, in remembering how disappointed her father had been to not fly, PJ knew exactly how he had "gone," a word that she now saw as truly apt. PJ remembered long periods of sadness in their home, a time when Chet was so forlorn that the air seemed thick with his sorrow. Though she didn't know exactly what had happened, there was no doubt in PJ's mind that her father had taken his own life. She didn't know how she could be so certain, but she felt more certain of that fact, that her dad had died by suicide, than she had felt certain the sun would set that day or that Panic was her sister and best friend.

Panic.

She looked at her.

Panic's eyes had grown wide and alert in this silence, like a trapped animal frozen with fear. Her hair seemed to stand up, eyebrows arched. She had come to such an upright position that she was perfectly straight in her seat. PJ knew her sister was smart enough to puzzle together the same thing she had, maybe not the suicide, but Panic knew he was dead. Everything about there being a place for them to go one day, a place where they might find him or where they could get to, something better than that damned valley, that horrible boxed-in land, that living coffin—some place he might have found to go—had been a lie they invented. PJ had invented it. Panic learned more than a young child should in that moment. All of the growing that PJ thought she would do over the next few years, the next decade, it all seemed to coil into her right in that moment.

Panic leapt from the loveseat like a wildcat sprung from a trap and she ran for the back sliding glass door. With a whoosh, the door was open, and she was gone. Only a jackrabbit could have moved faster.

"I have to go after her," PJ said to the room, but not to Betsy, whom she could not look at, and certainly not to Mrs. Perón, whom she could not stand for delivering this news in her callused and uncaring way. She was the harbinger of grief, the carrier of evil, as far as PJ was concerned.

PJ left through the sliding glass door and climbed the hill to where the eucalyptus stood. She followed the sounds of sobbing over the blowing Santa Ana winds. The noise resembled the same high desperation PJ had heard from the rabbit last spring trapped under the talons of a mother owl, the same cries in her dreams the night before, but PJ knew these sounds were Panic's. From up the hill, Panic let out the anguish of a new sorrow, more exposed and raw, than could be described; the place from where her grief started a new and foreign depth; the place where it would end, deeper still, maybe even to eternity; but how could they know?

PJ realized, as the crying grew louder, as she pressed each step toward her sister, that she was panting. Then, something else became strange in her thoughts. Her breath was more ragged than panting. She became alarmed to realize that she, too, cried. By the time she reached Panic, saw her arms thrust around the eucalyptus tree, holding onto its trunk as if it were their dad's midsection, she had fully joined her sister in her wailing. By then, PJ, too, found new depths of grief, and she, too, shared in such harrowing screams of sadness. Then, they fell into one another, lowering to the ground, desperately holding each other. PJ buried her face in her sister's hair, barely able to utter apologies, but nevertheless saying them through gasps, "I'm sorry. I'm sorry. I'm sorry." Soon, they both fell silent and listened to the wind pull at the tree branches above, listened to the sniffling of each other as they tried to make sense of the world. As their breathing calmed a silence grew between them so palpable, an absence of sound that became worse than the crying had been. They slumped against the tree's trunk, still wrapped in each other's arms, and fell asleep.

CHAPTER EIGHT

PJ woke to the sound of dirt bikes in the nearby hills. Their whining engines carved into her sleep, and she rolled her head to face Panic, undisturbed by the noise. For those few, brief moments of waking, she didn't think of recent events. She naively accepted the landscape around her. She and Panic often slept under the shade of a friendly tree or bush. Panic was huddled near to her, nestled into PJ's side. Looking at her sister's sleeping face, her parted lips and placid eyelids, the events of their waking day returned to PJ. She felt the bite on her hand throb with pain, maybe even infection as Panic had feared. As the events began to resurface in her mind, PJ remembered seeing Manny after school, how he described the fate of the rabbits, her embarrassment at not knowing where the rabbit's foot keychain came from. PJ remembered Manny's words "blood and fur," and how stupid she felt for not considering the lack of camouflage when they released the rabbits in the chaparral, stark white fur against the dark colors of the sumac and manzanita. She thought of Mrs. Perón and her pinched face. She thought of her dad. PJ wanted her to be wrong about her dad.

She gave that last thought some time to germinate. Maybe Mrs. Perón had been wrong. Maybe she didn't have all the facts. After all, Betsy had lied about other things when she talked to that woman. Maybe Betsy had said some things to her the wrong idea that he had died, only he hadn't, and he was living in Mexico or up in the San Jacinto

Mountains with Aunt Fancy. But then PJ remembered her mom's face, how Betsy had drained of all color in that moment. She wondered what Betsy did after they left the house. What Mrs. Perón did. PJ didn't know if Betsy ever rebounded from that moment because they left, first Panic and then PJ, following her up into the brush. Their mom had been in her waitress uniform already, which was a good sign. Perhaps she went to work after Mrs. Perón left. But PJ knew better. Something like this would cause a deep wallowing of self-pity. PJ hoped she hadn't wallowed her way into a bottle and was still floundering there. She could drink a lot by the time they made it back to their house.

Panic stirred. Her breath came out in a stutter, as if she were still caught in her grief, even in sleep. PJ touched her arm lightly and propped herself up on her side with her other arm. The dirt bikes were now far enough away that she could barely hear their buzzing engines. The landscape around them was filled with shadows and rustling; the Santa Anas continued to jostle everything about. As Panic awoke, PJ stared off lost in thought, not really focused on any one thing, maybe the mottled flecks of the granite boulder exposed beneath the oak nearby, or maybe the gentle lifting of fallen leaves stirring. Then she realized it wasn't the movement of leaves that had caught her eye. Not more than six feet from where they lay, a large diamondback rattlesnake had uncoiled and was slithering along the leaf litter coming toward them.

Growing up inland in Southern California, PJ had seen more rattlesnakes than she could remember. Snakes had been in their house, in her classroom, in the dirty laundry. Once they even found one wrapped around the tailpipe of Manny's dad's truck (it had been a cold winter and the creature only wanted to stay warm). PJ knew they were mostly big cowards, sliding away at the soonest opportunity when confronted by a larger animal. But a rattlesnake looking for warmth would cozy up to any heat source, which is what PJ was afraid of in that moment, because she and her sister snuggled up together in the shade of the tree became the heat source.

PJ reached her hand out and grabbed a small rock. She tossed it at the snake, and it coiled, its tongue flicking, facing the girls. PJ knew the snake could see them then. She couldn't know what the snake was thinking, but she knew her own thoughts: she and Panic were on the ground and rattlesnakes have terrible eyesight. To the snake, they could have been a roadrunner or a thrasher, worse, a threat.

The diamondback flicked its tongue and shook its tail with a chittering threat. PJ could hear her heartbeat in her ears, a loud thudding that overpowered the sound of the wind moving the branches and the leaves. Only her eyes moved. The rest of her body remained still as she scanned the area for a stick or a larger rock. Her glance swept the ground near Panic's legs then up by her torso, where she was sure she could reach a stone if one was available. Then she caught sight of Panic's face. Panic was awake, eyes wide and fixed on the diamondback too, already as alert and as coiled as the snake. Then, before PJ had time to even whisper her name, Panic sprung to her feet and pounced toward the snake shrieking.

PJ moved too, but by the time she was upright, Panic was already acting. Somewhere along her quick movement, Panic had picked up a rock about the size of a softball and she brought it down atop the rattlesnake's head. She screamed as she struck the snake. Blood and bone crunched and splattered. Panic struck again and once more, for good measure. Then she stopped, hunched like a crazed animal, and she slowly raised her arms for another blow. PJ was on the move now, going for her sister's arms as they lifted to hit the already-dead snake.

"Panic!" PJ yelled as she grabbed the smaller girl's arms and pulled her close. She felt Panic struggle to hit the snake again before she went limp in PJ's embrace.

Panic began to cry, softer than earlier. PJ held her and whispered to her, to herself, too, that it would all be okay. The danger had passed.

In Panic's thoughts, visions of Mrs. Perón's smug face swam forward. She saw her tongue flicker in and out like a snake. She saw her mom washed in shadow, as frail and vulnerable as the rabbits. Panic let out a final huff and pulled herself together. A sense of shame washed over her as she took in the snake carcass. She had killed an animal.

"I can't lose you, PJ," Panic said catching her breath as she turned toward her sister.

"I'm not going anywhere." PJ held her sister at arm's length and assessed Panic's face. She was part-mad, part-grief-stricken, but a grin spread across her crazed expression. She had bits of dried brown leaves stuck to the side of her face, and the rock still clutched in her hand. Bright red and grisly bits of snake brains stuck to her fingers. Panic's bushy, dark hair was extra disheveled and wild. Her eyes became demented, as her grin widened, her bravado almost comical.

Panic pushed away from her sister then and let out a howl like the neighborhood dogs released they heard sirens.

With PJ's heart still thumping in her chest and in her ears, she let out a cry of her own—one of exasperation and remorse. Then, because PJ also bordered on lunacy in that moment, she began to laugh without control.

"Oh my god," Panic said, watching PJ laugh. "You were scared."

"You were scared," PJ said. "I mean, you killed a snake." She ribbed her and laughed uneasy.

"No, you, chicken. Bock, bock, bock." Panic laughed. Then she did a little dance with her hands tucked into her armpits so that her folded arms flapped like wings.

By then PJ had stopped laughing and looked at her, moving in her circles, cutting up and goofing off, like a nine-year-old should. The weight of grief and conflict no longer pulled her down. This seemed to PJ more like how her little sister should be at nine years old, reckless, wild, and happy, instead of saving her older sister from rattlesnakes because they had fallen asleep in their grief without checking their surroundings.

"You killed a snake," PJ said again only this time with more awe than fear.

"No kidding," was Panic's reply as she wiped the gristly bits onto her pant leg.

PJ couldn't say what else she had been thinking at that moment, that Panic was only nine years old and shouldn't be taking care of her big sister. But she knew Panic would disagree; Panic would say she had handled herself pretty well, and she had. But she never should have been in that danger in the first place.

PJ considered the outcome and the ways it could have ended differently. Last summer, Mrs. Spencer's visiting grandson, an eight-year-old boy, was bitten by a diamondback rattler and PJ had been the one to carry him out of the hills. By the time she got him to Mrs. Spencer's house, the boy was already foaming at the mouth and throwing up. The situation had been one of the scariest experiences of PJ's life. It could have been similar for her now or for Panic. She couldn't push the thought away.

Panic examined the snake poking it with a stick. She scratched her head and said, "Sometimes they can still move around after they're dead. That's what Luis told me anyway."

"I think that's only true if they're cut in half. If their brain isn't smashed. Maybe you should leave it."

Panic turned toward her sister, a placid look on her face then. "I'm sorry it scared you, PJ. That I scared you."

PJ bit her lower lip. "Let's go home."

"Yep."

They walked down the hill, through the oaks and into their backyard.

As they walked, PJ said, "I don't know what Mrs. Perón is talking about, Panic. You know… about Dad? She might be crazy."

"Yep."

"She doesn't know us. She just met us."

"Yep."

"Listen, don't you worry. Things are going to be fine. I promise"

"I know." Panic said.

PJ took a long look at the deep blue of the sky. "How do you know?"

"Because now we can leave, PJ." Panic flashed her that look of determination.

"Oh, we can?" PJ asked and shook her head a little at the stubbornness of her sister.

"Yep."

The sliding glass door was still open when they got back to the house. PJ had no idea how long they'd been gone, but she knew the afternoon had grown late, judging by the length of the shadows. If she was right about the shadows, their mom should have been long gone to work by then—maybe it was almost 5:00—but true to form, almost as predictable as the sunset, they found Betsy half boiled on the sofa with the T.V. on, volume loud.

Panic took one look at their mother and sniffed. She walked on by and disappeared into the hall. PJ stood there for a long time, and then turned to face the T.V., to hear what they were saying about the PSA crash.

A woman with hooded eyes and a tight permed hairstyle leaned toward the camera from the newsroom, an urgent expression betraying her professional demeanor. She was speaking to the camera saying "… new development in the air tragedy of the PSA crash in North Park which killed 144 people. Philip Hogue of the National Transportation Safety Board says they are looking into the possibility that several other small aircraft may have been in the vicinity when the collision occurred, and they might be able to shed some light on this tragedy."

The T.V. screen changed to a man's face in close-up, his mouth near a microphone. He spoke slowly saying, "We have indications that, eh, besides the twin engine Cessna that was in the area, that there was possibly, eh, a Beach Baron and maybe a Grumman. And we're checking on, eh, any information that we are able to extract from those aircraft which would have been, eh, in the area at the same time but not necessarily in the immediate vicinity. If we get the radar plots we want, we'll know what the, eh—"

"PJ," her mom's voice slurred thick from the sofa behind her.

PJ ignored Betsy and continued to stare at the news report. The camera had returned to the reporter with the tight perm, and she said, "Hogue also said a new computer alert system was in operation at the Navy's Miramar Air Station and the alarm actually went off about forty seconds before the collision occurred. But the warning never reached the tower at Lindbergh Field—"

"This is important, too, you know." PJ heard Betsy's voice again from behind her, and so she turned to face her mother. Betsy had started to bring herself upright. She set down a bottle with a clunk on the make-shift coffee table and fumbled for her cigarettes. Vodka. PJ could see the Russian letters against the red label, though she knew it wasn't an expensive brand. She had no idea where the bottle of vodka had come from. Maybe her mom had stolen it. Maybe the lies about abuse were only the tip of the iceberg with this woman she called "mom."

"I can't imagine what you're thinking," Betsy said, and she pulled a cigarette from her pack and reached for her lighter. PJ glanced back at the T.V. They were now showing pictures of the wreckage, parts of the airline burned and torn like bits of paper you'd want to hide. In the smoldering debris, PJ thought she saw the shapes of luggage. She turned away, back to her mom. Betsy lit the cigarette and blew a cloud of smoke up and away from PJ.

"I always wanted to tell you, but;" she puffed on her cigarette again. "I got something for you. Something from him." Her eyes lowered. "He didn't leave it for me, just you." Then she reached down to the floor and brought up a small, red lacquered box with gold hinges. She set it on the table next to the ashtray and opened it. She pulled out a folded piece of paper.

PJ noticed right away that the paper was pink.

Betsy held out her hand, thrusting the paper toward her daughter.

What had the woman with the perm on the T.V. been saying, PJ wondered, trying to shift her attention to something else—anything else. What had she been saying about how that signal warning had gone off in Miramar? It never reached the pilots? That was it. How different would things be for so many people if they had received that warning?

PJ took the paper in her hands and saw that it was actually two slips of paper folded together. The outer sheet of paper was pink, a carbon sheet. She could see blue lettering through the thin skin of it. But there was another sheet of paper, too, a notebook sheet of paper. This one seemed thicker. She noticed the difference even before she had unfolded it. The papers in her hands seemed to take on a life all theirs. She turned them over in her hand, not ready to look.

She heard Betsy blow smoke while the news reporter on the T.V. behind her continued to recap the jet crash tragedy.

"Last night they talked about a possible third plane," the reporter said. "But they have ruled out that third plane today. The pilot of that plane has come forward to offer his account of the morning's events."

"Mom," PJ finally spoke, and Betsy seemed to straighten up at the direct address. "Do I want to read this?"

Betsy took another long drag from her cigarette and blew with an audible whoosh that sounded like the Santa Ana winds through the eucalyptus tree.

"I think you ought to. You're old enough now." She said this last part with a small nod, but her personal comment on her age made PJ mad. When had Betsy decided PJ was old enough for anything? No. PJ knew that she only held those pages then because Betsy had been found out, caught in her lie after so many years. She had allowed her daughters to think things about their dad that weren't true. She had kept something about him from them when that information would have. . . would have. . . well, PJ still didn't know what it would have done, but she had decided it was wrong for Betsy to keep this from them.

After a heavy sigh, she conceded it was okay to keep her dad's death from Panic. Such news—such terrible and sad and earthshattering news—can overwhelm a kid.

PJ unfolded the papers.

The outermost page was, indeed, a carbon copy of something official. She noticed along the bottom edge the printed letters that identified this as the "Recipient's Copy," this pink page, this dull pink paper in her hand. There might have been a white original and perhaps a yellow that went to the county office along with a certificate of death or some other, more formal document. The less official copy, this pink copy, had the same places for names and information that could have contained any myriad of responses. The blanks, before completion, were meant for anyone and any scenario, but these described her dad. Long lines held the careful, blue carbon-printed lettering of a hand that had scribed them with such care, the specific information there upon those lines, this part of the form, was exclusively for PJ. It stated so. "Name: Paula Jean Mc-Cormack," clearly pressed out in blue carbon lettering identifying her as the intended recipient of the form as well as the thicker notebook page it accompanied. "Deceased: Chester Thaddeus McCormack." His name cut into PJ like a sharp-edged knife, the blue hue of the words next to the black print of the fixed form 'Deceased,' those permanent letters that she knew could belong to hundreds, thousands of anyone elses, but they spelled out her dad's name. She marveled at the precision of the hand that lettered his designation, the great care they had taken to print each letter. How they might have wanted to get it right, as noted further down the form that the 'Itemized Personal Effects' included "one suicide note for next of kin, PJ (Paula Jean), a minor child." A minor child, she was nine years old then. Could the person writing this form in triplicate (perhaps even more copies), could they have taken such care to convey to PJ their great sympathy in the careful way they lettered the form, knowing that she might need to have that meticulous hand, perhaps the only careful hand in her life, spell out her dad's fate? PJ moved the pink form to reveal the words written in her dad's scrawl on the plain notebook page below:

July 14, 1973

Dear PJ, my little Wild Thing,

I don't want this to hurt you, but it might. Maybe not. I can't say that I understand much of this myself. Maybe if I did, I wouldn't feel this way. But here's what I do know: I know you love your little sister. The two of you have kept me going for a long time. But anymore, when I hear the noises (and I hear them always now) I'm afraid of what comes next. There's a part of me that knows they're just noises. Like, Chet, it's only a backfire, a thunderclap, a slamming door. But this voice sinks in other sounds, the ones I hear screaming for me to run, to hide, đi đi mau! You'll look that up one day.

But now, these voices can't make me hide anymore. There's no-where to hurry off to.

And so, I'll wave goodbye like when Max got in his boat and sailed away.

It doesn't mean I don't love you or that I won't miss you. It just means that I can't stay. The noises are too loud here. This can only be good, you know?

Well, you will. . .

It means that I won't let the sounds scare me anymore. More importantly, they won't scare you or Panic anymore, either, because I will take them with me when I go.

I don't deserve to make any requests, but if I could ask a favor, please take care of her. Please take care of Panic. She needs you. You're all she has, and she loves you best of all. She'll eat you up, she loves you so.

-Dad

PJ's entire childhood seemed to wither as she folded the papers. She looked back at Betsy lying on the couch; she had passed out again, sprawled there in her ragged pose. What was it she had said, PJ wondered? Something like, "He didn't leave it for me. Just you." The red box lay on its side opened near her outstretched hand. Inside were a few coins, a ring, and a mass card displaying the image of the Virgin Mary. Betsy hadn't received a letter. She had been married to Chet for over a decade. She'd given him two daughters, she'd written to him in Vietnam, written to his Army buddies, too. She'd been fierce and joyful, and also full of anger, but full of love, too. PJ remembered it; she knew she hadn't imagined it. And this man, this broken Army soldier, came back from a broken war and did the only thing he thought he could do.

PJ stood there watching Betsy drool on the couch cushion. Her breath quickened as she squeezed the letter in her hand. She imagined Panic smashing the snake with the rock, heard Panic's howl as more of a scream of agony then, in her mind, rather than the victory cry it had been in the moment. Without another word, or tender thought for her mom, PJ went into her room and packed. She didn't need to ask Panic to pack, because when she went to Panic's room, she found her, sitting on the floor with her bag, ready to go. And that's how they finally left. No goodbye. No big production. And also, no note for Betsy.

CHAPTER NINE

East Main Street glowed with neon signs below a star-winked night. A deep pink still colored the sky in the west, lighting the horizon with warmth and radiance; hope lingered there, beckoning PJ onward. They stood at the bus stop, two sisters on the precipice of change. Though few words had been exchanged since they left the house, they shared a profound knowledge about where they were going and who they would be when they got there—something far removed from the pain and heartache of what they'd already known in their short lives. Or at least this is what PJ had been thinking before the fear crept in.

PJ couldn't tell what scenario played in Panic's mind, but the one in PJ's mind contemplated many ways they could find themselves lost in the big world. She knew enough that the 63 bus would take them to the El Cajon transit station where they could catch the transfer to Santa Fe Station in Downtown, San Diego. That would be the ride to pay attention to, stay on high alert. PJ had only been that far once, and never at night, and certainly never without an adult. She had no idea when the Greyhound ran to San Jacinto—the far-away mountains that hosted the small hamlet called Idyllwild where their Aunt Fancy lived—but she knew she could purchase their tickets at Santa Fe Station. She knew the bus stopped in Idyllwild near Fancy's lodge; she had watched it deliver people to the mountains when she was younger. She also knew they had enough money. Panic's classmate, Leroy, had thrifty parents who took great pride in not owning a car, so they took the bus everywhere. PJ's family also didn't own a car, but it wasn't by choice. They had a car before dad . . . left? Died? She still couldn't accept the latter; maybe she never would. Maybe this was part of the reason Betsy had always said he'd left. PJ considered this, how Betsy had come to terms with his means of departure. In some ways, it seemed easier to believe he'd died rather than think he was out in the world refusing to come home, refusing to know his daughters or be with them, the way a family should be together. Then again, Aunt Fancy had kept her distance. They hadn't heard from her in a long while. This thought made PJ shiver despite the warm night air.

A long bench stood near the bus stop sign informing passengers of the bus schedule and route, the assigned number of the expected buses, and the arrival and departure times. The girls had about five minutes before the next bus would come and so they sat. An occasional car ambled up Greenfield Drive, perhaps dads coming home from a long day at work. When their dad came home from Vietnam, he had taken a job at the Greeley Slaughterhouse. He worked in the kill room, a place that gave him nightmares, PJ remembered. He and Betsy fought about his job because he had such a hard time going there each day, though PJ only knew this because of the scene that would transpire. Chet would cry and clutch his hair sinking low into the chair at the dining room table. But Betsy always managed to get him out the door to work the next morning. Sometimes, he came home with blood on his clothes. He was supposed to change his clothes before he left the slaughterhouse, but some days he couldn't wait to get out of there. He told PJ this when she gasped at his gruesome appearance one day. Now that she knew what had happened to him, PJ thought about his terrible job, how hard it must have been for him to go work each day at a place called "the kill room," to see the amount of death and blood there after already seeing what he might have seen in the war.

PJ remembered one exchange above the others.

"Change your clothes before you sit at the table, Chet," Betsy yelled at him from the kitchen as he slumped into the chair and gave PJ a look of weariness. In her mind, PJ could see Betsy at the stove, a toddler version of Panic perched on her hip as she stirred a steamy pot. "If you can't change, at least wash your hands."

"I'm tired, Betsy," Chet said. "Just let me sit. I can't be moved."

"You will move, mister, or you will hear the clack of this pot on your skull."

"You're not gonna hit me."

Then, before he could finish his wink at PJ, whack! Betsy had come across the room and hit him with the pot full of spaghetti sauce, which sloshed out and splattered the table and Chet's already red butcher's smock. All the while, Betsy held Panic perched on her hip.

Chet jumped to his feet, one hand on his head where she had struck and the other in the air poised to strike a swift backhand. Betsy stood her ground, a look of menace in her eyes that seemed to dare him to hit her. She even stuck her chin out a little as an invitation. But Chet hesitated and Panic began to wail. Some of the sauce, which had been hot enough to scald, painted the toddler's leg. Chet grabbed Panic and took her to the kitchen sink running cold water over her leg as Panic continued to cry.

"You get yourself changed up, Chet." Betsy said to his back. "Then we won't have to have such problems. You change your clothes and wash your hands like the rest of us."

It was odd to remember that as they sat at the bus stop beneath the fading light of their final night in El Cajon. PJ could not remember the last time her mom asked her to wash her hands. Besides the pancakes, she couldn't remember the last time Betsy had made a meal. She remembered Panic later clawing away from their dad so that she could toddle across the floor to be with Betsy.

"That's right, my JoJo," she said scooping up Panic. Panic's outstretched arms and straining face reached for her, and Chet stood, staring after the two of them. PJ remembered his blank look, like he'd forgotten where he was, blood and sauce and his slack jaw. He looked to PJ, then to the table. His thoughts were somewhere far away occupied by things that PJ could not imagine.

PJ assumed Panic had no knowledge of this part of their dad's life. She looked at Panic and wondered what thoughts occupied her as they sat at the bus stop. She watched her little sister kicking at the sidewalk with the toe of her shoe, her head turned in the opposite direction of PJ, facing up the road, maybe looking for the bus.

That's when PJ noticed a small group of bruises on the back of Panic's forearm. She knew that kind of mark; it looked like the result of being gripped too hard.

"What's that?" PJ asked, gently brushing her hand across the back of Panic's arm, though not exactly on the bruise—she wouldn't dare. Panic jumped at the contact and turned to look at PJ, a show of treachery flickering in her eyes.

"Watch it."

"Whoa, sorry." PJ tried to make her tone sound light, but her heart sank into her stomach. Had Betsy also been rough with Panic? All this time PJ figured it was only her. PJ often got lippy and talked back, got moody or slammed doors. Panic was mom's golden child, the one who could do no wrong. And she was fine with that, too. She did not want their mom to hurt Panic. But now that PJ had seen the bruises, faded purple and long, like the imprints of fingertips digging in where a hand might have grabbed and yanked to the point of agony, she wondered what else she didn't know about Panic and about their mom.

"Has she hurt you?" PJ asked then scooted closer to her on the bench.

Panic scooted and turned away again, looking up the road, though no headlights approached. She had tied her red sweatshirt around her waist before they'd set out and she pulled it from her middle then and slipped her arms into the sleeves. Despite the storm earlier in the week, it was still Santa Ana conditions outside, warm and dry, and PJ almost told her to take the sweatshirt off.

Maybe PJ didn't hear Panic's explanation. She knew all she needed to know to put the pieces together. Instead, she sat back against the bench feeling their hard lateral slats pressing into her skin through her thin shirt. Even though the night was warm, PJ also thought about putting on her sweatshirt. For some reason, the idea of an extra layer felt comforting.

As she pulled the sweatshirt from her bag, she noticed the rabbit's foot. PJ hadn't thought to tuck it into her bag before they left, and she wondered how it ended up there. She glanced back at Panic. Panic continued to face away from her, not daring to look back. PJ tucked the soft, pink keychain further into the bag and then pulled out Dad's sweatshirt. As she pulled the stretchy fabric over her head, she heard the distant sound of the approaching bus, loud and low with an easy rumble indicating it was slowing down and eventually coming to a stop to fetch them from the growing dark.

Panic turned to look at PJ as she stood up shouldering her bag. PJ also stood and looked toward the bus, looming in the dark. Its bright headlights watered her eyes. The windows of the bus were streaked with dust, like many other cars around town since the Santa Anas started blowing. Wildfires in the north, near Los Angeles, had brought smoke south to San Diego and everything was covered in a thick layer of grimy ash. The rain threatened but never fell. It would have been welcomed to their dusty valley, a necessary rinse of newness that never came. PJ always wondered why the plants never seemed to get dusty, but then, they evolved here right along with the wildfires. They were adapted to this life of smoke and heat.

Through the front windows, she could see the bus driver. He smiled as he came up alongside them, and then PJ could see him clearly through the glass of the side door. He tipped his head in a welcome as the door opened and the step lowered. PJ looked to Panic and then back to the bus driver. Shaking off her mounting fear, she reached into her pocket for the change she had already counted, then she stepped on the bus. She did not look behind her for Panic; she knew her sister would follow.

"Evening," the driver said in a cheerful manner that reminded her of the school's principal, Mr. Lubekey. The driver had black hair like Mr. Lubekey, too, only his eyes were small and close set. The name tag on his chest told PJ that his name was Herbie.

"Um, hi," PJ stammered. This was no time to clam up, but she found herself dumbstruck. Panic pressed into her back with an urgent nudge. "Yes, Sir. Can you tell me if this bus goes to the transfer station in downtown El Cajon? We need to get to Santa Fe station in San Diego."

"Yes ma'am, this here's the only bus that stops out this way. It only goes to one place, too," Herbie answered. His use of "ma'am" gave her some ease. PJ felt more grown up, like she could rise to this challenge, and take care of Panic on her own, out in the world. Herbie leaned closer to her and said, "It's thirty-five cents for you, but your friend is free because she's not old enough to pay." PJ already knew this, and she pulled out her change.

"Are you Herbie like The Love Bug?" Panic asked, and PJ started and shook her head at her little sister.

"The one and only," Herbie answered. "Disney got that name from yours truly."

Panic laughed and PJ hurried to get the coins counted. She held one quarter and one dime then slipped them into the coin slot. She was sorry to see the quarter go, a special bicentennial quarter that had been issued two years earlier. It had two dates on it, 1776 and 1976, which PJ loved. She had more like that one, though. In fact, most of their silver money (that's what Panic called their change, even the pennies) was in the form of bicentennial quarters. PJ had been collecting them whenever she came across one and she coveted them. She loved their shiny pictures of George Washington. On the back, he played a drum and marched in celebration of victory during the American Revolution. Manny had argued with her that the back was not a picture of Washington. He said that Washington would never have played his own drum but would have had someone play it for him, being as he was the president. PJ didn't care what Manny thought; she believed it was George Washington playing that victory drum for their country's independence. There was also something else near the drummer, the smallest ring of stars that PJ had ever seen encircling a flaming torch. In civics, PJ had learned that the stars represented the thirteen colonies. Manny couldn't argue with her about that because they had learned it together from a teacher.

PJ stood there for an extra second staring at the box where she'd placed the coin, until Panic gave her another impatient shove in the back, and she made her way down the aisle of the bus to find their seats.

Along the way, PJ took notice of the other people on the bus. A man in blue coveralls with grease on his face stared out the window. He didn't look at the girls as they passed. Another man peered out from behind a newspaper. He eyed PJ with suspicion before shaking his newspaper and then hiding his face behind it again. There seemed to be enough light in the bus for him to read, but PJ took the gesture as sinister, like a spy in Get Smart, a funny T.V. show about secret agents.

The sisters made their way to the back of the bus, which PJ thought was unoccupied. They tucked themselves into a seat near the rear. PJ took the window spot and Panic sat on the aisle. Looking across the aisle, beyond Panic, PJ saw that the bus row they picked was already occupied. An older woman with white hair and a serious expression sat in the row across from them looking directly ahead. Panic noticed the woman too, and she elbowed PJ and tilted her head toward the figured of the woman.

The old lady was dressed all in black, with a kerchief over her hair and tied beneath her chin as if she were in mourning or like the witch in the story "Hansel and Gretel." PJ always imagined the witch with a dark kerchief on her head. This woman also had on black gloves and her hands rested upon a small book in her lap. She stole a sideways glance at the girls and then straightened her posture and fortified her gaze forward.

Panic shrugged and looked at PJ with deep sadness on her face, like she understood the black clothes, the lady's solemn expression, forward gaze, and her rigid pose. PJ thought she understood too. She figured if this woman was in mourning, it seemed she had lost someone so recent that her clothes represented the grief she could not bear to express, like she was concealed behind a protective layer of black fabric and lace. Maybe she was even traveling from an actual funeral. But if so, PJ wondered why she wasn't weeping, dabbing her eyes, holding her breath.

The dark-clad woman caused PJ to wonder how she and Panic would express their own grief, now that they knew their dad's fate. Maybe they would never fully feel an appropriate sadness. PJ knew she felt some grief. But there was something else PJ felt too, below the grief, there was also a sense of relief. The idea that he had not really run away, he was not living somewhere else thinking about them each day, that he had not abandoned them in the way they imagined—this began to take shape in PJ's mind. It wasn't that suicide was better than abandonment;

it was different. She wanted to ask Betsy more questions about this new understanding, about what Chet had written in the letter. For the first time since they'd left, PJ felt the urge to turn back, switch buses or pull the stop cord and get off where they were, and walk back across El Cajon, back home. Then PJ remembered the finger-shaped bruises on Panic's arm. If Betsy had started to mistreat and abuse Panic, too, it was only a matter of time before it would get to the point like it did with the shoe. Then PJ would be the one reviving Panic.

She tasted bile in her throat at that thought. She knew she could not allow that to happen. Something their dad had said in the letter flashed in her thoughts: Take care of Panic.

PJ reached out to Panic and touched her arm, not in the place where she had seen the bruises, but near it. Near enough to her injury to say, I know this pain and I want to heal it and prevent it. At least that's what PJ wanted to convey. She found it odd to assume what gets transferred when abuse is shared. She thought of Panic seeing the plane crash. PJ couldn't see it like she did, but the deputy did; the man she spoke with at the sheriff's station. She had an entire moment with that deputy that PJ could not have understood, like they spoke their own language. The crash gave them a new vocabulary. But now, since the discovery of that bruise, there might emerge a new part of Panic's experience that could speak PJ's language, too, the language of pain and fear that Betsy had inflicted upon them. Though PJ never would have wished that on anyone else, she found some sense of comfort in knowing that she was not the sole victim of that infliction—and she felt guilty for the comfort, selfish for thinking it. But she did find solace in the realization that Panic might know her language now. In that moment, the relief PJ felt, though greedy and self-seeking, was greater than the sadness she felt that Betsy had hurt her too. It might have also been greater than the grief she felt about their dad.

Then, PJ got angry at herself for thinking such things and she pushed it away. Instead, she imagined how fearful Panic must have felt. She wanted to ask her about it, what had caused their mom to grab at her with such force that she would leave a mark, but she knew Panic would not talk. She was fierce and brave but also stubborn. She was the most stubborn kid PJ knew. The best PJ could do was get her sister out of there, and that's what they were doing.

She turned her attention to the window and watched streetlamps slip by as they drove. She saw a few kids shooting baskets at a lighted basketball court in a park, counted the long seconds it took the traffic lights to turn from red to green. She thought again about Aunt Fancy. The probability Fancy might not want them—a couple of busted up kids from a broken home—ran pretty high. Also, they might be a terrible and sad reminder about her brother, Chet, and how he had died. Maybe this was why they hadn't seen their aunt in so long, why she had stayed away, not kept in touch with them when PJ knew she loved them. She hadn't thought of that, and she chased the thought away. Instead, PJ thought of Fancy's cozy cabin in the woods. She had the best memories of visiting her place in Idyllwild. She remembered fresh baked bread, the kind that Fancy would prepare for a week, keeping a crock of slimy, bubbly dough warm in a dark place, transferring cups of the goo out and new flour in. The result was bread so sour it would cause your face to pucker with the first bite, but the salivation made you long for more and more, hot from the oven with a crunchy crust and warm, delicate webs of soft sponge on the inside. And the butter, too! Fancy churned her own butter. Made quilts and hand turned pasta and crocheted brilliant Afghans in all the colors of the rainbow, long stripes and granny squares and chevrons. Fancy always had fresh-brewed coffee on, any time of the day or evening, in case company showed up. And company showed up at her place all the time—this was how PJ knew she wouldn't turn them away. They were better than company; they were family. Fancy looked forward to company and welcomed even the roughest looking folks into her home. This was something Betsy did not like about Fancy. She would talk all the way down the mountain about Aunt Fancy's hippie friends and hippie lifestyle, loose and carefree. But Aunt Fancy seemed to be the happiest person PJ had ever known, so there must have been something to that lifestyle that gave her "that audacity," Betsy had called it. Audacity, indeed. PJ hoped that when they got to Idyllwild, Fancy would share some of that audacity with them. They needed some of that kind of living for sure.

As PJ was contemplating the meaning of audacity, Panic struck up a conversation with the old woman.

"Why are you dressed like that, all dark and funeral-like?" Panic asked.

PJ elbowed Panic but Panic kept her eyes on the woman.

The woman looked around the bus, as if she expected Panic had spoken to someone else. Then, when she made eye contact with Panic, her head pulled back in a slight gesture of surprise. "Do you mean . . . me?"

"Yeah." Now Panic leaned out across the aisle of the bus as if she expected the woman to reveal everything.

"Child," her lips were a thin, expressionless line when she spoke. "I've got no reason to tell you my business."

"It's okay. We're grieving too. Did you lose someone in the place crash?" When Panic asked her this, the man with the newspaper a few rows ahead of them turned his head and snuck a glance at them, then folded his paper. PJ supposed a bus was like a community discussion space, the public interior of the bus a sort of forum where strangers could talk.

"Do you mean the PSA crash last week? Heavens no." Now the woman's expression softened, and she turned her body in her seat to face Panic. "Did you lose someone on the PSA flight?"

"No ma'am. Our dad died."

The two of them faced each other for a long moment before the woman spoke again.

"My name is Marlene. What's yours?"

"I'm Panic and this is my sister, PJ."

PJ nodded expecting the usual questions about Panic's name, but none came.

"Nice to meet you . . . ladies."

"It's real nice to meet you too." Panic turned now to fully face the woman. She crossed her legs up under her body so that she was sitting in her folded pretzel shape, her back toward PJ.

PJ hoped Panic wouldn't tell Marlene they were running away. She entertained the fear of returning home only to be dragged off to the sheriff's station again. She'd also been thinking about how Mrs. Perón said that running away from home was against the law. Now, they were outlaws. Maybe PJ was even a kidnapper. The moment they'd stepped up on that bus, they had crossed some imaginary line that could not be uncrossed. But Panic didn't tell Marlene that they were running away. Instead, she started talking about the PSA crash like she had in the sheriff's station. She told Marlene all about seeing the smoke and the angels. This seemed to make the old woman excited.

"Angels going up to heaven, you say?" She clutched her book to her chest.

"Yes, ma'am. They were like ashes circling in the heat or like when the turkey vultures catch an updraft. Have you ever seen birds do that? They get all whooshy and swirly in the sky, like they might just soar up and up forever." Panic looked up at the ceiling of the bus. PJ looked up, too. Through the dark she saw an advertisement for Tab Cola conspicuous above the window.

Marlene didn't respond to the question about the vultures. PJ wasn't sure she heard Panic. Marlene had opened her book, even in the dark of the bus, and had started flipping its pages seeming to look for something important. PJ wondered what could be so interesting that she would want to read in the dark, but after Marlene started to speak again, PJ thought maybe she wasn't reading at all. She thought Marlene might have had that book memorized.

"Take heed that ye despise not one of these little ones; for I say unto you that in heaven, their angels do always behold the face of my Father." As Marlene said these words to Panic, she held the book open, but she didn't really look down at the page where her finger, cloaked in the black glove, pressed at the words. Instead, she watched Panic with expectation.

"Huh?" Panic's confusion was so earnest, PJ almost laughed out loud.

"Do you know who said that?" Marlene asked, first looking at PJ and then back to Panic.

PJ wanted to respond with sarcasm, you just said it, but she held her tongue. She had an idea who Marlene meant but she shrugged anyway. The sisters were not raised with any kind of beliefs, never even taught to say prayers. Betsy was not at all religious. PJ remembered seeing Manny's mom praying with her beads once, but it seemed more like a whispered song than a prayer. Then again, maybe that's all a prayer was meant to be: a song, but a special kind of song, one that went with a special set of circumstances and to a special recipient. Or was it like a letter? Maybe Chet's letter to her had been a prayer.

"Jesus said that," Marlene said, and her eyes sparkled in the low light. "He wanted us to know about angels. I believe that you saw them after the plane crash. I believe they were there to ferry the souls of those who were saved home to their palace in heaven." She smiled for the first time since she had started talking and she looked off above the girls' heads with a wistful gaze that was noticeable even in the low light.

The man a few rows ahead turned forward again and went back to his newspaper. The bus bounced along a rough patch of asphalt on Main Street before veering left onto El Cajon Boulevard. It sidled up to the curb and let on another two riders, two young men in dark coveralls carrying lunch pails. They stayed near the front of the bus sitting across the aisle from each other.

By the time the bus pulled away from the curb, Marlene had started to tell Panic all about Jesus. Marlene spoke about Jesus feeding the multitudes. PJ could tell Panic had her doubts about the story's authenticity. The sisters had known real hunger in their short lives.

"You mean he turned some bread and fish into a whole feast? How'd he do that?" Panic folded her arms and sat back against PJ. It was a good story, that much was true. PJ thought of the avocados and sweet bread they'd had that morning, how they had made that a feast, of sorts. Still, she didn't think they could have fed the entire neighborhood. Mr. Minkus could probably feed the neighborhood with his entire grove, but then he'd be out of avocados. She thought of Manny's family and the rabbits and felt sick all over again.

"Dear, you must have faith about these things," Marlene said. "Faith means that you believe even when you don't know where all the fish or loaves will come from. You know that you will be provided for because you know that Jesus loves you."

PJ's thoughts swirled between visions of Manny's mom clutching her beads and whispering her prayer-songs and Manny himself, grown and strong, so different from the boy she grew up with, his handsome face vivid enough in her mind that she could trace the outline of his chin. But then the image of Manny's mom took hold. PJ thought maybe Mrs. Gonzáles's faith would be enough to fulfill her family's needs, if that was all it took—a little faith. It was nice to believe that—that the Gonzáles family would be okay even without the rabbits—rather than think their family might be as hungry as she and Panic had been at times. PJ didn't wish that kind of hunger for anyone. Manny's mom had always given them things to eat, too. It was as if she knew the scarcity at PJ's house. And then, after a while, it was as if the girls knew that Mrs. Gonzáles knew they were hungry, so they would come around when times were lean. If she was honest with herself, PJ wondered if they had truly been after the scraps wood the night before. Probably not. Maybe Manny's mom was like Jesus, and she could turn bread and fish into a feast because she had faith. PJ hoped that Mrs. Gonzáles was like Jesus. She felt terrible for what she had done to the rabbits, but more now for how it had affected the Gonzáles family.

"Listen," Marlene said in a low voice. "I have some hard candy. Do you girls like candy?"

This question brought PJ to full alert.

"Yes, Ma'am," said Panic, sitting up, planting her feet on the floor.

"Well, I was saving this for my Sunday school class, but I can spare a few pieces. What we're planning for this Sunday is very special. Can I tell you about it?"

"Yes." Panic grew attentive.

"The children in my Sunday school class have been working very hard on learning about Jesus. They have all decided to accept Jesus into their hearts. This means they will be absolved of their sins, and they will be saved." She paused here and looked at PJ's face for a long moment before turning her attention back to Panic. "Can I tell you what that really means, though? It's actually quite wonderful. It's like a fairy tale."

Even PJ was intrigued now. She had no idea what it meant to accept anything into her heart. PJ often felt her heart thumping in her chest. She also knew that people referred to their heart when they were in love, loving someone with their whole heart or drawing cartoon hearts on their Pee-Chee folders in class. Still, PJ could not see how you could have someone come into your heart, least of all a man who lived a few thousand years ago. It had to be, as Marlene said, like a fairy tale. And how could he save people? That part caught PJ's attention the most. She thought of Lassie and Flipper and all the people they had saved.

"The best part is when Jesus comes into your heart, he will purify you. Make you clean and sparkling. As white as new snow. Then you will be saved." Marlene smiled.

There was the word again, "saved," and PJ leaned forward to look at Marlene. She saw her crooked teeth.

"And all you have to do is pray a few words. If you don't know how, I can teach you." She reached into her handbag and pulled out two cellophane-wrapped butterscotch candies, their bright yellow hue glowed even in the darkness of the bus. Marlene continued, "It isn't enough to simply say the words, though. You must understand them and try—as hard as you can—to believe them. So, let's pray together. I can help you."

PJ wondered if Marlene would give them the candy before teaching them to pray. She also wondered what the prayer would be like, if they would have to sing it in front of the men on the bus. She knew Panic would belt out "American, The Beautiful" in a second flat for that candy, but PJ had doubts she herself could do it, pray in public. Glancing around the bus again, she saw that the men had no interest in their conversation. It seemed okay to go ahead with whatever Marlene had planned. Besides, her mouth had already begun to water with the thought of that sweet and salty flavor of butterscotch, better than the starlight mints from the sheriff's station. She knew those candies. They were given out as rewards in grade school for a job well done. She knew that Panic knew them too; butterscotch was one of the only reasons PJ could still get Panic out of the house in the morning and off to school. She'd croon, Mrs. Ackerman's got a new bag of candy today because it's the beginning of the month.

"How do we pray?" Panic asked.

"First," Marlene began, "place your hands together like this." She brought her hands together, fingers steepled. "Then, you close your eyes and talk to Jesus."

"What do we say?" Panic asked, her hands already pressed together.

"First, you admit you are a sinner. That only means that you make mistakes. We all do that, right?"

Panic nodded. PJ nodded, too, so Marlene continued.

"Then, if you admit that you have sinned, you know that your heart is now . . . dark." She shook her head slightly when she said dark, like she didn't mean for it to sound bad, but it was bad. Darkness in your heart sounded like the worst thing PJ could imagine.

"Each time you make a . . . mistake, you take on more darkness." Marlene's words came with some care. "Sometimes the devil—do you girls know who he is? He's a bad angel that can manipulate you—sometimes the devil makes us do even worse things once we start making a few mistakes. This can cause our sinning to grow like a great big stone rolling down a hill, picking up all sorts of terrible things as it rolls." She seemed pleased with herself for her word choices, PJ noticed, not at all pleased with hearing Marlene's words.

An odd pressure flickered within PJ, like she should stop the conversation. The idea of darkness in her heart made her feel sick. It was those damned rabbits. PJ knew she had made a mistake by letting them go, but was it evil? It seemed to her like Marlene was saying PJ needed to admit she was evil, that maybe the devil made her do what she did the night before, but also that she had let the devil manipulate her. And if he could manipulate her then, he could manipulate her always, and he could manipulate Panic, her mom, Manny, and everyone.

PJ opened her mouth to protest but Panic nodded her head and said, "I know all about that kind of rolling rock." She looked at PJ with such a hopeful gaze. So, PJ nodded too.

"Don't worry, girls. The very good news is that Jesus can make your hearts pure again, no matter what. If you invite Jesus into your heart, he will purify your heart and make you white like fresh snow. Do you want Jesus to make your hearts white like snow?"

Marlene reached out her black-gloved hand to give them each a candy. Panic eagerly nodded then. But it was PJ who reached across to accept the candy. When she did, she saw Marlene's face with clarity. The old woman seemed spooky in that low light. Deep grooves marked her face with age. She wore the same pinched expression that Mrs. Perón wore, but with a touch of menace. PJ wished she had seen the woman with this clarity before they'd begun the lesson on prayer. Determined lines fringed Marlene's eyes—such gloomy eyes—surrounded by dark circles. Her wrinkles set her expression toward suspicion and distrust, and she glanced between the girls with cautious restraint. There was something else, too, in Marlene's face. PJ thought she looked greedy. Still, with Panic's hands earnestly pressed, PJ took the candy and gathered her own hands together.

She thought of recent news she had heard about taking candy from strangers. Halloween one year earlier, a kid in Los Angeles had been poisoned from his own trick-or-treat bag, cyanide in his Pixie Stick, though later it was reported the news was falsified. Still, Pixie Sticks had become off limits. Since then, you couldn't even trust a Sunday school teacher with butterscotch, especially not one accusing children of having hearts filled with darkness and being manipulated by the devil. Nevertheless, PJ had the candy and Panic smiled at her with hope, like this was the luck they'd needed.

"That's right; take it but don't eat it just yet, dears," Marlene tried to smile again. "First, let's pray. You can also hold your hands like this." Marlene interlaced her gloved fingers and clasped them together beneath her chin. PJ set the candy in her lap and laced her fingers together as instructed. Before Marlene continued, Panic grabbed one of the butterscotches and stuffed it in her pocket.

"Remember to acknowledge that you are a sinner first. This part is very important. Your heart cannot be made white like snow until it is first seen clearly for what it is."

That seemed odd to PJ. What was her heart if not pure, even if she had let the rabbits go, or lied to Mrs. Perón and the deputy about her mom, or even lied to Manny? Wasn't her heart still a place where she could love someone wholly, like she loved Panic or their dad? If it needed to be made pure again, PJ had to wonder if the fairy-tale-magic Marlene shared with them would do the trick, and, indeed, make her white like snow. PJ marveled at the possibility of such a cleaning, how easy and free it would feel, to not have guilt or shame. She could almost imagine that her mom hadn't hit her because she was bad or flawed, that their dad didn't leave—or even die—because of her. She could be white like snow, pure and fresh in a snowy, winter landscape with beautiful trees and lovely, perfect white hills of flawless powder.

"Now close your eyes and say these words after me."

PJ closed her eyes and waited.

"Jesus, I know I am a sinner."

Panic repeated the words verbatim then elbowed PJ and PJ did the same, though she kept one eye opened, looking toward the men at the front of the bus. Her voice came out in a ragged whisper. But Marlene didn't seem to care about the quality of the prayer, only that the words were said.

She went on, "I confess with my mouth that you are the son of god." The girls repeated her words, even though PJ didn't remember that part ahead of time. Marlene never mentioned that part early. It was also about then that PJ started to question how a person who had been dead for two thousand years could hear what they had to say from the back of the bus, there in the dark, driving up El Cajon Boulevard. The other thing she wondered, as she repeated those words that she did not understand, was this: if there was a magical deity named God, and his son, Jesus, had lived so long ago but they could still talk to him and he could still hear them, wouldn't he know what was truly in PJ's heart without her having to say anything? After all, if they were talking fairytales, why not go all the way and give Jesus the power to know what PJ did or did not understand about her sins, as Marlene called them. She began to have her own doubts. And she remembered Marlene said the devil could cause doubts. Was that what she said? But then something else happened, something PJ had almost expected and certainly had wished for. Her own hope grew at the possibility that she might wipe the slate clean and start anew, regardless of the many mistakes she'd made, those things that had darkened her heart. Maybe she really could get a fresh, new start, ready to wholly accept whatever came next in this life, free of regret or shame or fear. Then PJ remembered the candy. If the fairytale was true, could she still accept that candy in her lap knowing she should not have taken it from a stranger in the first place? Could she still get 'saved,' as Marlene had called it?

"Please come into my heart and make it white like snow," Marlene finished.

Despite her doubts, PJ said the words that Marlene told her to say. She said them in unison with Panic, and then Panic opened her eyes and looked at PJ, smiling. She turned back to Marlene and said, "Thank you." Then Panic took the candy out of her pocket, untwisted the cellophane wrapper, and popped the butterscotch into her mouth.

"Now, you are saved. And white like snow." Marlene sat back in her seat with a contended look upon her face, though without enough warmth in her expression to erase her deep grooves of distrust. Still, she rested contentedly and returned her gaze ahead.

PJ sat motionless for a moment watching Marlene as the streetlamps along the drive washed her face in light, then dark, then light again, over and over as they moved up the boulevard. Marlene did not look at the girls again and she did not speak to them again. Before long, she reached up and pulled the stop cord with her gloved hand and the bus moved to the curb. When Marlene got up to move down the aisle, Panic gave a small wave of her hand, but either Marlene didn't see or chose to ignore her.

A few minutes later, the bus pulled into the transfer station and all the men in the front stood and got off the bus. Panic hoisted up her bag. PJ joined her in the aisle and then they made their way to the doors at the front of the bus. They were greeted once more by the friendly face of the bus driver, Herbie.

"You girls can catch the transfer to Santa Fe Station in about ten minutes. I'm going to give you a transfer slip, so save your coins. I saw the way you looked at that shiny quarter." He winked at PJ and handed her a slip of paper. "Remember, your friend is free."

"She's my sister," PJ said taking the slip.

"Is that so? Well, look out for each other, you hear." And he nodded his head at them.

"Thank you," PJ said.

"Thanks," Panic said, too. PJ could hear the candy, thick with syrup, in her sister's cheek.

They stepped off the bus into the station. The air had cooled, and night was heavy upon them. As the bus pulled away from the curb, PJ saw the sign on its front flip from '63' to 'Garage.' Herbie was also done for the day, like the other men getting off the bus, only he was headed back to the garage to dock the bus before going home, or wherever he went when he wasn't giving out free transfer slips.

PJ looked at the slip of paper still in her hand. It had been a nice gesture.

They made their way to the turnstile where they would catch the downtown transfer. When they set their bags down there, PJ noticed the man with the newspaper again. He sat on a bench nearby and nodded at them, like he knew the girls now that they had shared a bus ride. PJ positioned herself between him and Panic keeping one eye on him and the other on the road watching for the arrival of the transfer bus she thought would not come soon enough.

CHAPTER TEN

The driver of the next bus, a thin, grey-haired man, took the transfer slips from PJ without making eye contact then waved them onboard. As they made their way up the aisle, PJ noticed the emptiness of the bus, the dim recesses of void. No passengers occupied seats they shuffled past. No strange women in mourning clothes sat waiting to pray with them. They were alone, she and Panic. Then, as they selected their place—about halfway into the bus, moving into the seats on their left so Panic could watch the pedestrians along sidewalks—as they sat and eased into this strange place, a final passenger came up the steps into the bus and handed the old man his fare. It was the newspaper man from the earlier bus. He nodded once again toward PJ, that same assumed familiarity of his gesture that made her feel uncomfortable.

PJ could see the newspaper man with more clarity, then. He sat one row ahead of the girls, but on the opposite side of the bus. His sweater vest had the diamond pattern of blue and red argyle connected by a thin line of yellow. Hunched shoulders framed his posture. He wore a hat, which PJ thought looked like something a spy would wear. In the station lights through the window, PJ easily saw his curly hair, brown and greasy, cascading from beneath his hat along the back of his head. The man took off his hat then to reveal a bald spot on his head. He ran his hand along the smooth crest of his skull then turned around in his seat to face them.

"You girls headed home?" He asked. His eyes moved from PJ to her duffle bag. Through the dark, PJ could make out an attempted smile on his face.

"Yep," PJ looked from the man to the old bus driver. She squeezed Panic's hand, hoping her sister would remain quiet. She should have talked with her about the way she carried on with that old woman on the last bus. But for some reason, when she saw the man's face, she softened. Her eyes had adjusted to the dimness, and she could better see his eyes, kind and round. His expression, one of concern and interest, seemed to reassure PJ, though she didn't know why. His lips were pressed together in a resolute line of firmness as if he were puzzling about something important. His eyes shined in the low light, and he didn't seem menacing like she first thought. Contrary to his bald head, his face was rather young, almost boyish. Maybe he was one of those men who lost their hair early, PJ thought. She was reminded of Manny.

"Good of you to take care of your sister that way," the man said as his eyes fell upon Panic. "Maybe you take care of each other, huh?" He nodded his head then turned back around in his seat unfolding his newspaper the way he had on the first bus. Even with the lights dim and night creeping in, the man's attention stayed on the pages of his paper.

The door of the bus hissed shut and the driver pulled away from the curb. By then, PJ had eased up on Panic's hand and so Panic pulled away and turned to face the window. PJ also looked out of the window. It had been a long time since the girls were out of El Cajon. The scene that moved along outside the bus was strange and new; bright neon lights illuminated store fronts and street corners. They passed a group of women in colorful, tight dresses, high heels, and fur jackets, most of them smoking cigarettes and striking poses like they were on the pages of a New York magazine. But they weren't quite highbrow, those women in their dark stockings and red lipstick. Even from afar, PJ could see the dirt of their clothing, the worn places where time had not been kind. She figured they were prostitutes, or hookers as they were called on T.V., except the hookers on T.V. were cleaner, more like caricatures of these real women along the curb. PJ thought these women looked genuine. They stood tall and waved and called out to cars passing. They were brave, too, more so than the women in Hollywood only playing hookers in television sagas. No. PJ thought these women had to be about the bravest women there were, but by the time she'd settled on that idea, the scene out the window had changed, replaced by vacant sidewalks and dark storefronts.

The bus rounded a corner, and a long, well-lit avenue came into their sights. PJ knew this part of El Cajon Boulevard. They were well into La Mesa, and they would soon move into the collage area by San Diego State University. She wondered if they would go through North Park near the PSA jet crash site at Dwight and Nile. Surely that location would be cordoned off, but PJ wondered all the same. If they did end up there, she'd have to distract Panic, who remained so rapt by the passing scenes that she might have forgotten to blink since they got on this second bus.

What was Panic thinking, PJ wondered. Was she afraid to be away from home? PJ didn't want to admit to her own fear, but she also felt afraid. The words of the newspaper man played on repeat in her mind for the last several miles: Good of you to take care of your sister that way. A new sense of duty began to mount. She could care for Panic at home, but out in the world, there were too many unknowns. What if Fancy wouldn't have them? What if they couldn't find their way to her place? Or worse, what if Fancy blamed them for their dad's death. All of this loomed in PJ's anxiety.

The rising shapes of tall buildings grew closer in the distance and PJ could see that they were headed toward downtown San Diego. They passed motels and restaurants, occasionally stopping to let a person on or off, but always the newspaper man stayed on board, always focused on his paper, no matter the darkness.

The light was not so dim that PJ couldn't make out the newspaper man's threadbare jacket over the back of the chair next to him, tweed and faded, khaki in color; its arm she could see most clear, adorned with an oval leather patch over the elbow. She wondered who he was. Could he be someone's father? Could he leave his kids? Could he end his own life, rob his children—children PJ only guessed at—of knowing him later and forever? Maybe he knew a thing or two about family and that was why he had seemed so concerned when he looked at the two of them, huddled in the bus. Or maybe he didn't have children; maybe he had his own terrible childhood and could imagine what it would be like to feel so overcome with fear and grief that running away proved better than staying. Maybe he was also a runaway, like them, but now he had grown up and knew, in retrospect, the difficulties they might face. PJ invented many scenarios about the man. But really, the man didn't look like he had children his own.

Her thoughts returned to her own dad and her throat constricted. The letter, folded up and secured in her jacket pocket, seemed to burn there with an uncomfortable heat. She recognized the anger as it crept into her thoughts. Betsy had kept his death from them for so long. All this while, she imagined her dad had escaped to Mexico or else hid at Aunt Fancy's house in the mountains, that they might someday see him again and ask him why he left, or if they were the reason he left for the burden they brought simply by being his children. But now she had a different explanation: this letter, along with a new version of events even then revising her foundation. Betsy had called him a coward, said he'd been afraid of the noises, mostly in his head. The ghosts he'd picked up in Vietnam haunted him unto his death. But was cowardice the thing that compelled him to end his life? PJ wondered then about the burden of children; how much work she had to do to take care of Panic. She thought about the things she had done to bring food home to take care of her sister—recycling bottles, yard work, the avocado harvest. But Panic was also a big help.

Panic.

Her sister's name sparked a memory like the flicker of a lighter to a cigarette. Panic was a nickname their dad had given to the infant Josephine—Baby Jo—many years ago. PJ was about five years old then, but Panic wasn't even walking yet. And then the flicker of recollection caught fire and PJ's mind flooded with images of tiny Josephine cooing and giggling, unaware.

Their dad, Chet, sat in his recliner chair, a cigarette smoldering in the ashtray on the magazine table nearby. The glass disk of the ashtray hid beneath a mound of cigarette butts, some of them reigniting with the red heat of the tip from the cigarette that he had set down. He had set the cigarette down so that he could pick up the baby, Panic. Only she was Josephine then, named after their grandmother, Chet's mom. PJ remembered their grandmother mostly from photographs, but she knew she had short, red hair, bottle-dyed and pin-curled, and she always had a cigarette in her own hand or mouth. Josephine, the baby, had pink skin and brown, silky curls atop her very round head. The image of her infant sister grew clearer in PJ's memory as the bus slowed for a red light. She remembered what Panic wore that day, a plaid jumper, red and green, maybe for Christmas. Her tiny fingers were no bigger than some of those cigarette butts, and strangely as curled, the way cigarettes are if they're smoked and stubbed out early, and then they bend in all sorts of fantastic ways and shapes. Only, it didn't seem right to compare the baby's fingers to the cigarettes, smoldering in the ashtray as their dad hovered over Jo and made happy cooing noises to her.

Then, the sound came. Bap! Bap! A car puttering down the gravel road had misfired and caused the din. Bap! Bap! PJ could hear it in her memory as clearly as if it were the bus they rode then making the sound. She tried to push away the rest of the thought, but it came, nonetheless.

That simple sound—then the rush of action! Chet jumped from the chair; coiled cigarette butts erupted, burnt and bent; tiny hot embers, too, streaked upward, like fireworks before they exploded. Their dad's body lunged as he dove for the dark place behind the sofa, but not before the cloud of ash, like solid smoke, burst around him and hung in the air of the living room above PJ's head. She sat on a braided rug near the plush chair, a smallness all her own then, holding her captive in the tenth of a second when Chet thrust. She gaped at the suspended poof that held her baby sister up with the ash and smoke, up with the white curling fingers, some hot with fire and burning before they arced then fell to the hard floor. And Josephine, a tiny baby, seemed to hover there, suspended in the air, but not long enough for PJ to reach her, not held aloft long enough before she could get beneath her, before Baby Josephine reached the floor with the burning embers and the coiled cigarette butts and the terrible sound of pain and wailing that came after. By then, the flash of their dad had completely vanished, hidden from the noise.

After that, the baby flinched when he held her, remained alert and wide-eyed at his cooing. And so, he took to calling her Panic.

●

Panic felt an urge in her bladder. She whispered, "PJ, I have to go."

PJ looked like she had just arrived on the bus, and she glanced around, disoriented, coming back from some trace-like thought.

"Now?" PJ whispered.

"Yes."

"We can't stop the bus, Panic. And if we get off, I don't know when we'll get another bus." She looked out the window at the dark and unknown city around them. "Plus, I have no idea where we are right now."

"Okay." Panic squirmed, trying to find a more comfortable position. "I think I can wait."

"Okay?"

"Yeah, sure." She settled back into the bus seat and turned her head to look out the window again, hoping for something distracting. She saw people walking dogs, glass store fronts, bricks and signs and doors, but nothing spectacular. It would be a long stretch.

Twenty minutes later, they pulled into downtown San Diego. Tall buildings climbed from each side of the road, each seeming to reach higher than the last. They reminded Panic of the oaks along their street back home, thick and solid, only here the sky hid behind the towering buildings. They did not offer the same protective feeling of the oaks along Forester Creek. In fact, even though PJ sat beside her, Panic felt alone, like she'd never connect with another person again. She pulled her sister closer to her side. PJ welcomed the contact and leaned into her sister. Both girls' eyes remained skyward out the window of the bus, in awe of the grand cityscape expanding around them.

Along the sidewalks, litter blew like tumbleweeds between parked cars and newspaper stands. Steam rose from manholes. Dark recesses appeared to swallow the city lights that hung above the streets like sentinels of dying hope. A group of men stood around a trashcan lit by the glow of a small fire within. From the red traffic light, Panic had time to discern their shadowy faces, hard-worn and gaunt. Three of them encircled the can rubbing their hands and looking into the flames. Where did they live, Panic wondered, but by then the light had changed green and the bus moved off away from the men at the corner, and Panic's question hung in the intersection forgotten like the names of the streets themselves.

Before long, the waterfront appeared, and the bus turned right along the embarcadero. Navy men, sailors in white uniforms, walked together in small groups away from the docs and toward the glow of the pubs and nightclubs facing the harbor. As the bus drove near one such establishment—The Tiki Lounge—Panic could make out the sign: "Come as you are! No dress code required." Panic wondered what types of outfits might inspire such a sign. A long line of sailors stood waiting at the door. Another sign boasted, "Live, Nude Girls." At this, Panic pulled her sleeves down over her hands. Within a few minutes, they pulled into Santa Fe station and the bus driver called out, "Final stop." Panic and her sister gathered their things and made their way off the bus.

The man with the newspaper was already off the bus, hat once again on his head and newspaper tucked beneath his arm. He was walking away up the sidewalk and Panic remembered how he had talked to PJ in El Cajon. Panic asked, "did we know him?"

"No," PJ answered.

Panic followed PJ into the station, with its high arching façade and Spanish mission-like appearance, a single lofty belfry rose to the sky. The stucco walls were dim and hosted a series of archways. Huge wooden doors stood ajar, and the girls walked through them into a gigantic interior room with dark wooden ceilings complete with additional arches and carved balustrades. Heavy wooden chandeliers adorned with lightbulbs that flickered like real candles hung from beams along the sidelines of the ceiling. Benches lined the floor. It was magnificent!

But PJ was all business and hurried Panic along.

Across the room they saw a sign for the Amtrak train company and a sign for the Greyhound bus company. They walked across the large room hearing their footsteps echo as they moved. Panic noticed a family, a man and woman with two children, seated near a set of luggage. They spoke in hushed words. A group of nuns stood together arranged in size from tallest to shortest like they had assembled by size on purpose, their black and white habits framing them like the nesting dolls she'd seen at the public library over the summer. They stood near a group of men, not unlike the newspaper man from the bus, each with a magazine or news-paper held a short distance from their faces. They all clustered around a sign that read "3A." At the far end of the station, a portly man with a thick mustache pushed a flat broom and pulled a wheeled trashcan along behind him as he swept, occasionally pulling a long pole from the can to poke at a paper cup or napkin on the floor. The stick speared the rub-bish, and the man brought it into the can and deposited the item, easy. One of the wheels on his can squeaked as he pulled it along.

Panic made a beeline toward the restroom sign and PJ followed. The insides of the restroom matched the station itself, each stall an arch with a wooden door in the style of the Spanish mission. After they had taken care of business and washed up, they made their way back to the station floor to purchase their bus tickets.

As the girls reached the window for the Greyhound, Panic no-ticed the shade was drawn down and the signed read "closed." The hours upon the window showed that the ticket booth closed at 6:00 PM and reopened at 7:30 AM. Glancing at the large clock, she saw that they had missed the ticket sales by over an hour. Her stomach lurched and she felt sick. She turned to face PJ, hoping her older sister had a solution, but PJ merely had squinted at the sign as if she couldn't quite make sense of it.

"They're closed?" Panic asked.

"Looks like it. I didn't even think about that."

At once, a man's voice called out, "First-class passengers for Santa Barbara. Tickets at the ready, please." His cap and suspenders offered the quintessential look of a train conductor. The businessmen folded their newspapers and tucked away their magazines and then shuf-fled toward the "3A" sign. Next the conductor called out, "All other passengers now, all aboard. All aboard." The rest of the people waiting, the family and the nuns and a few others, all formed up a queue and then moved through the opening. The only person left in the station was the man with the broom and wheeled trash can.

"Well?" Panic asked her sister.

"I don't know." PJ looked around the vacant station, up to the tall ceilings and heavy chandeliers, then back to Panic. "We can wait here over night. I bet they have trains that come and go all night. We can buy our bus tickets in the morning when the ticket booth opens."

Panic's shoulders slumped. Her eyes fell away from her sister, and she felt dejected. She sagged away from the window and toward the closest bench where she swung her bag and plopped herself down. PJ crossed the floor and joined her sister on the bench. She sat on the other end of the bench, though, maybe to give Panic some room. Even though she didn't like that PJ was far away, it seemed reasonable. Let her have her space. Still, PJ was the big sister and should have anticipated something like this.

She wondered what else PJ hadn't thought of. How could she anticipate everything that might go wrong? Panic knew she couldn't. and just when she started to think this had been a terrible idea, the newspaper man from the bus appeared in the opened doorway from where the girls had arrived. Panic knew it was him because he had on that same hat and tweed jacket, and even from across the station, she could make out his curly hair. Everything about him was the same expect that he no longer held a newspaper. Now, he held a taut leash attached to a straining, small dog. The dog pulled so hard on the leash that its claws skittered across the floor as they made their way into the station. The man noticed them sitting on the bench across the room and he made his way toward him.

The voice of the conductor from the train going to Santa Barbara called out once again, "Final call. All aboard," before disappearing through the doorway to the unseen train.

Panic noticed the small dog headed toward her and her disposition improved at once. She sat upright on her bench and giggled like a hopeless fool. The dog seemed to be locked onto her and continued to pull the man in the direction of the girls, but with its focus set on Panic. When the man and the dog got near, she stood from the bench and kneeled. The man dropped the leash. The dog bounded toward Panic, at once reaching her and nuzzling and licking her, as Panic giggled and squealed.

"Her name is Lucky," the man said, "and I'm, Driscoll. Harvey Driscoll. But everyone calls me Driscoll." He tipped his hat at PJ and nodded, though she did not rise to greet him. Panic, however, continued to rollick with Lucky. Up close, PJ could see that Driscoll was a lot younger than she'd first thought.

"I thought you might have missed your bus or train," Driscoll continued. "I also thought you girls could use a little kindness, so I brought you something from home." He reached into his jacket pocket and pulled out a candy bar, a Hershey's with almonds.

"Wow! Thanks mister." Panic said, now sitting cross-legged on the floor with Lucky in her lap.

PJ did not reach for the candy. "No, thank you."

"PJ," Panic hissed at her sister.

"It's not right," She gave the younger girl a menacing look then turned back to Driscoll. "Honestly, Harvey Driscoll, thank you, but we're fine." Even as she said it, she knew they weren't fine. PJ felt afraid and tired, and she knew they were so far from home.

"I understand." The man said, pocketing the candy bar as Panic's expression shifted to disappointment. "Like I said, you've got to take care of your sister."

That wasn't what he had said earlier, PJ remembered. He had said it was good of PJ to take care of her sister; there was a difference. But right then, PJ didn't feel like having an argument with a grownup. But was he a grown up? Up close, he looked like he could be a senior at her high school. Still, she wanted him to go away and to take his dog, too, so that she and Panic could figure out what they were going to do next. But she found herself looking at his face with more interest. He had a large nose, but it wasn't ugly, like it had been broken. His round eyes had a kind depth to them that seemed a little sad or troubled, or both. Maybe it was loneliness, PJ guessed. Maybe that was really why he had come back to the station.

The train to Santa Barbara blew its whistle and started its departure. The noise from its wheels strained along the metal rails of the tracks and it shrieked a high-pitched whine as the train carried the nuns and businessmen and small family away from the station.

"I'm sorry to have bothered you girls." Driscoll nodded. "Come on, Lucky." He gave the dog's leash a small tug and Lucky sprang from Panic's lap and joined the man by his heels. Then, he turned and walked away without looking back.

Panic stayed on the floor, pouting. The man with the large broom came up them and stopped sweeping. He looked at the girls and then watched as Driscoll disappeared through the opened doors.

"Aren't you kids going with your daddy?" the man asked. His blue coveralls had stitched pockets and a loop that held an amazing number of keys. His mustache covered his mouth.

"What?" PJ asked looking at the man and then looking to the vacant doorway where Driscoll had left the station. "Um, no. He wasn't our dad. We don't know that man."

"Well, what are you doing here, then?" the mustached man asked.

"We're waiting for the Greyhound ticket office to open so we can go to our aunt's house in the morning." PJ explained.

The mans mustache seemed to protrude. He looked at the ticket window, and then back to PJ. He looked at Panic on the floor. Panic was not looking the man but was still sulking, flicking her shoelace with her finger, and staring idly at the fingernails of her opposite hand.

"Well, you cain't stay here," he said. "We got a no loiterin' rule and I gotta enforce it."

"What do you mean?" PJ asked. Now Panic looked up.

"I mean, you cain't stay." He took out a handkerchief and blew his nose, then he stuffed the handkerchief back in his pocket. "I'll be locking up, forth with. Y'all can use the little girl's room and get yourself a drink, but then you gotta leave." He took his pole out of the can and poked at a crumpled-up newspaper, running it through with the tip of the stick, which PJ could see now boasted a three-inch spike. He plucked the balled-up newspaper off the end of the stick and tossed it in the can.

"Soon as I'm done, you gotta go. Go on, now." And he nudged Panic with the tip of his shoe.

In an instant, Panic was up with her fists in front of her like she might fight the man, but he only laughed. "She's tough, that one. Good. That's real good." He pushed his broom past them muttering to himself, "She'll need to be tough." Then, "soon as I'm done. Soon as I'm done, you gotta get."

"What now?" Panic asked PJ.

PJ started gathering up their things. She handed PJ her duffel bag and made her way to the door. "I saw a place outside where we can wait."

"Outside!" Panic burst out and the sound of her voice bounced around on the emptiness of the station. Then, she lowered her voice and caught up to her sister saying, "We can't sleep outside . . . in the city."

PJ continued to walk as if she hadn't heard her sister. She made her way through the doors and out into the cool air of evening. The Santa Ana winds had died, and the chill of the harbor nipped at PJ. Panic reached her sister and shivered visibly.

"It's not ideal," PJ said.

"You're telling me," Panic responded.

Along the edge of Santa Fe Station, on the opposite side from the train tracks, they found an alcove recessed in at the base of one of the many arches of the building. They scooted into a corner there and huddled close to each other. From where they were, through a small opening, they could not see the passers-by on the sidewalks in front of the station, and that suited PJ fine. This also meant that the passers-by could not see them, and this was the way she needed it to be if they were to remain safe for the night, tucked away from the blowing garbage and wandering sailors.

CHAPTER ELEVEN

A different kind of cold held the air of downtown, so different that the temperature of inland seemed a dream, like something PJ had only made up from earlier that same day. She shivered and held Panic closer to her, drawing her sister's warmth into her own body and trying to breathe hers back into their huddled mass. Minutes could have been hours and PJ wouldn't have known the difference. She stared at the stucco wall and waited for the day to come, not knowing how late the hours had grown nor how cold the night had become. She did know how tired she felt. The weight of the day, or maybe the entire week, pressed down upon her. She fought against the heaviness of her eyelids, fought against the memory of Mrs. Perón, and of her mother hitting her with the shoe, and of the kicking rabbit in her arms, its sharp bite on her palm.

The sound of an arriving train broke the monotony of her stare at the stucco wall. She listened to the chugging as it grew louder, heard the metal screeched against the rails, almost felt the vibration of the horn as it blew when the train entered the station. Panic must have been sleeping, because the noises roused her and she pulled away from PJ and looked around with sudden attention, sleep still lingering on her weighty eyelids.

"Who's there?" Panic said to no one.

"It's a train; it's nothing. Go back to sleep." But PJ knew the young girl would not be calmed.

"I have to go again."

"Just go here," PJ said. "No one can see you."

"What?" Panic asked. "No way. Yuck."

"Well, where then?" PJ asked, but Panic was already standing and gathering their things.

"Um, the station, of course."

"It's closed."

At this, Panic looked at her sister for a long couple of seconds then she laughed out loud. "The station's is open," she said. "We caint loiter in thar." Panic mocked the voice of the mustachioed janitor. She put her finger above her upper lip and pretended like she had a bushy mustache herself.

"No. It's closed. He said."

"Everyone knows they don't close train stations, silly. At least not this one."

"Who's everyone?" PJ stood next to her sister. She wanted it to be true, needed it to be true, even. PJ felt so cold and her back hurt from sitting on the concrete outside in the damp air so close to the harbor. But her sister didn't answer her. Instead, Panic moved around her and made her way back toward the station entrance.

The doors were closed, but when Panic pulled on the large, wrought iron handles, they gave way, opening to the large room of the station once again. The chandeliers glowed a warm yellow and the air rushed out to greet them with a soft warmth. As they entered, PJ decided they would stay in the station all night, if they could get away with it, maybe sleep in the bathroom stall. They made their way to the restroom and once again walked into the arched stalls with the great wooden doors. This would do nicely, PJ thought. When they were done, they both held their hands under the faucets for an extended length of time, letting the hot water warm their hands and turn their skin pink.

Panic grinned at her sister's reflection in the mirror and said, "Told you so."

"You were right," PJ said.

"Say it again," Panic laughed.

"You were. Only, let's have a look one more time to make sure that janitor is gone, okay?"

As they made their way out of the bathroom, they were surprised to find Harvey Driscoll, the newspaper man from the earlier bus, standing in the middle of the train station looking all around, seeming alarmed. When he spotted them, he went directly to them.

"Oh, girls, am I so glad I found you," he said before he reached them. Lucky has escaped and I thought she might have tried to find her way back down here to you. I don't suppose she's turned up here, has she?"

"Oh no!" Panic answered in alarm, but PJ remained quiet, looking around the empty station.

"We haven't seen her, Mr. Driscoll." Panic turned to PJ, "Have we PJ?"

"No, we haven't seen her." She frowned at her sister.

"Well, it was a long shot, but she did seem to like you a lot. She doesn't often wander so I thought she might've had a reason for wanting to get away, to get back down here." He nodded at Panic and wrung his hands, then looked around the station. "Well, if she turns up, please keep her close by and I'll check in after I go around the neighborhood. Would you do that for me, please?"

"Sure," Panic answered.

PJ raised her eyebrows at Panic wondering what her sister thought they would do with a dog, even if they did find her, but before she could protest, the man turned and left in a hurry.

"That was dumb, Panic." PJ scolded her sister.

"You're dumb." Panic shot back.

PJ was reminded of how young her sister was, but she pressed. "We can't help him find his dog. We shouldn't even be talking to that man."

"What's your problem? It's not like I offered to help him look." At this, Panic stomped to a bench and threw her bag down before plopping herself next to it and crossing her arms to glower.

PJ rolled her eyes and then followed her sister to the bench where she also sat. Panic's feet were dangling from the bench, and she kicked them back and forth like swings on a swing set. PJ watched Panic's feet before she said, "I'm sorry." She tried to explain that she was tired and cold, and maybe even a little scared.

"Don't be scared, PJ." Panic turned to face her sister. Her feet stopped swinging. "Tomorrow, we'll be at Aunt Fancy's house, and everything will be okay. I just know it will be. You'll see. We're almost there. Look at how far we've come." She gestured to the station.

PJ stared at her little sister's face. Small eyelashes curled from her lower lids in faint curves clustered along the creamy pink of her skin. Her upper lids hosted thicker, darker lashes that crowned her eyes. Panic's eyes—iris brown and lighted from within by golden flecks—appeared to be in constant wonder. Panic's nose hadn't changed much since she was a baby, its slender bridge arched to a round nub that turned slightly upward at its tip. She saw the tiny scar on Panic's cheek and wondered if it happened when she was a baby, when her dad had dropped her with the smoldering cigarettes. Sprinkled across her nose and along her cheeks were tiny freckles that PJ always thought matched the stars, if not a star map in this galaxy, then from a galaxy somewhere. And her smile was infectious, like nothing PJ had ever known, containing the ability to cheer her gloomiest day, lift her deepest depression, heal her sadness with a curl of her lips or a blast of her giggles. She even thought maybe Panic could turn bread into a feast for the masses—but this was a silly thought, really.

"Did you hear that?" Panic asked a second time, when PJ swam back from her thoughts.

"Hear what?"

"A bark. I'm sure I heard a bark. Listen."

And sure enough, it was a bark, a soft chirp of a bark, some-where off the platform side of the station where the newly arrived train now sat silent. Panic stood, looking toward the door where Mr. Driscoll had disappeared, in the opposite direction of the bark. He was not there. She gave PJ a quick glance before she bolted out through the opening beneath the 3A sign toward the direction from where the bark came. PJ didn't have time to gather their things. She left them right there on the bench. The station was deserted anyway. And she chased after her sister.

Once outside, PJ looked around the tracks, took in the great train engine and cars before her. She scanned the left side of the plat-form and the right side. There! Panic disappeared over the tracks in front of the large train. PJ jumped off the platform to follow her sister. She thought she heard a voice yell something from behind her, but she could not give up chase. As she rounded the opposite side of the train, she saw Panic standing on its other side, holding Lucky in her arms. Lucky was licking Panic's face and wiggling with delight. Then, the voice PJ only thought she had heard became clear: "Stop, you kids!" PJ turned to see a different conductor—this time a heavy man with a dark suit and a blue hat with a stiff brim—round the train shaking his fist. He stopped and caught his breath, placing his hands on his thighs and coughing.

"Sorry sir," PJ offered. "I had to catch my sister."

"And I had to catch Lucky," Panic added quickly.

"You kids aren't allowed back here at all," the conductor said, returning himself upright and breathing more steadily. His face was red which almost matched the color of his red sideburns and thick eyebrows. "This is a very dangerous place for kids. Come on out now."

Panic came alongside PJ, Lucky still licking her and wiggling in her arms. The two girls walked to the front of the train. They passed the conductor, climbed back onto the platform, and headed into the station. All the while, the conductor followed. Once at the bench with their stuff, the girls sat, Panic securing Lucky on her lap. The conductor looked over their bags and harrumphed.

"You two all by yourself?"

The girls said nothing.

"I'll have to call the authorities, if you haven't got your parents with you."

"We're waiting for our bus," PJ said.

"Well, you aren't allowed to wait here and you're too young to be on your own anyway," the conductor said, but before he could say anymore, another voice joined in.

"It won't be necessary to call anyone, sir." Mr. Driscoll spoke as he came up behind the girls. "They're with me, of course." Lucky jumped out of Panic's arms and ran to Harvey Driscoll. She made a path of tight circles around his legs until he reached down and clipped her leash to the link on her collar.

"Well, they were out on the tracks and that's no place for kids. Do you know what can happen out there with these engines moving all around? You need to keep a closer eye, you hear."

"Of course. I'm so sorry," he said, and he tipped his hat. "Harvey Driscoll. My friends call me Driscoll. I was supposed to pick the girls up and I ran late tonight. You see, my dog got away from me and made her way here quicker than I, and well, as you can see, she's quite fond of these children." He gestured at the girls in a wide, sweeping motion with his hands that made PJ feel like she was on display.

"Well, they can't be here alone."

"So, I've heard," Driscoll responded. "We'll just be going then." Now he pointed to the girls' bags and then gestured for them to follow him. Panic and PJ gathered their belongings and turned to walk after Driscoll as he moved toward the door. Lucky's claws clicked along the floor tapping as they went.

Once outside, PJ said, "We can't go with you, Mister Driscoll."

"Just Driscoll, sweetheart, no mister." he said, "and you don't have to." He took a breath and looked around. "I only wanted to make sure that man didn't call the cops on your girls. I don't know your story, but I'm gonna guess you don't want the fuzz in on it."

The way he said 'fuzz' made Panic snort with a quick giggle.

"It sure is cold though." His eyes settled back on PJ. "You could stay over at my place, crash for the night, and get back over here early to get your bus or train or whatever. I know you girls have already missed it or you would've been long gone. Am I right?"

"Yep," Panic said as she bent down to pet Lucky.

PJ shoved her sister, but not hard.

"Listen, kid," Driscoll said, as he took out a cigarette and lit it. "I get it. Things are rough at home." He eyed her cheek where the bruises were still conspicuous. "You gotta get out. I know the drill. I'm happy to help. Really." He held out his cigarette pack to offer one to PJ and she shook her head. "Also, what I said earlier about you taking care of your kid sister is true. I really respect that. It's hard work, the kind of work I know something about."

"PJ, it will be okay," Panic said in her comforting way.

"PJ, is it?" Driscoll asked. "PJ, I gotta kid brother. He's away at my grandma's, but I usually look out for him the way you do her." He nodded at Panic. "Let me help, please. I'm a quick block away from here. I'll walk you back first thing."

PJ didn't know what to think. She felt cold and scared, but she also knew they couldn't go back into the station until the morning. Plus, he had a nice dog that Panic really liked. And they had each other. She thought about her mom, passed out on the couch before they left, the letter she had kept from her all these years, how her dad's absence had been a lie, his death a secret.

"I've got cocoa," Driscoll said, which sent Panic into a spin. She yelped with glee.

"How far?" PJ asked.

"Yes!" Panic sang, and even though PJ hadn't said yes, she started walking along with the man, his dog, and Panic.

"I'm only less than a block away. I travel San Diego County for work so living this close to the station makes my commute easy. It's a nice place. You'll see."

True to his word, Driscoll's walkup was only a short walk from the station. He lived over a store that sold army surplus goods. The window at street level boasted canvas sacks and food rations displayed in the sidecar of a motorcycle within no motor. Knives and machetes hung near a sign that claimed these to be "Survival Gear." In the darkest corners of the store, PJ could make out the butts of rifles. The stairs that led up to the apartment were narrow and went between the Army surplus and another store PJ never saw. Once Driscoll opened the door and flipped in the light switch, the interior of the apartment came to life.

The amber light within displayed dark wood paneled wall- and obscure artifacts. An old grandfather clock sat opposite the door. A large string-art picture of the Golden Gate Bridge in San Francisco hung above an orange sofa where Lucky charged and landed playfully waiting for Panic to join her. The carpet was orange, a shaggy spread that covered the entire floor of the small living room. The room was accented with wooded tables topped with stacks of books and dirty ashtrays. One table was a giant wooden spool. A stereo system sat against a wall atop cinder blocks, and stacks of records were either strewn about or stacked neatly leaning into the blocks. On the opposite wall, through a curtain of hanging beads, a small kitchen was conspicuous. But it was a peculiar table lamp near the opening to the kitchen which caught the girls' fascination. Panic saw it first and commented, "Look at that!"

The lamp, figure of a bronzed angel—a cherub, like a fat baby with wings—sat perched upon a regal pedestal blowing an invisible kiss off of its outstretched hand. On its own the chubby angel would have been nothing special, but the entire figure was surrounded by dozens of hanging strings of beads that were channeling droplets of oil running down their length, catching the light as the oil cascaded.

"Wow," PJ said, going toward the lamp. Panic was already there touching the dripping oil.

"Oh, you like that?" Driscoll asked. "That's a mineral oil rain lamp. Got it at the secondhand store but the chain was broken." He pointed to the cap at the top. "It's supposed to hang from the ceiling, but I couldn't fix the connector and it's pretty heavy so, now it's a table lamp."

"It's so pretty," Panic said.

"Cool," PJ admitted. She continued to look around and stopped in front of the wooden clock. She found it interesting with its deeply carved groves and intricate patterns of acorns, leaves, and flowers. Panic joined Lucky on the couch and started petting the small dog. PJ made her way to the albums on the floor, and she started to look through them, not really giving them much mind but feeling like she needed to do something with her hands.

Meanwhile, Driscoll had disappeared through the beaded curtains. The clanking of the beads rattled with the crackle of plastic-on-plastic. When he returned a few moments later he announced that he had started heating the cocoa. He stopped at the beaded curtain and gathered it up, tying the strands together, securing them to a fastener along the wall. PJ hadn't noticed the fastener before, but she thought it was a clever idea. She figured the sound of the beads colliding would get annoying after a while. She watched Driscoll move around the room, then down the hall, where she imagined she might find his bedroom if she were to follow him. He stopped about halfway down the hall and opened a cupboard.

"I only have one extra blanket so maybe you two can share," he said from the hallway, his voice muffled into the folds of unknown spaces.

"Sure." PJ turned over the album she had picked up so that she could see the front. Warren Zevon. She had no idea what that meant; was it a band or an artist? "Thanks for having us. It's very nice of you." She hoped she sounded older than she felt.

"No problem, seriously." By then Driscoll's voice was clear. He was right next to her, and his closeness startled her. "Sorry," he said, as if he knew he had frightened her. He reached out with the blanket and handed it to her. "She's already out," he said, with a nod toward Panic.

PJ stood and went to the couch. She placed the blanket over her sister. Lucky curled next to Panic and tucked in her tail.

"I'm going to get those drinks going. I hope you still want some."

"Sure," PJ answered, though she felt exhausted and would have welcomed the opportunity to fall in next to Panic and the dog and shut her eyes. Instead, she followed Driscoll through the apartment, but stopped short when he went into the kitchen. She could still see him, though, opening cupboards, pulling out mugs.

Driscoll had taken off his hat again exposing his bald head. PJ thought it made him look a lot older and she wished he would put his hat back on. She didn't know why his baldness made her feel uneasy, but she didn't like it. She didn't like how he had been so close to her a minute earlier, how trapped she suddenly felt within the walls of his tiny apartment. Though he was only going into the next room, she was glad he went. She looked at Panic on the orange sofa nuzzling the dog in her slumber. For a fleeting moment she thought she should gather up her sister and their things and leave, slip out the door, maybe even take the dog with them. But then, Driscoll hadn't done anything to give her a reason to flee. Hadn't he been kind and generous to open his home to them? He certainly didn't have to welcome them.

The small, fat angel surrounded by cascading mineral oil along the small beads seemed to glow at PJ from the end table. She studied its tiny face and wondered how children became models for angels. Panic might be an angel, PJ thought. Panic had said they would be okay, and so far, they were. Tomorrow they would be at Aunt Fancy's, and everything would be fine. She'd tell Aunt Fancy all about that strange oil lamp. Only, maybe she wouldn't have to tell her because that lamp seemed like the sort of thing that Aunt Fancy would have. PJ thought Aunt Fancy's lamp would be properly hung from the ceiling the way it was designed instead of resting on a table.

"Why don't you come in here and help me with this cocoa?" PJ heard his voice from the kitchen, and she knew he meant her and not Panic. She got up and moved into the kitchen, ducking beneath the tied back bead curtain.

Driscoll had two mismatched mugs of steaming liquid on the counter before him. He poured milk into one. When she stood before him, he reached around her leaning his body into hers. She stepped back.

"Sorry," Driscoll said quietly. "Tight space." He stepped around her and opened the refrigerator then turned back to show her a clear, glass bottle. "Do you want some of this?" he asked with a sly squint. "It's super groovy."

"What is it?"

"A little peppermint schnapps." He didn't wait for her to answer but instead tipped the schnapps into the two mugs without the milk before capping the bottle and sticking it back into the fridge. Then he lifted one of the mugs and handed it to her. She took it, though with some hesitation. She knew what schnapps was, of course. Betsy drank anything that had booze in it, but PJ had never had a drink of alcohol herself. After seeing what it had done to her mom, she wasn't sure she wanted to find out what it would do to her. Driscoll clinked his own mug into hers. Then he said, "cheers," and tipped his cup for a sip.

PJ smelled her cocoa. She laughed uneasily.

"I can see you're a tough customer," Driscoll said, and he set his cocoa down and took a step closer to her.

"I've never had schnapps before. That's all." PJ took a step backward and felt her heel hit the baseboard behind her, the back wall of the kitchen preventing her retreat.

"You never know what you like until you try it." As he said this, Driscoll took another step forward. His eyes closed halfway. He stepped again; this time his hips pressed into her lightly at first, then with more force. He took the cup from her hand and set it on the counter as he pushed his body into hers against the back wall of the kitchen. "You don't have to drink it if you don't want to. I won't make you do anything you don't want to do."

PJ's heart exploded in her chest. She took a deep breath, smelling the mint on Driscoll's breath; she felt his warm exhale. He moved his face very near hers as she opened her mouth to speak. As she formed the words to protest, he put his mouth on hers, muffling whatever she had thought to say. His lips parted and his wet tongue stuck into her mouth. She gagged.

"Shh." He said, though he didn't need to silence her. PJ's thoughts swirled into such a gripping fear, she could not speak. Her fear pinned her to the wall. But it was the wall that brought her back. Her hand flat against the cold wall, fingers splayed out along the floral wallpaper.

"Driscoll, stop."

"You don't want that," he said. "I know what you want. You've been telling me since we were on that first bus together."

"No," PJ said, pushing against him.

"Playful, right?" Driscoll laughed.

PJ shoved as hard as she could. Her face flushed with heat.

"You stop that now or I'll make it hurt," he said, and he thrust his pelvis into her harder, biting her hard on the shoulder.

"Ouch!" She cried out.

"Oh, I like that," he said. "Tell me when it hurts."

In a flash, he moved his hands to his belt buckle, pulling his fly open with a quick motion. He shimmied his zipper down. PJ felt Driscoll's erection against her hip, heard his breath as he leaned forward and smelled her hair with an audible whiff. Then he breathed heavily down her shoulder. The heat of his body moved like a vile wave against her. His cold hands slipped under her shirt along her back, then under her bra strap, then he pressed his left hand sharply into her back and he brought his right hand around the front of her and squeezed her breast.

PJ's own breathing stopped; she was aware she held her breath. Fear consumed her, fear of what was happening and fear she might scream, that she might scare Panic. She did not want to scare Panic.

Panic. My god, she thought, what if he goes after Panic next. What could she do?

But she didn't have a chance to complete the thought. Within a moment, all hell broke loose.

At once, Driscoll's head thrust forward as if jolted by a powerful force. Mineral oil splattered on PJ's face as she heard her sister's scream-ing voice—Panic's most courageous call—let out a howling cry.

Almost dreamlike, PJ had instant knowledge of what had hap-pened. From out of the smallest corner of her vision, she had seen the thrust of the angel and its beaded strings of mineral oil, hurtle toward the back of Driscoll's head as he attacked her in the kitchen, saw his head jerk unnaturally as the lamp hit him in the back of his skull, felt his body go limp against hers as she took in her sister's war cry, and she felt his body slide unconscious away from her. Only after it was all over, did Lucky start to bark.

"Let's get out of here!" Panic yelled, and before PJ could think anything through, she grabbed their bag and jackets, and the two girls rushed out the door and into the dark stairwell, down the stairs, then out and away from Driscoll's apartment.

They ran until their lungs burned, until the air could no lon-ger escape through their heavy panting. But Panic was relentless; she dragged them further still. Panic grabbed PJ's hand and pulled her along, past dumpsters, along a dark alley, through the intersection PJ thought they'd crossed on their way to the train station. They had slowed as they sped along the sidewalk near the train station but only enough to catch their breath and regain footing. But then, that couldn't have been right. PJ didn't actually know where they were or which direction they head-ed. The streets were darker than she remembered with tall buildings towering above them, closing in on them. Then, all at once, the skyline opened, and she saw before them the arch of the Coronado Bridge; it crested above them like an archway to heaven. Below its concrete blue ribbon, the dark water of the harbor danced with the reflection of lights and boats. They ran still, as far as they could, through a construction zone, past chain link fences, all the while the image of Driscoll chased them, pursued them along the waterfront, moving their feet until, at last, they reached the piers and could go no farther. Panic pulled PJ behind a cement column, and they ducked down and wrapped themselves up into each other, huddling, shivering and not daring to make a sound.

After a long while, PJ looked up at the Coronado Bridge thinking back to that day last week when she and Panic had climbed the boulder and looked out over the valley taking in the view, the visibility carrying them all the way to that bridge and beyond. Of all the possibilities and of all the lives between their valley and that place, she imagined only horror then. Only horror awaited anyone, she thought, as she clutched her little sister.

A distant sound of foghorns blew, and PJ wrapped Panic tighter in her arms. She couldn't think about what might have been or what still could be. She knew then that the worst thing that would happen to her could not be her father's death or her own abuse. PJ had found the worst thing in the world, the thing that terrified her more than any other thing, the real possibility that something might happen to her sister.

Because of Driscoll, their plans had changed, and PJ knew it. They couldn't go on to Aunt Fancy's now; that much was plain. There was too much out of their control. So much more could go wrong, and PJ could not take that chance. They had not been prepared for the world outside of El Cajon, and maybe never would be. PJ knew they had to go back, but she didn't yet know how. Her plans had been short sighted, but she only had the limited resources of her limited world. Looking up at the Coronado Bridge, PJ knew they were a long way from home then, a long way from their gravel road and their crazy, broken mom.

Panic had burrowed into her side and there remained still and quiet. She had acted courageously, that was certain, but PJ could not know what thoughts lurked behind those bright eyes, now shut against the darkness of the night. She had seen a lot in those few days, witnessed so many people's lives go up in the blackest smoke of a jet crash, watched her mother beat PJ to unconsciousness, uncovered the death of her dad—their dad. And what she saw tonight—PJ could not even image the fear her sister had felt to go after that man like she had. How could she know what her sister had prevented? PJ could never thank her enough for what Panic did, but she could also not replace the memory. Then, she thought, it could have been Panic in that kitchen. She cursed herself for her mistake. Why had she agreed to go there, and to take Panic into that terrible apartment? The man deserved his fate and she hoped he felt that bump on his head in the morning. They had no way of knowing if Driscoll was dead and PJ was fine with not knowing, but she wasn't sure if Panic would ever be. After all, Panic could never forgive herself for the rabbits; she could never forgive PJ either.

An image of Driscoll flashed before PJ's eyes, his buckle coming undone as he forced her against the wall. Then she saw her mother's drunk rage as she pounded her with the shoe. The moment the oil lamp swung through the air, and the sound of the thud against Driscoll's head. His body as it fell slack, collapsing to the floor. Panic's hallowed war cry. Marlene and Manny and the jet on T.V. on fire and descending at such a terrible angle. These traumas swirled together, and PJ shook her head. These recent events confronted her like a movie screen she could not turn away from. In a surreal way, it started to seem like everything had happened to someone else. The images played over and over but grew further distant.

She rubbed her eyes hard and looked back up at the bridge spanning the harbor. It really was something to behold from there, or from anywhere you could see it in San Diego. The concrete columns rising exponentially from the water, the shape taking on a bell curve, while at the same time rounding the road the motorists followed through the sky. Her eyes followed it from Market Street up and over the harbor and back down to Coronado Island, then back to Market Street again. Over and over, she gazed across the span of the bridge allowing the act to hypnotize her into submission and eventually she slept curled in a ball, huddled against her tiny hero, a nine-year-old girl who might have murdered a grown man to save PJ from a fate she couldn't imagine, certainly one she never thought she would have to imagine. A chill crawled into PJ then as she dreamed of a destiny darker than what awaited her at home. She slept in fits and shudders.

Panic woke her with one word: "Cop."

CHAPTER TWELVE

"Hold it right there!" The man's voice said even though the girls were sitting on the ground. "You kids are trespassing. This is a construction site."

"We were just waiting for our bus, officer." PJ explained to the security guard in the blue suit. She noticed right away that he wasn't a real cop. "We got lost, is all."

The officer eyed Panic then asked PJ, "How old are you, young lady?" A shiny badge glinted sunlight at her.

"Seventeen," PJ lied.

"And you?"

"I'm eleven," Panic said, picking up the queue.

"And you say your mom's expecting you on the 58 this morning?" He pressed his lips together as he looked between them, his face shrouded in skepticism.

"Yes, sir." PJ said. She made note of his name, Skoner, spelled out below his badge. "We were at our dad's house, Officer Skoner. They're divorced."

Skoner squinted between them then seemed to soften. "My folks were married 52 years," Skoner said. His eyes relaxed. "I'm sorry, kiddos. That's rough."

Boats moved slowly on the water behind the towering figure of the cop. A strange seabird—not a gull or piper but something bigger and darker—perched atop a channel marker. It tipped its head sideways to eye the water below. The cop scratched his forehead, lifting his hat in the action.

"Where's she work?" He asked.

"Sir?" PJ asked, forgetting what she had told him.

"Your ma. Where's she work?"

PJ thought fast. "A café in uptown called Chicken Pie Shop." It was all she could think of. She knew the Chicken Pie Shop from years back when they used to go there, before their dad left. No. Before he died. A rigid lump formed in PJ's throat, and she balked. She opened her mouth to speak again but no words came. She had a moment when she thought about telling the cop everything that had happened, how they had finally decided to leave because Betsy had lied to them about their dad, how her mom hit her with the shoe, even about the ugly thing that had happened with Driscoll and how they left him, unconscious, maybe even dead, upon the floor.

"You're a long way from the bus station." Skoner tilted his head at Panic. His eyes narrowed again.

"My sister likes the boats."

The man looked out at the water. His lower lip curled in contemplation as he scrutinized the harbor traffic. "Okay then," Skoner nodded. "I'll drop you at Santa Fe, myself. You'll make the 8:35 if we hurry."

"Sir, we're fine to get there on our own."

"Won't hear it," he said. "Besides, I'm off work now and headed that way."

Panic nodded at PJ. She said, "We're lucky you came by Officer."

And they were lucky. Not only did the security guard believe their story, but he decided to let them walk back to the station after PJ told him that Panic feared strangers, even nice police officers.

"Thank you," PJ said. She made wide eyes at Panic hoping to convey the need for her to be quiet about the details of their night. The last thing she needed was Panic sounding off about the jet crash and all the angels flying away in the smoke, and then the terrible situation with Driscoll. "We just need to know how to get back to Santa Fe Station, is all."

"Oh, sure," Skoner said, and he pointed up the road and told them to follow that same road—he called it Kettner—all the way past Broadway. "You can't miss it. It's a straight shot."

When Skoner set them on their way, he gave them a warning about staying out of construction zones, and he waited until they were well down the street before he returned to the construction area. PJ turned back often to check if he was still there.

The girls found their way back to Sante Fe Station and inside to the bus depot window. They asked about the fare for the 58 bus. The night before, they had used transfer slips so PJ was unsure how much it would cost to get them home.

"You give the driver your money," the woman behind the glass responded. She had dark skin and a dark, wedge haircut with bright earrings of dangling, pink hoops that hung from the sides of her head. "Make sure you have the right change."

"It was thirty-five cents in El Cajon," PJ said. "But the driver gave us the transfer and so I'm not sure how much it is, ma'am."

"It's thirty-five, sugar," the woman nodded, her pink earrings bouncing slightly with her head. "Do you have a few dollars? I can make change if you need it. You'll need seventy cents if you plan to transfer." She flashed a smile at PJ.

PJ thought of the bicentennial quarters in her pocket; how she didn't want to spend them. She slipped three single bills through the opening at the base of the window and the woman's hand went to a belt on her waist where she clicked a silver device that housed columns of coins. She thumbed a lever and stroked out several quarters, dimes, and nickels, then handed the change back to PJ through the window.

"One thing, dear, before you go. You wait around in here until 8:30. You hear?" The woman nodded her head and raised her eyebrows at the same time giving PJ a stern look. "I know it's broad daylight outside, and all that, but this is not the neighborhood for kids to be running around. Stick close until 8:30, then. Okay?"

"Okay. Thank you." PJ swept up the change and jingled it into her pocket.

They had enough time to use the bathroom again and have a long drink of water at the drinking fountain—Panic had two drinks—before the clock struck 8:30 and they made their way to the curb near the sign for the 58 bus, that same place where they had stepped off a different 58 bus the night before. It wasn't long before the flat front of the 58 pulled up to the curb and the girls clambered on along with many other people at the station that morning.

When the sisters climbed onto the bus, PJ noticed the increase in occupants compared to the evening bus. Folks of all sorts with different outfits filled the seats. They found a bench near the back where they could sit together. Once settled, PJ knew she needed to have a talk with her sister.

"You haven't said anything about dad."

Panic looked out the window, craning her neck up at the tall buildings and answering as if she were directing her words to the sky. "What's there to say?"

"Well, for starters, what do you feel?"

"Nothing, I guess." Panic leaned back and took a big breath through her nose then closed her eyes and let it out. "Tired. I guess."

"I'm tired too," PJ said. "I always thought that he would come back, though. I'm still thinking it, even now."

"PJ, don't"

"Listen, I have to tell you about him. I have to talk about it. You're the only one who knew him besides mom and she's not really available."

"It's just that—"

"No," PJ spoke loud at first then looked around the bus and adapted a hushed tone. "No, Panic. I'm all alone with what I remember, and I need you to hear me on this. Maybe not always, but now. I need you to listen." She paused. "I miss him." Tears welled up in her eyes and Panic swam in and out of focus until PJ blinked the tears away.

At last, Panic said, "It's just that I didn't really like him." She looked at her hands, her eyes downcast. "I don't remember him like you do. To me, he was scary and I–" She stopped short and looked at PJ.

A lump had formed in PJ's throat and her chest burned to hear Panic speak this way. She wanted nothing more than to pull her sister close and sob into a deep embrace, but she needed to hear this new information. If she expected Panic to be a good listener, she had to listen, too. PJ breathed as if the weight of the bus pressed the air from her lungs. She nodded for Panic to continue.

"No, it's nothing," Panic said, and she gave her head an urgent, quick shake.

"What? No. Please, Panic. Please tell me." When PJ said her name, the image returned of her baby sister nestled and cooing in the lap of their dad, then hitting the floor with a dull thud. Bent cigarettes falling, the ground collecting burning embers and butts around a terrified Panic. The small scar on Panic's cheek seemed more pronounced.

"Do you think that man back there, the one I hit, do you think he's okay?"

Although she knew her sister deliberately changed the subject, PJ automatically remembered Driscoll's hands on her, his body pressing her body into the wall. His gross mouth. "I don't care if he's okay or not."

"I know, but am I still white like snow?"

"Like what?" PJ grimaced at the strange nature of her sister's question.

"Like the lady on the bus told us. Marlene." Tears formed in Panic's eyes and rolled down her cheeks. "I want to be pure, like snow, like white snow, PJ."

"Sure, Jo. You're the purest kid I know." PJ reached her arms around her sister and drew her close. "There's not a thing wrong with you. Not a thing."

"But then, I need to tell you something else." Panic pulled her head away from her sister and looked her square in the face.

"Well?" PJ waited.

"I took the shoes, PJ!" she blurted.

Again, PJ grimaced a little trying to connect with what her sister said.

"Mom's espadrilles. It was me. I played dress up, is all." Tears spilled from her wide eyes. "I didn't mean for you to get in trouble. I didn't mean for her to hurt you."

At first, PJ couldn't make sense of the younger girl's words; they came too fast and included too much information in such a short span. But once it dawned on PJ, she saw the true anguish then in Panic's eyes. Panic had taken the shoes their mother had later weaponized, a weapon that seemed to set the entire week into motion. An innocent act from a child playing dress up. She remembered hearing Panic's voice before she lost consciousness, "It is your shoe, Mama."

The bus turned left and chugged up a long hill. It was near the top of the hill before PJ spoke again.

"There's nothing wrong with dress up, Panic. A kid's gotta play." PJ pulled her sister into another embrace, holding her close for as long as she could, reassuring her that she was still pure like snow. The bus rumbled along, and buildings obscured the windows in flashes as they passed. Though PJ knew the world around her was filled with noise, the only sound she could hear was the breathing of her little sister in her arms.

"I was glad he left." Panic said from within the muffled embrace. She pulled away from PJ and, this time, looked out the window. "I know we have to go back, but I hate that place."

"Then don't go back to that house. Go back to our hill. Go back to our fort. Go back to the wash where we relaxed in the sun last weekend and laughed and laughed. We can go back there whenever we want." PJ believed that, too. She knew that no matter what happened or where they ended up, they would always have that rustic paradise where they could go and be as wild as the land. She thought again of their valley, what it looked like from their air, from Chet's flying lessons.

As if reading her mind about their dad, Panic said, "My clearest memories of dad are not good memories."

"How so," PJ asked, but part of her did not want to know. PJ placed her hand on Panic's shoulder, and she gently patted her. She thought of her own memories of Panic and Chet together, images of Panic and Chet walking along the sidewalk, Panic and Chet in the recliner, Panic and Chet at the kitchen table. These were snippets of recollection, fragments of time that told no story, only flashes of situations that came to PJ in a montage of consideration. Daughter and father, not good memories or bad ones, simply pictures, like the ones Betsy kept in the old photo album with the yellowed, sticky cardboard, holding photos covered in clear plastic sheets. The one image that skewed the refrain of the montage was the infant Panic shooting through the air, Chet diving behind the sofa, and then something new that PJ hadn't thought of in a long time or maybe ever: a baby with a cast on its arm, on her arm, Panic's arm. A real memory formed then; not one from a photograph in an album.

"He pulled me by my hair because I wouldn't get out the car for kindergarten." Panic said with a steady tone, as plain as if she were reading the words from a book. "It was my first day of school—kindergarten—and I must have been afraid to go in, so, he pulled me out of the car by my hair. Heidi Hill was there laughing at me the whole time."

The words did not fully develop meaning in PJ's mind. She looked at her sister's wild hair, brown and bushy and impossible to tame. She looked at Panic's placid profile as the younger girl continued to stare out the window, calm eyes, her fixed expression of resistance. But as she looked at her sister, more images surfaced in PJ's mind, pictures of Panic yelling at Chet, Panic running from Chet, Panic being pushed into the side of the car, her tiny toddler form rebounding off the fender and falling backward to the ground. PJ shook it away. It was too much. She turned her head and scanned the bus, saw the backs of people's heads, the rushing of the scenery along the street going by at a pace she found exhilarating and fast. She figured they must be uptown already, well on their way home. A billboard advertised Seagram's Seven and 7-Up; graffiti obscured the logo of the 7-Up bottle. Cars merged in front of the bus, bright blue and silver, a convertible with its top down, the woman driving holding her headscarf in place with one hand while clutching the steering wheel with the other. And more images came to PJ then: Chet's face red with anger, Chet's hands clenched in fists and hammering away, Chet's belt swinging, Chet's loud voice and his rage.

When she looked again at Panic, PJ saw that her sister's attention fused to the scenery outside the bus, too. PJ noticed sister's tiny, round scar, the one that had marked Panic's cheek for all these years. They'd never had chicken pox like Manny and Luis had, evidence of the disease on the boys' brown skin in small round dimples and indentations. Manny had one chicken pox scar on his eyebrow that interrupted the line of his brow hairs. Panic's scar, PJ almost knew, was from that day when Panic flew through the air and hit the ground with a thud along with so many lighted cigarette embers. A new realization formed. The scar could have come at another time when their dad might have deliberately burned her with his cigarette. Could she believe that about him? Could she imagine her dad would have hurt Panic on purpose? Panic: the very name stood as a reminder of the unease in their world, of the unreliability of memory.

"I don't want to call you Panic anymore," PJ suddenly declared. Before Panic could respond, she added, "Dad gave you that name and I don't like what it means. If you don't like Josephine, we can come up with something different, but it's not going to be Panic. Not anymore."

Panic had started to open her mouth to say something, but she shut it again. Instead, she just sat and looked at her sister with her big, expectant eyes.

"Jo," PJ said. "Jo is a fine name, strong and good."

To this, Jo nodded. The bus turned a corner.

"Listen," PJ went on. "I don't know how Mom's going to be when we get home so let me do the talking, okay? We might be in a lot of trouble for being gone all night."

"Okay."

"If she gets angry, you have to let me take it. You clear out."

"But—"

"No. You clear out. Got it?" PJ gave her sister a stern look. "Things are going to be different now, Jo." When she added her sister's name—her new name—she stressed the word by physically leaning into it when she said it. "I'm not sure how I can make it happen, but I know I can. It's going to be different." PJ promised this not only to her sister but also to herself.

For the rest of the bus ride, they remained quiet. At one point, Jo fell asleep leaning onto her sister's side. She was difficult to roust when they reached the transfer station in El Cajon, but PJ managed to get her up and on to the next bus. By the time the girls stepped out onto the corner of East Main and Greenfield, the afternoon sun once again fell hot upon the world. It was strange to think that they had just had the cool air of the Pacific Ocean on their skin a few hours earlier. Strange, also, to think that they had been away all night. PJ knew Betsy would be in a state. She would be furious, for certain.

They walked the length of Greenfield before turning into the sparse network of dirt roads that crisscrossed the foothills of La Cresta and Shadow Mountain, up Forester Creek. When they got to their long gravel road, they saw Manny's dad's pickup truck disappear around the bend ahead of them, the dust it had kicked up already settling on the miter and aggregate of the road.

"What should we say?" Jo asked.

"Not 'we,' but me. I'll do the talking and I'll just tell the truth. I mean, we just found out our dad's dead." She swallowed dust and grief. "I think taking off was the right thing to do. Maybe the only thing to do.

If she's mad, I'll take it. You're going to make yourself invisible. Promise me again."

"Okay."

They were thirsty and hot, and the day's heat beat down upon them with unrelenting ferocity. The early afternoon sun cast short shadows from the pepper tress that grew along the road. PJ took the far left and let Jo walk as close to any available shade that found the road. Their bags felt like lead weights, and their skin was wet with sweat. Each step seemed to drag with a little more hesitancy, but it wasn't their fatigue that mired them. Instead, the fear of the wrath of Betsy weighed heavily upon them both, mounting as they approached their home.

When they found themselves facing the dark oaks that framed the front of their small house, they stopped and stood, staring at the entryway shrouded in shade. Though the shade beckoned them with its promises of coolness, they stood firm in the blazing sunlight for a few moments longer.

"I can't stand her hitting you," Jo said. "The other night I couldn't move. She had that shoe, and I couldn't move. The next day, do you know what I thought? I thought, I'll kill her, PJ. I am brave enough to do that. I thought that, that I'd kill our mom if it happened again."

PJ examined Jo, her squared shoulders and tilted chin. Instead of tears, Jo had doubled down on her bravery. She seemed to want her sister to see how she could be strong and bold.

"You won't have to kill anyone," PJ said. "All that's over now."

"You can't just decide it's over."

"I can. Just did." PJ nodded resolute in the bright spark of Jo's eyes. She considered her sister her favorite person. She loved everything about her from her wild hair to her boney shoulders, and now her fixed mouth. "It's time for me to be the brave one."

"What are you going to do?" Jo's eyes grew wide. She stared back at PJ, then looked at the house, then back to PJ.

"Something I should have done last week. I'm going to tell Mrs. Perón the truth about what happened. No more covering Betsy's tracks.

And I'm going to take care of us. If we have to be here, I'm going to make this place safe for you. For both of us."

"But what if they put Mom away?"

"I'm going to give her that choice. I think she'll see it my way."

"Okay," Jo said.

They finally walked into the shade of the oaks and up the front steps to the door. Just like they had on the previous Saturday when Mrs. Stanislaw had brought them home from their first attempt to run away, they held hands as they went through the door and into the house, prepared to face whatever waited.

The hallway was cool and quiet. No lights greeted them. The hard tile of the floor echoed the closing of the door behind them. They set their bags down and went into the living room. There, on the couch in the exact same place where they had seen her the day before, was Betsy, curled up and sleeping, a low whistling sound through her nose marked her exhalation. The bottle PJ had seen her with the day before was now empty and horizontal on the floor, along with a few other bottles, cigarettes, the red lacquered box. The T.V. flashed pictures on the screen, its audio turned all the way down, while images of soap opera starlets with red lipstick and thick, blue eyeshadow moved across the screen.

"Mom," PJ said softly. "We're home."

Betsy rolled and flopped onto her back and the whistling noise turned into easy snoring. PJ looked at her little sister and shrugged, then thumbed toward the bedrooms and off they went leaving Betsy passed out on the couch where they found her. They went into PJ's room and took the sleeve of saltine crackers from PJ's duffle. As they started to crunch on the crackers, PJ thought about the week they'd had. She remembered the rabbits in the darkness, saw them in her mind's eye hopping about but not really going anywhere. Then, she remembered how mad Manny had been at her and how worried she felt about what losing the rabbits had cost his family.

"I'm going to get a job," PJ said. Jo had started flipping through one of the National Geographics and only glanced away from the magazine for a moment to look at PJ. But PJ didn't care if her sister was paying any attention. She wasn't really talking to her just then anyway. Instead, she planned out loud what was going to happen next and just how it would take shape. "I'm going to go down to Best Spot Café with mom and get a shift after school. Then, I'm going to go to the grocery store and make sure we have food here. How are you supposed to get through school with an empty stomach? You're already half a foot shorter than the rest of the kids your age."

"Am not," Jo said and now she tossed the magazine she'd been reading at her sister.

"I'm serious, Jo," PJ said. "You need to eat. Pillaging avocados and eating crackers is not the same as fruits and vegetables and meat."

"Ugh, don't say meat. I'm starving!"

"That's my point. You are actually starving. But not for long. Not if I can help it. And I think I can help."

The two sisters stared at each other for a long time but finally Jo picked up another magazine and started munching crackers again. PJ also pulled a magazine from the stack. She took out her notebook and, flipping the glossy pages of the National Geographic, began writing down ideas for her civics project.

"I thought it was quiet back here." Betsy's voice alarmed them both when it arrived at the doorway. The two sisters froze and stared at their mother as she swayed a little and steadied herself on the door jamb. "You're home early from school, I think." She yawned and scratched her hip.

PJ thought about what Betsy had just said: home early from school. Did she even know they were gone? Something inside of PJ started to grow white-hot like she was being lit on fire with rage. She couldn't take her eyes off the woman in the doorway, their mother, the lady who was supposed to care for them more than anyone. And she didn't even know they were gone? It seemed preposterous to PJ. If she didn't know Betsy as well as she did, she wouldn't have believed it. But she did know Betsy and she knew it was true that their mother didn't know they had gone, the danger they faced, the potential for harm they had encountered.

"I need a shower," Betsy said, as she moved away from the door and down the hall.

PJ stood and moved toward the door. Jo reached out, brushing PJ's arm with her fingertips as her big sister went into the hall to follow their mom into the bathroom.

"I need to talk with you, Mom."

"I bet you do, PJ, but I need to get to the restaurant." Betsy was turning the water spigot on in the tub by the time PJ came into the bathroom behind her. The smell of stale booze lingered in the air in Betsy's wake. Her stooped form shook slightly and when she stood fully upright; her hands came to her lower back, and she rubbed small circles where PJ imagined it might ache because Betsy had slept on the couch, had weighted tables too long, had carried too many lies.

"I need to talk to you about where we were and what happened." PJ steadied herself, resolved to say what needed to be said not only for her sake but also for Panic.

"Back over at that Stanislaw woman's house again?" Betsy said reaching into the stream of water to check its temperature.

"No. Mom, this is important. Can you look at me?"

Betsy shook the water from her hand and did not answer PJ.

"We ran away. We ended up in downtown San Deigo."

Besty glanced over her shoulder at PJ, a look of apathy on her face. She turned back to the tub.

"I'm going to tell Mrs. Perón what's been going here. I'll tell her the truth about how you hit me last week, and the other times, too," PJ said to Betsy's back.

The older woman's shoulders hunched as she reached forward and turned the spigot to shut the water off. She stood upright again then turned to face PJ. Her eyes narrowed, and her brow grew severe. "How dare you," she sneered. "How dare you talk to me like that."

"Mrs. Perón said I could tell her the truth and she would listen, and you would get in trouble." PJ fought to keep her voice steady but heard the betrayal in her quaking tone. "Jo has also agreed to tell the truth."

"After everything I have done for you—"

"What have you done?" PJ demanded. "We steal avocados and beg for sweet bread so we can eat. We lie to the neighbors and our teachers about how much food or money we have. And somehow you always end up with enough to drink but we never have enough to eat!"

"You ungrateful, little brat. You horrible bitch." Betsy slurred her words, her ire rising, but she did not move toward PJ to strike her. Not yet. "You have no idea what I have gone through for you."

To this PJ just shook her head. It occurred to her that Betsy believed she had made great sacrifices for her daughters. Maybe that was true many years ago, but it had been a long time since then.

"You think you're so smart," Betsy went on. "You think that just because your dad killed himself, but left you a letter, that you have it all figured out now. Well, let me tell you something about your dad!" Betsy raised her arm then and gathered a fist, stepping toward PJ, but PJ was quick, and she caught Betsy's arm as it swung forward. PJ held her mom's arm in midair, their eyes locked onto each other's. Then, with strength she didn't know she had, PJ pushed her mom backward and she collided with the contents of the countertop sending cosmetics and toothbrushes flying.

"That's all. No more of that. No more hitting, "PJ said. "From now on, things are going to be different." PJ stood taller. She stepped backward to the doorway of the bathroom, and she could see down the hallway from her periphery. She knew Jo had come out into the hallway when she heard the racket and she felt stronger knowing her sister was close by. "No more hitting. No more skipping groceries. We're going to get a phone, too."

"Oh, are we?" Betsy leaned into the sink. Her expression told PJ that she was both flabbergasted and exhausted, but also wracked with resentment.

"Yes," PJ said.

"Or else?" Betsy folded her arms, rubbing her elbow where it had rammed the countertop.

"Or else I'll tell Mrs. Perón the truth about what happened."

"She won't believe you. You're just a dumb kid."

Jo's voice came from behind PJ in a shrill, purposeful yell. "She's not dumb. She's my sister and she's the only one who's been taking care of me." And then Jo leaned past PJ so that she could get her upper body inside the doorway, and she shouted with her mighty voice, "I'll tell Mrs. Perón too!"

The look of astonishment on Betsy's face told PJ that Jo's words had landed with impact. Betsy shifted her weight and sat down atop the closed toilet lid. She put her head into her hands and started to cry.

In the reflection of the bathroom's vanity mirror, the two sisters looked at one another, their faces awash with dread. PJ wondered if she had gone too far by grabbing her mom and pushing her. But there was no turning back now. Besides, PJ knew the outcome of what would happen when Betsy's wrath was unleashed. Only now she would get to find out what would happen when Betsy's wrath was abated.

"Mom," PJ whispered.

"PJ, don't." Betsy sobbed.

"No, Mom, listen. Please." PJ moved into the bathroom and put her hand on her mom's shoulder. She didn't know the last time they'd had physical contact when it wasn't violent, but this felt like the thing she should do at that moment. "I don't know what it's been like for you, but I do know what it's been like for me and for Jo."

Betsy looked up at Jo through yellowed eyes. Her face was red and swollen. Jo nodded and also moved into the bathroom. She put her hand on Betsy's other shoulder.

PJ continued. "I don't hate you, but I am tired of this, and I need to do something else besides just let you hit me and drink all the time."

"I have to drink," Betsy said with a quickness that did not surprise PJ. Her eyes filled with desperation and fear.

"I'm not asking you to stop."

Betsy looked down at the floor and said through a constricted voice, "I'm just so mad, you know?"

"I know." PJ patted Betsy. "I am too. But it all changes right now."

Betsy tried to move closer to her then, but PJ pulled back.

PJ took in the gray roots of Betsy's hair, then the color of the grout along the tiles in the shower, a dingy white that had spots of dark mold near the faucet. She glanced at Jo. Then, she turned and left the bathroom, left her mom and sister there in that small room, left them within those four walls. She walked down the hallway, through the dark living room, past the empty cans scattered on the floor, the piles of cigarette butts in the ashtrays. She went to the back sliding glass door and pulled open its heavy drapery. The brightness of the blue sky and buff hills beyond overcame her vision. For a moment she squinted, then closed her eyes and breathed deeply. She slid the door open and stepped outside into the sunlight.

The warmth found her skin and she welcomed it. The scent of sagebrush, acrid and sweet at the same time, accompanied the eager call of a mockingbird trilling a song that belonged to another. Nearby, a tarantula hawk with strange purple and orange wings dragged the upside-down body of a large hairy spider across the ocher dirt and into a hole beneath a boulder. When PJ pulled the sliding glass door shut behind her a group of tiny finches flitted from the manzanita nearby. The sound of their beating wings rose in unison and then faded as they fled. PJ made her way toward the large eucalyptus, out beyond the live oaks and the dry riverbed where she and her sister had made a world of imagination better than home. She thought about her dad and thumbed the note still in her pocket. She came to a stop in the shade of the towering eucalyptus. There, she sat and scanned the chaparral for an improbable white rabbit, one she hoped might overcome the odds.

EPILOGUE

June 1987

PJ came through the front door and tossed her keys and purse down on the table in the entryway. She flipped through the mail before calling out, "I'm home." She set down the mail, and then untied her waitress apron and set that on the entryway table as well. She made her way into the living room and found her mother sitting on the couch in front of the T.V. Betsy nodded a little but did not take her eyes away from her show. "Do you need more juice?" PJ asked. She picked up the old woman's empty glass and headed for the kitchen. As she filled the glass with orange juice, PJ continued to speak to Betsy, though she could not be sure how much her mother understood. "Earl Pichette came in today. Said his chickens had been eaten by coyotes—every last one. Mary said that it was a sign of the times and that he ought to get his eggs at Vons like everyone else. Then Walter came back for his old job. Jerry laughed and laughed but gave it to him just the same." PJ came back into the room with a juice in one hand and a sandwich in the other. She set each down on the T.V. tray in front of Betsy. "Today's a big day. You sure you don't want to come? It would mean a lot to Jo."

"Can't," was all Betsy could manage.

PJ knew better than to push. Besides, she didn't want anything to spoil Jo's special day, her graduation.

"Where is she now?" PJ asked Betsy and Betsy's eyes flitted to the slider. "Naturally." PJ slipped off her waitress shoes, thick rubber-soled beasts heavy on her tired feet, and laced up her hiking boots before setting out into the back yard. She found Jo near a monkey flower bush, sitting in the dirt, her lanky body bent forward as she moved her pinky finger between flowers pollinating them by hand.

"Save some work for the bees," PJ said as she came up beside her.

"I always do," Jo said, and she looked up at her sister squinting against the bright sun.

"Time to get dressed, I guess. Don't you think?" PJ asked as she squatted down beside Jo.

"Just about."

"Got your speech?"

"Yep," Jo said, and she exhaled hard blowing her long bangs out of her face.

"It's going to be fine," PJ said.

"It isn't the speech I'm worried about." Jo grimaced when she said this and pointed her small pinky toward her sister.

"Me? There's no need." PJ took in the mature face of her little sister, now seventeen years old, beautiful and strong, with eyes so full of acumen and wonder. The wonder had always been there, of course, even back when she was Panic. Over the years, though, her intellect had grown and sharpened, and she'd become a keen mind all of her own—little Jo, not so little anymore.

"I was thinking about how it's going to be in a few months, when I'm at Stanford and you're here. And she's here."

"We've been over this. It's not for you to worry about. Besides, you think I can't handle her? She's a lot easier these days, isn't she?"

"Yes, but— "

"But nothing. Go on inside and get your shower or we'll be late."

"Okay." Jo took another big breath. "PJ?"

"Yeah?"

"When she's gone, you'll come to Palo Alto?"

PJ didn't like to think about this outcome, though she knew it was inevitable. They'd taken Betsy to several specialists over the last year. She'd even had a liver biopsy. The results were fairly decided. Betsy had cirrhosis of the liver and she wasn't expected to live much longer. When the prognosis first came, the girls tried to keep the booze from her, dumping it down the drain and hiding the car keys, but Betsy always found a way to get a drink. Before long, it just seemed easier to bring the booze to her, to monitor her intake, to keep her safe under their protective watch. Really, it was PJ who did the watching. Jo had school and extracurricular activities and so much work to do to clinch her scholarship to Stanford. She had been given a full ride, housing, a student internship, and a stipend that would cover her needs. Plus, she would be one of the first students to participate in a new field of study that moved beyond ecology, one that would examine global climate change. Jo would have her dreams fulfilled. PJ was so proud and so happy for her sister. The last thing she wanted was for her to worry about Betsy. And PJ had taken care of their entire family for so long that with Jo away, taking care of only Betsy would be easy. Mostly, their mom watched T.V., kept quiet, and had a little orange juice with vodka to keep away the delirium tremens. It was heartbreaking to see her slip away, but the alternative was worse. Screaming, gnashing teeth, and flailing about as if having convulsions; PJ knew how to avoid such episodes. And at least Betsy would remain near family until the end.

"I'll come when it's time," PJ finally answered. "But you know Betsy. She's not giving up any time soon."

This was how they had come to regard the woman that occupied the space in their home and in their lives. She was not quite an invalid and not really their mother either. It had been a long time since she was anything other than a name: Betsy.

"Time to get ready," PJ said, and she rose up with Jo following close behind.

•

Later, at the commencement ceremony, PJ scanned the crowd for familiar faces. She saw a few teachers she knew from her own time at Granite Hills High School. A group of women about her age also looked familiar but PJ couldn't be certain. She spotted Manny Gonzáles with his wife Stacy. They had a small bundle with them, a new baby, though she didn't know if they'd had a boy or a girl. The yellow blanket revealed nothing. She knew they were here to see Luis walk for graduation and it made PJ feel a sense of pride for him, too. Luis was going to Grossmont, a junior college that had started a new program to help students from middle income families transfer into the University of California system. Jo had told her all of this, but she never mentioned that Manny and Stacy had had a baby. No matter. It was good to see the whole Gonzáles family together, smiling and happy, on such a joyous occasion. She saw Mrs. Gonzáles give a small wave in her direction and PJ waved back, the memory of pan dulce reminding her of a kinship and gratitude that was always there.

Soon, the music started up and a procession of burgundy clad graduates filed across the lawn of the football field, their regalia flowing in the breeze. They formed up a well-rehearsed walk then sat in rows facing the podium. Some graduates turned to wave to their families. Some held their mortar board hats against the breeze. Jo and a few others sat on the stage with the teachers and administration. When Mr. Lubekey stepped to the mic and gave it a tap the feedback set PJ's teeth buzzing, but the noise was soon squelched, and all was calm again. Mr. Lubekey began his speech by thanking the families of the graduates, and then the teachers, and finally the students. He talked about their hard work and determination. At last, he said what PJ almost held her breath waiting to hear: "Ladies and gentlemen, it gives me great pleasure to introduce this year's valedictorian, Josephine McCormack."

Applause erupted as Jo stood and made her way to the podium. A random voice surprised PJ and shouted out, "We love you, Jo!" To this, Jo responded directly into the microphone, "I love you, too," and everyone laughed. It warmed PJ's heart to see how much this community loved her sister. When PJ was in school, she had very few friends. She was so busy working and taking care of her family that there wasn't much time for school let alone any type of social life. But this wasn't about her. This was Jo's moment in the sun. She chided herself a little and then returned her focus to Jo. PJ wanted to drink it all in, to have this moment imbedded in her memories forever held with such clarity that she could recall today whenever she wished. Her sweet Jo in the bright sunlight of success surrounded by love and applause—heaven to PJ.

And then Jo began.

"It isn't enough to say thank you, though this is what we say. How many times have we uttered these words and thought to ourselves, when will they be enough to convey my truest gratitude? In its history, the word 'thank' is related to 'think' the same way that 'song' is related to 'sing.' For instance, I think of you in gratitude, since you have done this deed for me, and this means 'thank you.' But, as proud Granite Hills Eagles, we have learned that words and thoughts are not enough. We have learned to back up our thoughts with action. And so, as graduates, we thank you today and honor you, our teachers, our families, our friends, and each other, for what you have done for us these four years.

"And I wish to offer an additional thanks to someone very specific in my talk today. I have often asked myself: will this thank you be enough to convey my truest gratitude? A wise man once said, a life well lived is thanks enough. I have lived and will continue to live well, and I hope you will too."

Jo found PJ in the crowd, and she pointed then blew a kiss. Then, she looked down at the podium and she held a long moment in silence before she continued.

"I must apologize but I must remind you now of a sad day in our history. The date is September 25th, 1978. I can say this date and many of you already know what I intend to talk about. Some of you are nodding your heads."

And, indeed, heads among the crowd were nodding.

"For those of you who need the reminder, this is that day in our history, in the history of all of San Diego, when PSA Flight 182 crashed into North Park and killed 144 people. Some of us knew people who were killed, some of us saw the crash, all of us saw it played repeatedly on the news, on our T.V. sets, in our living rooms, our classrooms.

"I saw the crash that day and it changed me. I saw the smoke from far off and I knew what happened there. Like the rest of our graduates today, I was just a kid, but I decided then that each moment is precious, and time should not be wasted.

I remember the people we lost that day and I thank them for their lives. Let's give them a moment."

Jo paused and closed her eyes. Then she moved a strand of hair from her face.

"Eagles, we back our thoughts with action, right?" The crowd clapped.

"And each moment is precious." She found PJ in the crowd again. "I didn't arrive at that epiphany all at once, and—believe it or not—seeing that plane crash wasn't the most traumatic thing I saw that day."

PJ's heart skipped a beat. She sat forward in her chair and thought back to the plane crash, her sister in the chaparral, Betsy with the T.V. She hadn't thought about what had happened with the shoe in a long time. She didn't know that Jo was going to tell everyone about that day, and she held her breath fighting tears and fear.

"I won't go into the details, but I want you to take my word for it. If I tell you that I saw something more terrifying to my young eyes than watching that plane crash, and right in my own home, please take my word for it. It was certainly terrifying for me."

Mrs. Gonzalez looked back through the crowd at PJ, and she nodded.

"But my story has a hero. And so many stories like mine do not. In fact, I am standing here today because of my hero, my sister, Paula Jean McCormack. Some of you know her as PJ. That's how I know her: PJ, my sister."

Now, more faces turned and looked at PJ. A few people clapped. PJ wanted to duck or hide but she held fast. This was Jo moment, she reminded herself again.

"PJ decided after that plane crash that things were going to be different in our house. When she first told me that she was going to take charge, make some changes, I couldn't imagine what she meant or how she would pull it off. She was just a kid, too, but she did it. Each day, she made a positive contribution to our home, and each day I felt a little safer and a little more relaxed."

Jo connected with PJ in the crowd again and she looked directly at her. PJ's face was hot, and her ears rang. She wanted to climb beneath the bleachers and hide, abandoning her earlier idea to commit the entire occasion to memory. She wanted to run away so that Jo would stop talking about her and that day, and the days that followed.

But her little sister continued. She softened and her smile grew conspicuous, even from the bleachers. "She doesn't want me to tell you about this because she didn't do it for recognition. She made sacrifices so that I would be safe, so that I could get my schoolwork done, so that I could have a square meal, so that I could participate in 4-H and band and the science club.'

A few kids in the science club cheered and the crowd laughed which gave everyone a little ease.

Jo continued. "I often associate the PSA crash with that moment in time when everything changed at our house, when I finally started to feel safe and at ease. I got my first A after the PSA crash. I had my first sleepover. My first crush. These things might have happened anyway, but not without my sister making the change happen, building a safe environment for me, making sure I was okay."

Manny Gonzáles turned around in his seat and found PJ. He nodded in her direction and PJ reddened again.

"And it wasn't for nothing. You see, each time I saw my sister go off to work after school instead of to the library to do her own homework, I thought this can't be for nothing, and it made me work harder. Each time I saw her saving quarters for the laundry I doubled up on my reading. When she collected the bottles for recycling, I researched scholarships. When she made my lunch, I studied an extra two hours for my exams. I paid her back with my efforts to improve myself, to be the best person I could be. PJ wanted me to succeed in school and so this is what I did for her. So, when I made the Vice Principal's list, I did that for her. When I made the honor roll, that was for her. When I was invited to be class speaker, it was all for PJ, and as I go off to Stanford, that's for her too. Because it isn't enough to say thank you. We back our thoughts and our words with action. I learned that from my time here at Granite Hills, but I learned it most of all from my sister.

"And so, my fellow graduates, as you go out into the world to do . . . whatever it is you choose to do after you leave this place," she gestured around the football field, but PJ knew the place Jo meant was the entire valley of El Cajon. "Take the time to consider your heroes and how they have made sacrifices for you. How will you say thank you?"

As Jo moved away from the podium, the level of applause was appropriate. The speech wasn't spectacular. It might not even be remembered by those in attendance, except by PJ who heard nothing else for the remainder of the ceremony until they called Jo's name and handed her a diploma.

After Jo walked, PJ watched the grasses along the hills dance with the breeze as she pictured her sister, head down, scrawling out math equations.

The lush foliage behind the high school displayed a multitude of colors, the muted ocher of chaparral broom, the striking scarlet of the monkey flower, and the white heads of flattop buckwheat. PJ knew the jackrabbit there and the sidewinder. She chased the roadrunner and quail and held court with the crows as they cawed on about the day. A woman now, but the girl in her still held that place dear and believed in the magic of its wild. Somewhere in the boulders up higher still, there remained a fort made of particle board and chicken wire where the sisters had raised one another amongst the sagebrush and scrub oaks. Gazing at the greens and yellows of the hills, she heard a faint whisper, a call of sorts, beckoning her to come. She thought after the ceremony she might encourage Jo to take a much-needed hike with her. She thought back to how it once was her utmost wish to leave this place. Now, that same feeling was her greatest cause to stay, to remain here, inland. She'd never again have cause to escape El Cajon except of her own free will. PJ knew someday that moment would come, and she would leave this place. But for now, she would enjoy the sun-tea of summer, the swarming bees on their move to a new hive, the simple ways that life here paused and leapt and rested beneath the shade of the oaks and the eucalyptus on the hill, beyond the sprawling neighborhoods, the advancing concrete, and the inevitable change.

END

ACKNOWLEDGEMENTS:

I am deeply thankful to all who have contributed to my journey, whether mentioned here or not. I appreciate the numerous advisors, friends, and colleagues who have generously dedicated their time to provide constructive feedback and encouragement over the years. I would like to mention a few of you by name:

I extend my deep gratitude to Steel Toe Books and its editors, John Gosslee and Andrew Ibis, for their invaluable support and direction. Receiving the STB 2023 Prose Prize is an honor.

Special appreciation goes to Stephanie Grey, Connie May Fowler, Brian Leung, Martha Southgate, Abby Frucht, Trinnie Dalton, Tom Howard, Suzanne Barefoot, Karen Ford, Carla Lafleur, Liza Nash Taylor, Melissa Scholes Young, Megan Vered, Arielle Bernstein, Patty Park, Lindsey Green-Simms, and Angela Martinek, whose guidance and encouragement shaped my writing.

Thanks to Wordcrafters in Eugene, Lane Literary Guild, Fiction Club (Ruby, Jen, Ellen, Mike, Jeff, Ryan, and Sylvia), Vermont College of Fine Arts, and Townsend Journal (the latter published an early version of chapter one).

My sincerest appreciation goes to my family, especially to my partner, David Vazquez, and our children, Gabriella and V, for their unwavering love and support—you are my endless well of inspiration and strength. A final and humble thank you goes to my literary confidante and cherished reading companion (and niece), Samantha Havens. In many ways, this book is a tribute to our shared passion for literature, mental health, and family. Always read ahead, Sam. Always.

ABOUT THE AUTHOR

Rhonda Zimlich teaches writing at American University in Washington, DC. Her writing focuses on history, grief, and intergenerational trauma, with an occasional ghost story. She is the recipient of the 2020 Literary Award in Nonfiction from *Dogwood*, a Journal at Fairfield University, and the 2021 Fiction Award from Please See Me. She received an honorable mention in *America's Best Essays*, 2021, and is a 2023 recipient of a Maryland State Arts Council grant for writing.

RHONDA ZIMLICH